The
Last
Piece

ALSO BY IMOGEN CLARK

Postcards from a Stranger

The Thing About Clare

Where the Story Starts

Postcards at Christmas (novella)

The Last Piece

IMOGEN
CLARK

Published by Lake Union Publishing, Seattle

www.apub.com

Amazon, the Amazon logo, and Lake Union Publishing are trademarks of Amazon.com, Inc., or its affiliates.

ISBN-13: 9781542020770
ISBN-10: 1542020778

Cover design by Lisa Horton

Printed in the United States of America

The
Last
Piece

PART ONE

1

ENGLAND

LILY: mum's disappeared ;-)
JULIA: ???????!!!
FELICITY: What?
LILY: am at the house now. she's gone!
JULIA: gone where?
LILY: on an adventure
JULIA: hahahaha
FELICITY: Will someone please tell me what is going on?
LILY: mum's gone to greece
JULIA: nice one
LILY: i know ju - cool huh?
FELICITY: When? How? Why?
LILY: this morning - by plane - don't know
FELICITY: Well did Dad know?
JULIA: has she left him? ;-)

LILY: *hahahaha - no she's coming back on Friday*
FELICITY: *What?????*
LILY: *thats what dad said*
FELICITY: *But she's having Hugo today.*
JULIA: *not any more she isn't!!*
FELICITY: *Very helpful Ju. Shit. Got to go and sort childcare.*

2

Felicity Nightingale hurled her mobile phone on to the freshly made bed, raised her hands to her forehead and gently massaged her temples with her thumbs. She forced herself to breathe steadily through her mouth until her heart began to beat a little more slowly. Wasn't it a pressure point, the temple? How hard did she have to press before she did herself some damage? She pressed a little harder.

The garish green display of the clock radio read 7.37. On Mondays she dropped Hugo off at her mother's at 8.00 on her way to the train station. That was the arrangement and had been since she first went back to work. It never varied, week in, week out, which was just how Felicity liked things. She knew where she was with an arrangement.

But now what was she meant to do? Her mother couldn't just disappear off to Greece without so much as a by-your-leave when she was supposed to be taking care of her grandson. It was ridiculous. And highly inconvenient.

To make matters worse, the nanny had gone to a funeral. Supposedly. Felicity wasn't entirely convinced that this was true, but Marie-Claude had chosen to clear the time off with Richard and not her (a fact that made her suspicious on its own) and Richard had just taken her request at face value and agreed.

Felicity knew that if she had spoken to the nanny herself her intuition would have sniffed out any lies, but Richard seemed far less adept at spotting untruths (which was quite ironic in the circumstances). Either that or he really didn't care one way or the other. This was probably more like it. They both knew that making alternative childcare arrangements for their son would tumble into her lap come what may, particularly as he was in London again and not due back until Friday. No – this lack of her mother and their arrangement was very much Felicity's problem.

Quickly she ran through her options as she traced a neat red line of lipstick around her mouth. She could call in sick, but she was supposed to be at an important board meeting and she wasn't about to miss the opportunity to be in attendance, even if her opinion was rarely sought or considered. Feigning illness was not on the cards.

She could ask her sister Lily to have Hugo. Lily would just absorb another child at her glitter-encrusted kitchen table without even batting an eyelid and it would suit Hugo, too. He loved spending time with his Aunt Lily and all his cousins, although Felicity had noticed a distinct decline in his table manners after a day spent at their house. Lily was unhelpfully relaxed about that kind of thing, but Felicity felt very strongly that it was important he knew how to hold a knife and fork properly. Her son might only be four, but it was never too early to learn basic etiquette and very hard to undo bad habits.

Her sister's lack of table-manner training wasn't what was putting her off, though. If Felicity asked Lily to help, then Lily would tell Julia and that would doubtless lead to one of their little 'twin chats' behind her back. Even when they'd been children themselves, Felicity had hated it when her siblings did that. It always left her feeling excluded and alone.

Time was ticking on. If she wasn't careful she was going to miss her train. It was no good. She was all out of options. She would have to leave Hugo with her father.

Felicity let out a deep and heartfelt sigh as she thought of the number of instructions she would need to provide him with to get him through a day with his grandson. For a start, her father had no idea what children should eat and would supply ice cream at 10.30 a.m. if Hugo asked him for it. There would no doubt be messy play, commenced willy-nilly without a thought for Hugo's clothes, even though she knew that her mother kept a little plastic art shirt for exactly this eventuality. And she would have to make it crystal clear that the park was totally out. Her father could not be trusted to watch Hugo properly. Last time they went, Felicity had caught Hugo at the very top of the climbing frame with her father just standing at the bottom and egging him on. God only knows what would have happened had he fallen from that height. In fact, Felicity had had nightmares about the various possibilities for days afterwards.

She checked her reflection in the mirror, smacking her newly painted lips together, and removed a stray blob of red from the corner of her mouth with the tip of her little finger. Perfect. Then she reached for her mobile and rang her parents' house. At least, she thought as she waited for it to be answered, she could quiz her father about what on earth was going on with her mother.

3

Julia sat in a traffic jam and laughed out loud. This was all too perfect. Never, in Julia's entire thirty-five years on this planet, had her mother done something so spontaneous, so, well, just plain out of character. Taking off to Greece without saying anything first? It was unheard of. Where was the rota of who would call in on their father, which pre-cooked meals he would eat when, which plants needed watering by how much and full instructions on the television programmes to record in her absence? She hadn't even left them the phone number of where she was staying. It was all so deliciously unlike her.

And poor Felicity. Julia obviously hadn't seen her face as the situation unfolded via WhatsApp, but she could picture it nonetheless. Priceless. She knew she shouldn't mock – she loved Felicity, despite all her flaws and insecurities – but what she wouldn't have paid to be a fly on the wall at the moment when her sister's carefully laid Hugo plans had all come crashing down around her.

She had half-expected to receive a distress call from Felicity herself, but it appeared that she fell quite a long way down the pecking order when it came to the care of her nephew. Lily had probably just whisked him up along with her five and saved the day calmly and without fuss. If she'd been in a different mood, Julia might have allowed this to niggle at her. Just because she had no children of her own didn't mean that she was incapable of looking after one. In many ways, and definitely in Felicity's eyes, the fact that she was a GP should have served to bump her up the rankings somewhat, and yet her phone had remained tellingly silent. Still, Julia couldn't get herself in a steam just because she was languishing at the bottom of her sister's 'go to' list. She was too far intrigued about what her mother was up to.

She pulled the car into her parents' road, the road where she had lived until she left for university. Even though she had now been gone for longer than she had been there, it always felt like coming home and she absorbed the familiar houses, the pavements where she'd played and the copper beech tree that leaned dangerously across the street, still threatening the telephone wires as it had done for decades. The warm evening light shimmered through its branches as she came to a stop in her parents' driveway.

Felicity's A5 cabriolet was already there – of course it was – with Hugo's child seat jammed incongruously into the back. In her sister's shoes, Julia would have swapped the car for something a little more practical, but Felicity's priorities had always been different from hers.

Julia edged her Clio in next to the Audi and climbed out. The house was beginning to look a little shabby, she thought as she locked the car. It had always been more of a much-loved family home than a show-house, but now Julia noticed that the aged silvering tarmac was crumbling in places and the grass, which had previously been restricted to the edges of the drive, was now growing in a thin stripe up the middle. They should have a word with their parents about getting someone in to keep on top of the basic maintenance, or it would turn into a massive job when the time came to sell. The horror of selling the family home briefly did battle in Julia's head with the practicalities of maintenance, but she shook the thought away. There was no need to think of selling yet. There was plenty of time left.

She walked up the drive, looking beyond the dandelions that poked through the ragged lawn like miniature Catherine wheels, and let herself into the house.

'Hi,' she called as she hung her keys on the hooks by the front door through force of habit.

Felicity had told her parents that the world was no longer as it had once been and that they must keep their door locked at all times and definitely not leave their keys where anyone could see them from outside.

'And feel like a prisoner in my own home?' their father had scoffed. 'No. Let the burglars come. It's not like we have anything worth stealing.'

That was probably true. The twenty-first century had largely left her parents untouched. Their television was ancient, their antiquated video recorder sitting beneath it, VHS tapes scattered around, each with a Post-it note attached saying what was currently on it. The tapes had been recorded over so many times that the pictures must surely wobble by now. Could you even buy VHS tapes any more? Julia had no idea – maybe she should investigate. The three of them had once clubbed together to buy their parents a new DVD player for Christmas but then Julia had found it in the garage some months later. It was still in the plastic packaging.

'We're in here,' her father's sonorous voice called from the sitting room.

He was sitting at the round table in the bay window, a jigsaw set out in front of him. He had his reading glasses on, his distance glasses perched on his forehead, giving the impression of two sets of eyes, rather like an alien. Bifocal, or, heaven forfend, varifocal lenses, were more than he could contemplate. Hugo was sitting opposite him, noise-cancelling headphones over his ears like mufflers and an iPad in his hand. He didn't look up, so Julia assumed that he was unaware of her arrival.

Felicity was tapping furiously into her phone. 'Just got to send this email . . .' she muttered to no one in particular.

Julia strolled over to her father and planted a kiss on the top of his head.

'Hi, Dad,' she said. 'How are you? Coping okay on your own?'

Felicity threw her a warning look, although Julia wasn't sure what she hadn't been supposed to say.

'I'm getting along just fine, thanks, Julia, or I would be if I could just locate this piece. I've been hunting for it for three days now. I'm beginning to think that your mother's hoovered it up.'

The front door banged again and the noise levels went up as lots of little voices rang through the house.

'Only me,' called Lily.

'In here,' Julia and her father chorused.

The twins Leo and Luca appeared first, sandy-blond heads that didn't quite reach the door handle bobbing along together until they arrived at Julia's side and each pressed themselves into one of her hips like a pair of slightly grubby bookends. Lily trailed behind her boys, the baby strapped to her chest by what looked like nothing more than a cotton scarf.

'In here, please,' she said to the remainder of her brood, but no more children appeared. 'Okay, but don't go near the road.'

The front door creaked open again and then slammed shut.

'Hi, hi,' said Lily, spinning her head from one side to another to spray her greeting at her collected family.

Julia felt a little burst of love for her twin, as she did each time they met. It was like an electrical impulse over which she had no control, but signalled that all was suddenly right with the world. Lily looked as wonderful as ever, her skin fresh and dewy and her china-blue eyes bright and clear. Whatever Lily had found to give her such deep contentment, Julia wished it could be bottled and sold by the gram.

'Would you like some squash?' her father asked the twins with a conspiratorial wink, and Hugo's ears seem to prick up despite the headphones.

'Yes, please,' the twins chorused.

Felicity let out a sigh of exasperation. 'Squash is so bad for them, Dad,' she said, as though her parental duties extended as far as her nephews.

Lily shrugged. Her children existed mainly outdoors, tracking the movement of the sun across the sky by way of a timepiece and stopping only when hunger called them back in. A bit of sugary naughtiness would do them no harm from time to time.

'Well, I can hardly give the twins some and not Hugo,' their father stated reasonably.

'Better not to have mentioned it at all then,' replied Felicity under her breath, and then added, 'Oh, all right. Just this once.'

Their father got to his feet, Julia noticing just a ghost of stiffness in his movements, and pointed his arm, sword-like, at the door.

'Come on, troops! To the kitchen!'

The menfolk left, leaving the women alone.

Felicity spoke first, an urgency to her voice that suggested she wanted to get everything said before their father returned. 'We need to find out what Mum is up to and how long she'll be gone and then we can set up a rota between us to sort out his meals. You know how shocking he is in the kitchen and he can't live off ready meals for more than a couple of days.'

Julia thought that he probably could and that many did, if her patients were anything to go by, but one of the advantages of all three of the Nightingale girls settling in their home town was that it was no problem to pop round in an evening with a little bit extra of whatever they had had for supper. In fact, she thought, it might be very pleasant to cook here sometimes, rather than at home, and share the meal with her father. She wondered idly why this thought had never occurred to her before and she made a note to suggest it to her mother when she got back from wherever it was that she'd gone.

'Obviously, it's going to be harder for me to drop everything, what with Hugo . . .'

Julia resisted the urge to glance at Lily.

'But I can do my best. And things'll be easier when Richard gets back tomorrow.'

Richard was away again, then? Sometimes Julia couldn't help but feel sorry for her sister, not because her husband was away so often but because of how exhausting it must be to be so stoical about it. Felicity appeared to accept her husband's absences as if they were a penance for some former misdemeanour, rather than an irritating fact of life.

'Well, I'm just up the road,' said Lily simply, 'so it's easy to pop by.'

Julia doubted that it was easy to pop anywhere with five children in tow, but Lily made everything look so effortless that you could just be sucked in by it and forget the logistical challenges of her life. Felicity clicked something on her phone and started squinting at the screen. She should probably get her eyes tested, Julia thought, but Felicity would never admit that her eyesight was slipping.

'I'm here today,' Felicity recited. 'Meeting late tomorrow, out of town. Wednesday is the third Wednesday so we're all around. Thursday is a bit vague but perhaps she'll be back by . . .'

'Who'll be back?' asked their father, kicking the door open with the toe of his slipper and then turning on the spot to push it wide with his back. He was carrying a tray on which sat three glasses of purple squash and what looked like four gin and tonics, the bubbles fizzing delicately. Ice cubes clinked as he set the tray down. 'I took the liberty of preparing a little something for us all,' he said, taking the largest of the gins and holding it aloft. 'Cheers!'

'Mum, of course,' replied Felicity. 'And I can't drink that. I'm driving.'

'Well, one little gin won't hurt,' replied their father, lifting a glass and offering it to Felicity, who looked as if he were passing her a glass of Novichok. Julia reached out and took the glass from him.

'I'll have one, thanks, Dad,' she said, and took a long gulp. The lemon tasted sharp on her tongue.

Lily handed the squash out. The twins, not much older than Hugo, seemed to manage the glasses with no difficulty, but Julia noticed Felicity watching her son, ready to pounce should a drop spill.

'Shall we sit down?' asked Julia and moved towards the well-worn sofas. For a year or two, when shabby chic had been all the rage, they had almost been in vogue, but now they just looked tired. They were still comfortable, though. Buy well, buy once was one of her father's mottos.

They all took a seat, Felicity perching next to Hugo, Julia and Lily and the baby taking the other sofa, their father in his armchair and the twins sprawled on the floor at their feet. Hugo, apparently feeling disadvantaged by sitting with the grown-ups, slipped down to roll around with them. Julia noticed that he left the iPad where it was, and that Felicity shot out a hand to make sure that it was safely in place and didn't fall. The boys immediately fell into a game of rock, paper, scissors.

'So, Dad,' said Julia. 'What's this all about? Where has Mum gone exactly?'

'And why?' chipped in Felicity with more aggression than the question merited.

Julia threw her a warning look, which Felicity ignored.

'Your mother has gone to Kefalonia until Friday,' their father said.

Julia noticed that his gaze was focused on the heads of his grandsons, seemingly to avoid meeting his daughters' eyes.

'An opportunity arose for her to go and she decided to take it,' he continued. 'With my blessing,' he added, in case this was in any doubt.

'Lucky Mum,' said Lily, shifting the baby in her lap and lifting up her shirt. The baby's head disappeared under a tent of white linen. Her father didn't flinch, but Julia knew that he still found breastfeeding to be a painfully intimate activity and one that he would rather not be witness to, despite Lily's practised discretion.

'What opportunity?' Felicity asked, clearly not as easily fobbed off as her sister.

'She received a letter inviting her and she decided to go,' their father replied. 'Personally, I think it's wonderful that the world is now so small that we can do these things so easily and I wholeheartedly support her decision.'

This sounded to Julia like a pre-prepared speech, and for the first time it crossed her mind that there might be more to her mother's trip than met the eye. Her father nodded then, and took another mouthful of his gin as if to signal the end of the matter.

Lily's mouth turned down a little at the corners as she considered this, and then she threw Julia a look that told her that her twin was content to let this be enough for now.

But now, Felicity was digging in. 'But what do I do with Hugo on Thursday? Mum knows that Thursday is the nanny's day off.'

'I can have him,' said Lily.

'As can I,' said their father, sounding just a little put out. Felicity could be so insensitive at times. Now she sniffed at all these offers of help as if they were an unwelcome solution to the fundamental problem of what had caused their mother to leave.

'You haven't had a row, have you, Dad?' asked Julia gently. 'She's not gone off in a strop?'

Their father settled his gaze on her now, his dark eyes full of mirth, the wrinkles around them deepening a little. 'No strops,' he said simply.

This, it seemed, was all they were going to get, no matter how much Felicity huffed and puffed. Julia found that she quite liked the intrigue of it all. Their mother was safe, which was the main thing, and no doubt someone would tell them what it had all been about eventually. They would just have to be patient.

'Well, I think it's very odd,' sniffed Felicity. 'And what about food, Dad?'

'What about it?' replied their father. 'I'm sure I shall require to eat some whilst your mother is away.'

Lily suppressed a giggle, and began to fuss the feeding baby to try and disguise it. Julia bit her lip. Was there anything funnier than Felicity being frustrated by their father?

'My point exactly,' Felicity pressed on. 'So, I thought we should draw up a rota and then one of us can come round each evening and bring you your dinner.'

The humour flooded from their father's face and he set his jaw as he had done if one of them had challenged him when they were girls.

'I may be older than you, Fliss darling, but I'm hardly incapable. Granted, the preparation of dinner has generally fallen to your mother to date, but I watched a very interesting television programme last night with one Jamie Oliver. He made food preparation look very simple. I thought I might have a go myself. It'll be a nice surprise for your mother when she gets back.'

'Good on you, Dad,' said Lily. 'I've got a couple of his recipe books. I'll bring them round and you can see if there's anything you fancy.'

Their father sat back in his seat and nodded happily, as if his becoming an excellent chef was now all but guaranteed.

The front door banged and Lily's two older boys returned, squabbling about who had been faster. Where the twins were fair, Frankie and Enzo had their father's Italian blood with dark hair and skin that toasted to a rich hazelnut colour at the first sign of sunshine.

'They're hungry,' said Lily, rolling her eyes. 'They're always hungry. I'd better take them home and get them fed.' She unhooked the baby from her breast and then, retying the scarf sling over one shoulder, she slid him back into his cocoon. 'Come on, you two,' she said to the twins. 'Home time.'

Then she picked up her gin and tonic and downed it in one, avoiding looking at Felicity who would no doubt have a view about the ethics of alcohol and breastfeeding. Hugo looked as if his world might end if his cousins left.

'You must come and play very soon, Hugo,' she added and his smile reblossomed.

Lily had a way of putting everyone at their ease. It was such a skill and when they'd been handing it out Lily must have gone round twice because she definitely seemed to have got more than her fair share.

Julia kissed her father on the cheek and then trailed after the rest of them outside. Felicity followed, closing, and locking, the door behind her.

In the garden the three of them stopped for a mini post-mortem whilst Lily's boys chased each other around the lawn.

'It's all very strange,' said Felicity as she fastened a complaining Hugo into his seat, an operation that required almost a contortionist's skill on her part, given the size of the car. 'But I think everything's okay, don't you?'

It was rare, Julia thought, this element of doubt in her eldest sister. Only when the three of them were alone together would Felicity ever let her guard down, and there was no guarantee that it would happen even then.

'It's fine,' replied Lily. 'It's certainly weird, but Dad seems happy enough. I wish he'd tell us what's really going on, though.'

Julia agreed. It was obvious that their father was holding something important back. He had mentioned that their mother had received an invitation, but who had sent it, and what was so alluring that she had dropped her life with them and raced over to Greece at a moment's notice? Still, one thing was clear. There would be no answers for any of them just yet.

4

GREECE

Cecily looked out of the window and across the wing of the plane. The sky beyond was the purest blue, but if she tilted her head to look below her all she saw was a thick blanket of grey. They truly were above the clouds. It felt a little bit magical, almost on a par with being over the rainbow, a secret place where wonderful things might happen.

She wanted to tap the arm of the woman in the next seat to tell her, too, but then she supposed that perhaps the stranger might see things differently and so she focused on the clouds instead, spotting which parts were thicker, which more fluffy-looking.

She must have been above the clouds before – this wasn't the first time she had been in an aeroplane, after all – but somehow she had never noticed. The weather was a little disappointing, though. She would have preferred to peer down at a tiny world beneath them. Where would they be now – somewhere over France perhaps, or Italy? Her mouth pulled itself into an involuntary little smirk. She was on her way to Greece. Then she remembered why, and a tiny wave of panic washed over her.

She wriggled herself down into her seat, trying to block out the sound of the whimpering child a few rows behind her. The sound set off a chain reaction in her, resulting in a twinge of guilt. By disappearing without a word, she had let Felicity down and her conscience was pricking her uncomfortably. Still, she felt sure that the problem of what do to with Hugo would have been sorted without too much difficulty. Norman was perfectly happy to look after him on his own and having his grandson in the house would keep his mind busy and stop him overthinking. Cecily hoped that that was what had happened, but there was little point in worrying about it now. She was on a plane 36,000 feet above the earth and her daughter's childcare arrangements were no longer her concern.

She closed her eyes and tried not to think about the letter nestling in her handbag. In truth, she had thought of little else in the days since it arrived and it made her feel . . . she wasn't entirely sure how, but it wasn't pleasant. Still, there was nothing to be done whilst she sat on the plane. Everything would no doubt become clearer when she arrived at the hotel. She just had to be patient. So instead, she forced her mind to think about what she had packed, whether she had brought enough knickers and how she might wash the dirty ones if she hadn't.

'Any drinks or snacks?' said a voice to her left, and she snapped open her eyes. The air steward, resplendent in a yellow jacket with white trim around collar and cuffs was staring at her expectantly. His skin was an unusual colour, as if he'd been dipped in maple syrup.

'I don't know,' Cecily said. 'What do you have?'

The air steward did an excellent job of not actually rolling his eyes at her, but she saw his chest rise as he took a deep breath before answering. 'We have a wide range of hot and cold drinks, sweet and savoury snacks, meal deals and alcoholic beverages,' he said, just about managing to maintain a civil tone.

Cecily, in her fluster, only heard the final option. 'A gin and tonic, please,' she heard herself say. 'And some nuts?'

What time was it? Was this an appropriate order? She had no idea, but the person across the aisle was sipping Stella Artois from a can so at least she wouldn't be alone. She had a quick look at her watch. It was gone midday – not too shocking. And she was on a holiday of sorts. Wasn't she entitled to relax a little, let her hair down?

'Ice and lemon?' asked the air steward as he retrieved a tiny bottle of Gordon's from one of the drawers in his trolley.

Cecily nodded. Decision made. Well, that wasn't too hard, was it?

With her plastic cup resting lightly on its little paper coaster she resumed staring out of the window. Yes, Norman and Hugo would be getting along just fine without her. Hugo was such a funny little child, so solemn and contained, but with a quirky sense of humour that bubbled to the surface once in a while and took you by surprise. He wasn't a bit like Lily's kids, who were basically feral. But then Felicity wasn't a bit like Lily so it was only to be expected.

Six grandsons. What a blessing. And would there be any more? Only time would tell. Felicity had struggled so hard to have Hugo that it seemed unlikely she would go for a second. Lily and Marco might try for a girl, she supposed. Julia showed no sign of settling down with anyone. Girls were having babies later and later these days, Cecily knew, but there must come a point at which one decided it was no longer feasible. Julia would surely be getting quite close to that cut-off, particularly if you factored in the time it took to find a suitable partner. And who knew what news was awaiting her in Greece? But she mustn't go jumping the gun. This could all turn out to be the wildest of wild goose chases.

When the pilot announced that there were ten minutes to landing, Cecily's stomach began to turn somersaults. She had never negotiated an airport by herself before. Usually she had Norman at her side to take control. What order did things happen in? She could never remember. Was it baggage reclaim first or passport control? Not that it mattered. No doubt there would be signs in English as well as Greek. The plane was full of English holidaymakers and surely not all of them spoke Greek. She had learned a little at school, although that had been Ancient Greek, of course. Was there much crossover between the two languages, she wondered? Not that she could remember much of what she'd learnt, and certainly not anything that might translate to 'Where do I reclaim my suitcase?'

She reached forward and took the letter out of her bag, slipping it out of the envelope and unfolding it carefully. Her eyes skimmed to the part she wanted to check.

'Please go to the Travel Connect desk and they will direct you to the minibus that will bring you to the hotel,' she read for the umpteenth time. Would they actually be expecting her? There had been no chance to send a reply in the timescale, so she just had to trust that everything would be just as the letter suggested.

When it had arrived three short days before, and Cecily had first read its contents, it had taken her an hour or maybe two before she could do anything other than just stare at it. Norman had been out with his rambling friends and Cecily had sat herself at the kitchen table and reread it over and over until she knew its contents off by heart. When Norman returned, all pink-cheeked and muddy, she had simply passed the letter to him without explanation.

'Oh,' he said when he read it, and then, 'Oh my.'

Cecily said nothing, Norman having captured her thoughts precisely.

'Will you go?' Norman asked simply.

'I don't see that I have much choice,' Cecily replied.

'But Monday? It's very short notice.'

Cecily shrugged. 'It is what it is. I'm not sure that there's much I can do about it. I rang the travel agents and they say there's a flight on Monday morning. Shall I book a seat?'

There was, of course, a chance that Norman would have objected, raised the obvious concerns about her venturing across the globe on the say-so of a letter received out of the blue and containing only the sketchiest of information. But she had known that he wouldn't. How could he?

As the wheels of the plane unfurled and it hurtled towards the runway, Cecily refolded the letter, placed it carefully in the envelope and slotted it back into the pocket of her handbag. The invitation had been made. She had accepted it. Nothing could be more simple.

5

The Hotel Aphrodite was an hour's drive from the airport, or so they told Cecily at the Travel Connect desk. They had been expecting her, which was a relief, and the lank-haired girl ticked her name off the list with an extravagant flourish, as if she were the very last to arrive and it was now a job well done. In fact, another four people appeared after her and they all clambered into the minibus with their luggage and then sat back and watched the unfamiliar countryside take shape beyond the window as they drove along increasingly narrow roads.

After a while they reached the coast. The clear turquoise water shimmered beneath them and the cliffs rose up from the roadside, the earth a vibrant zingy orange. It looked like a page in a travel brochure. Cecily had always assumed that those images were manipulated somehow, the colours turned up to make the scene even more appealing, but it seemed not. Kefalonia really did look like the pictures and it was breathtakingly beautiful. She wished Norman was there to share it with her but she could tell him all about it when she got home. And in a way, it was quite nice to be striking out on her own.

She leant back against the headrest. So far so good, she thought. The next test would be whether the hotel had a room for her when she tried to check in, but Cecily took comfort from the fact that she had been on the minibus list. It was all working just as the letter said it would.

They made several stops on the way for people to get out. One couple, who were dressed alike in matching waterproof jackets despite the azure sky, muttered under their breath that their accommodation didn't look much like the picture on the website as they descended the stairs. Cecily smiled to herself. The British abroad were a race apart.

Eventually there was just her and one other woman left on the bus. Cecily, keen to avoid a conversation when she had so many gaps in her knowledge as to why she was here, did not make eye contact, but she could feel the woman staring at her and sensed her desire to start a conversation.

'Are you going to the retreat?' the stranger asked her, when it became obvious that Cecily was not going to engage unprompted.

Cecily nodded and gave her a thin smile.

'Have you been before?' the woman pressed on, undeterred. 'I come every year. It's marvellous. Just what the doctor ordered. I usually just go to a couple of yoga classes and then spend the rest of the time by the pool. One year, I did the detox programme but the food is soooo goood . . .' – she stretched the words out and let them roll around her mouth as if she were actually tasting the food there and then – 'that it would be a crime not to eat it, you know what I mean?'

The woman was carrying more weight than might be considered good for her but Cecily was heartened by the information. She would have survived on rabbit food for the week if that had been required, but she was grateful that it wouldn't be necessary.

'That's good,' she replied simply, and hoped it would be enough.

As the minibus drew to a halt the woman let out a huge sigh as if arriving home after a long journey, then sprang down the steps and disappeared up the path and into the building, her suitcase bouncing along behind her. Cecily sat where she was until the driver came and eyed her quizzically.

'Aphrodite Hotel?' he asked in a heavily accented voice.

Cecily nodded and he gestured to the door. She was going to have to go inside, but still she hesitated.

He raised his eyebrows. 'You go in,' he asked, 'or I take you back?'

'I go in,' she said, repeating his pidgin English back at him, but actually at that moment she would have returned from whence she came quite happily.

Once she had her case, the driver clambered back into the minibus and drove away, leaving Cecily standing on the doorstep of the hotel like a wartime evacuee. It was an attractive building, two storeys high with expansive arched windows, each with a little Juliet balcony in front, and painted a greyish pink, like the underside of a mushroom. Tall urns planted with yuccas and other softer foliage were spaced evenly across the frontage, and the terracotta roof tiles were set off perfectly by the deep blue sky. It looked smart and well kept, which was promising.

Cecily took a deep breath. If everything went wrong, at least it was a nice spot to be in for a week. She could have a little holiday here and then just go back home and do her best to forget all about it.

But she wasn't going to get anywhere if she didn't actually go inside. With her heart in her mouth, she pushed open the front door.

The reception was bright and airy, the floors and walls all a cool white marble with yet more healthy-looking plants in huge pots positioned tastefully in the corners. The desk was at the far end and Cecily headed for it, the wheels of her suitcase clattering noisily across the tiles.

The man on reception smiled expectantly. 'Good afternoon,' he said in English.

Her fair hair and skin always seemed to betray her nationality.

'My name is Cecily Nightingale,' said Cecily. She hoped that this would be enough, as she wasn't sure of any of the details of her stay. He nodded as if he knew precisely who she was, and Cecily relaxed a little.

'Ah, Mrs Nightingale,' he said. 'Did you have a pleasant trip?'

'Very pleasant, thank you,' replied Cecily brightly.

'You are here with the retreat, I understand. We have a room booked for you overlooking the sea. I hope this is good.'

Cecily nodded. 'Lovely,' she said.

'The costs are all dealt with, but if I may take your passport . . .'

Cecily dug it out of her handbag and handed it over. Costs all dealt with. What did that mean? Was she to stay free of charge? That was very kind, but perhaps it would have been better if she paid her own way. She was already feeling exposed and a long way from where she felt comfortable. This generosity just compounded it. But now wasn't the time to question things, she could see that. There would be time to clarify the situation when she had a better idea of what was what.

Formalities completed, the man called a boy who took her suitcase and led her up some stairs, along a corridor and finally to her room. He opened the door and then stepped aside to let her enter first. It was a beautiful space, again decorated mainly in white with pops of blue and pink in the cushions and bedspread, and a tall glass vase containing a single woody stem of purple bougainvillea. The window did indeed look out across the sparkling Ionian Sea.

Cecily dug in her purse for a tip for the boy, but he did not wait for one and simply let himself out, closing the door quietly behind him.

What would happen next? she wondered.

She had been summoned. She was here. And now she would just have to wait.

6

ENGLAND

Lily scrolled through the online university website. You could do free courses in so many different subjects. Consumer Behaviour and Psychology. An Introduction to Cryptography. Digital Wellness. What even was that? An Introduction to HR. Maybe she should take that and then she would be able to impress Felicity with her newly discovered knowledge. Actually, what was the point? She probably wouldn't understand it and she definitely wouldn't be able to pick up from a free course what Felicity had learned from nearly fifteen years in the job.

Perhaps she should try something that neither of her sisters knew anything about. Her eyes settled on a course entitled 'The Importance of Play in Everyday Life'. Well, Felicity definitely didn't know much about that, Lily thought wryly, and then reprimanded herself. Her sister had many other strengths. Lily clicked on the link. An image of a middle-aged woman waving her arms in the air and grinning as if she had just been given the answer to the secret of life filled the screen. Lily ran her eyes down the programme and saw that most of it was what she considered to be common sense, and yet the course would take three hours a week for seven weeks to complete. What could there possibly be to talk about for all that time? There was so much about life that Lily didn't know.

'You should stop worrying about it,' her husband Marco had said once in one of their very many conversations about what Lily considered to be her inadequacies. 'You don't have to go to university to understand life. Look at me! I'm a success, no?'

Lily had to agree. Marco had come to England from a village outside Ancona to work in his uncle's pizzeria when he was just sixteen, and now he ran a small chain of his own restaurants.

'You are a success,' she said. 'Of course you are, but no one in your family expected you to do anything else. I am the only one in my family not to go to university. It's different for me.'

Marco had shaken his head. 'What you have, it's more important. We made children and you care for them. This is the most important job in the whole world. Felicity has only Hugo and she gives him to someone else to look after and Julia has no one. Tell me, what would you rather have, our babies or a boring job in an office?'

When he put it like that Lily knew he was right, even though she winced a little when he criticised her sisters. What upset her, though, was not that she hadn't gone to university, but more that she couldn't have gone. She didn't have the grades. She just wasn't smart enough.

In many ways she was lucky to be alive at all. Lily had forced her way into the world, uninvited, at thirty-one weeks, born just a scrap of a thing at two and a half pounds in weight. She had been rushed to an incubator where she had been ventilated and fed through a tube and it had been touch and go, her mother told her. More than once they had thought that they would lose her but Lily had fought on, and little by little she had grown stronger until she was able to breathe on her own. But this premature start to life had meant that she had reached the various developmental stages later than was expected, and some she just hadn't reached at all.

And where was Julia, her twin, whilst all this was going on? Julia was still safe and warm in their mother's womb. Through what many had termed divine intervention, her mother's body had relaxed after it had expelled Lily, her muscles no longer contracting. By the time Julia finally emerged, pink and healthy and able to breathe unaided, Lily had already been on the planet for seventy-one days.

The press had loved the story. Miracle twins born nine weeks apart. Their proud parents had posed for a photo with both of their girls, Lily waif-like next to her younger but stronger twin, and a feature had appeared in the newspaper. The history of their births had been a talking point ever since. Twins who didn't share a birthday. What a thing.

Their mother said it was wonderful that they each had their own special birthday and didn't have to share, but Lily had never felt like that. As far as she was concerned, she should have been born on the same day as Julia and hated that she had to celebrate alone, as if she wasn't worthy of the 'real' day. Julia had always been happy for Lily to share her birthday and Lily knew that she was expected to feel special for having two birthdays, like the Queen, but nothing about it had ever felt special to her.

When the twins had gone to school, one in age five uniform and the other in the smallest sized everything that still had to be taken in, it had quickly become apparent that having their real birthday wasn't the only advantage that Julia had over Lily. Lily had been late to read and write, struggled with her times tables and never really got the hang of maths. So when Julia went to university to read medicine, Lily had done a qualification in childcare and become a nursery nurse. Not that this was something Lily regretted. She'd made a far better nursery nurse than Julia would ever be.

Still, she couldn't help but feel a little cheated out of the life that she might have had if she had only managed to stay in place for a couple of months longer.

So, instead of following a career like her sisters, Lily had chosen a different path, and had babies. Lots of babies. And the success of Marco's business meant that she was in the luxurious position of being able to stay at home and bring them up herself. As it turned out, neither of her sisters seemed to be particularly good at breeding and Lily knew that both Felicity and Julia envied her her simple choices. Couldn't life be ironic sometimes?

Lily closed down the computer and checked the time. The baby would be up from his nap in twenty minutes and then they would wander along to collect the boys from school and playgroup. There was just time to ring her mother first. Lily liked to talk to her mother most days. She was different from Fliss and Jules there, too. Apparently, Felicity only rang to make arrangements for Hugo, and Julia almost never rang. Lily got as far as finding her mobile and retrieving the number on speed dial when she remembered. Her mother wasn't there. She was in Greece.

Lily's shoulders slumped. Her mother didn't use a mobile phone, having refused to embrace the one they had bought for her.

'If I'm in then I'll answer the phone,' she'd said, 'and if I'm out you can leave a message on the answerphone and I'll ring you back. It's worked perfectly well like that for thirty years. I see no reason to change things now.' And she hadn't. But now she was going to be gone for almost a week and Lily had no way of getting in touch. The thought of their separation stabbed at her chest. She didn't even have a number for where her mother was staying, although her father probably did.

So Lily dialled her parents' house and waited for the phone to be answered. Her father would probably be at home but as the ringing went on, seven, eight, nine times, Lily's heart sank. The answerphone clicked on after ten rings. Then, just as she was about to give up, her father lifted the receiver.

'Nightingale here,' he said in his deep voice. Felicity had told him not to answer with his name as it gave cold callers a perfect way in, but still he did it.

'Dad, hi. It's Lily.'

'Hello, Lily. Your mother's not here,' he replied by force of habit.

'I know that. She's in Greece.'

'Ah, yes. Quite so.'

'I was ringing to make sure you're okay. Do you need anything at all?'

'No, thank you. I am perfectly fine. Plenty to be getting on with, you know. I promised your mother that I'd tackle the shed whilst she's gone. It's got into a bit of a state. I've been to the tip twice already today.'

'Don't overdo it, will you?'

'I'll have you know that I'm hardly decrepit!' Her father sounded a little put out.

'I know that, but you are seventy, Dad. Marco will do the tip run for you. It's no trouble.'

Her father gave a little harrumph.

'And have you been to the shops? Do you have plenty to eat?'

'I have,' he replied, but then his tone changed to something considerably lighter. 'It's amazing what you can get these days. I found a recipe that had something called pak choi in it and blow me but they had it in Tesco.'

'That's great, Dad. Did you get some?'

'I did!' He sounded so proud. 'So I'm having beef noodle broth for supper. I've always loved Asian food, although your mother's less keen. She says it's too wet. I recorded this programme and I've

32

written everything down. I'll watch it over again before I start. I'm really looking forward to it actually.'

'And have you heard from Mum?'

'No. Not yet. She'll ring when she's good and ready, I expect.'

This surprised Lily. As far as she knew her parents were never apart, never really had been across the forty plus years of their marriage.

'What's this all about, Dad?' Lily asked now. 'Is Mum okay?'

There was a brief but discernible pause at the other end. 'She is. This is just something that she had to do. I know it must look odd to you girls but I'm sure she'll talk to you about it when the time is right.' Another pause. Lily opened her mouth to say something else but then her father continued, 'Don't ask me any more, Lily. It's for your mother to explain.'

'All right,' replied Lily. 'But you're okay?'

'I am perfectly fine. And now, if you'll excuse me, the shed is calling.'

Lily smiled down the phone. 'Well, enjoy your beef noodle thing. I'll ring again tomorrow.'

'There's really no need, Lily. I'm perfectly all right on my own.'

You might be, thought Lily, but I'm not.

7

Julia was tempted to order another drink before Sam arrived but she had no reason to be nervous – not really. And she wanted to keep a clear head. She didn't want to forget anything or agree to anything by accident.

The bar was quiet, as she'd hoped it would be, and she took her glass and made her way to a table by the wall, away from any thoroughfares. It was unlikely that anyone would be eavesdropping on their conversation but she would rather not take any chances. It was going to be a weird enough discussion without worrying that a stranger was listening in.

She had butterflies. It had been so long since she'd been excited about anything enough to give her actual butterflies. It was like being a girl again. This buzz had even woken her up in the night, which was unheard of.

But then, every so often, her adrenaline became mixed with a different emotion as it pumped through her veins: panic. Somewhere at the back of her mind the little voice of reason kept chirping up. What are you doing? How will you afford it? Do you think you can cope? Really?! And what will everyone say? What will Lily say?

Julia hadn't told Lily. She told her twin everything and yet somehow she had managed not to mention what she was planning;

not in any detail anyway. They had mooted the possibility at various points over the last five years but only in a 'pie in the sky' kind of way. To be fair, Lily had been surprised but not against the idea, and Julia was sure that she would still support her, but she wasn't taking any chances. Now that she had decided that this was definitely what she wanted, she felt the need to get all her ducks in a row before she told anyone. Except Sam, of course. Sam had been brilliant about the whole thing so far.

And there he was, strolling into the bar and scanning the room until he spotted her. He raised an arm in casual salute and then went to the bar. A minute later Julia saw him laughing with the barman. He was pushing his thick dark hair away from his face as he spoke and then leaning forward as if the pair of them were sharing a secret. She rolled her eyes. Sam was flirting. Now! When they had so much to discuss. God, the man was incorrigible. She couldn't blame him, though. The barman was kind of cute in a clean-cut sort of way.

By the time Sam finally wandered across to her his pint was already half drunk.

'When you've quite finished . . .' laughed Julia.

'Sorry. Got distracted. I'm all yours now though,' he said, settling himself in the chair opposite hers. 'How are you? All good?'

'Fine, thanks,' replied Julia. 'Except my mother seems to have disappeared.'

'For real? Have you contacted the police?' His grey eyes were wide and for a moment Julia got a flash of the boy she'd known at school.

'Well, she's not disappeared as such. We know where she is. Kefalonia. We just don't know why she's gone.'

'How very intriguing. Has she left your father? Is she having a tawdry affair with a Greek waiter like in *Shirley Valentine*?'

This possibility hadn't even crossed Julia's mind. She considered it now and rejected it. 'No. Dad seems to be in on it but he's keeping schtum. It's all mightily perplexing. Fliss nearly had a fit.'

Sam smirked.

'She wasn't best pleased, but mainly because Mum was supposed to be looking after Hugo and hadn't told her that she wouldn't be there.'

Sam raised his eyebrows. He might have made some comment about the preciousness of Hugo, but he didn't need to. They both knew what he was thinking. 'Well, it's all happening with the Nightingales at the moment,' he said simply, and he was right. It was.

Julia took a swig of her wine. It had gone a little warm and was less enjoyable as a result, but she could make do for the time being. She was eager to cut straight to the business in hand and not get distracted by the dramas of the rest of her family. She put the glass down decisively as if to signal a change in the conversational direction.

'So,' she began tentatively. 'Are you sure about this, Sam? You haven't changed your mind? If you have then that's totally fine. I'll completely understand. But please tell me now, so that I know.' She looked straight into his eyes, searching them for any modicum of doubt, but found none.

'Of course I haven't. I didn't just say yes on a whim, you know.' His tone was bordering on the offended.

'No. I know that,' Julia added hastily. 'But it is a big decision, the biggest really. And I don't want you to feel pressured in any way. I just want to give you the chance to back out now . . . before it's too late.'

Sam leant across the table and took Julia's hand in his. His hands were cool, chilled by the glass that they had just put down. 'Dearest Julia. I have known you almost my whole life. I love you like a sister and I am thrilled and honoured that you have asked me to do this incredibly special thing for you. I have thought about it carefully and I can categorically say that I'm not going to change my mind.'

Julia let out a sharp breath. 'You don't know how pleased I am to hear you say that,' she said.

'And are you sure?' he asked her.

Julia's eyes looked up to the ceiling, as if the answer to this question could be located in the rafters. She chewed on her lip as she pushed the idea around in her head yet again. 'Yes,' she said in strong, clear tones. 'I am single. There is no Prince Charming waiting in the wings for me. I have a good job with good benefits. I have my own home. I have lots of friends and family nearby and I am thirty-five. Unless Mr Right puts in an appearance very, very soon I'm going to be older than I want to be. So yes. I'm sure.'

'Great!' said Sam, and he raised his glass to toast the decision. 'To two becoming three,' he added, nudging his glass against hers.

A rush of excitement flooded through Julia from her hairline all the way down to her toes. This was really going to happen. Well, maybe that was a little bit premature, but it was at least closer to happening than it had ever been in her life before.

8

GREECE

Cecily had unpacked her suitcase. She'd hung her skirts, dresses and cardigans in the wardrobe and laid the rest of her things neatly in the drawers. It had taken her less than ten minutes and now she sat on the edge of the bed and looked around her tidy, solitary room. She couldn't think when she had last been in a hotel without Norman, if indeed she ever had. It was an adventure and she ought to be feeling intrepid and independent but in fact, all she felt was small and vulnerable. She had done as the letter had asked her and so had put herself on the line for potential rejection and humiliation. The thought of what might happen next made her stomach knot.

She reached into her handbag and retrieved the letter that had sent her chasing off across the globe. She had read it so many times already, but again she let her eyes rest upon its contents. Its style was very matter-of-fact; just the bare bones of what had happened, which was enough to convince Cecily of its authenticity, and practical information about the arrangements for the meeting. The invitation, such as it was, gave nothing away about its author, which in itself might have made Cecily feel even more trepidatious if she had allowed herself to think about that, but its contents were clear enough. 'If you would like to meet to discuss this then come to the hotel as suggested below.' That was it. There was nothing to suggest that it had been a difficult or emotional letter to write and it revealed none of the details that Cecily craved, but there was nothing she could do about that. She would just have to wait.

She stood up, paced across the room to the window and looked out across the rocks to the sea beyond. The sunlight made the water twinkle as the waves danced across its surface. Her stomach growled ominously and the sound made her realise how hungry she was. What with all the busyness of travel she had barely eaten anything since breakfast. Maybe she should wander downstairs. There was bound to be someone who could explain how the retreat worked and point her in the direction of dinner. She remembered the woman on the minibus, who had mentioned that the food was the thing that brought her back again and again, and her mouth watered.

With that decision made, Cecily quickly changed out of her travelling clothes and put on a cotton skirt in a pretty floral print and a short-sleeved blouse. Her arms and décolletage had turned a honeyed brown in the early part of the summer at home, but her legs still held on to the pasty hue of winter. Not that anyone here would be looking at her legs, but she still liked to look her best. Perhaps she could get some sun on them over the next few days, colour them up a little? She slipped her feet into her sandals, picked up her bag and key card and left the room.

The reception area was much busier than it had been when she'd arrived. Women wearing yoga leggings or sarongs were hovering about the space. Each seemed to be holding a cocktail glass. Cecily scanned the space to see where the drinks were coming from and spotted a table of glasses filled with bright orange and red liquid. She headed that way.

A woman was standing behind the table handing out the drinks. She was tall and slim with cascades of ebony curls that threatened to totally swamp her features. She was dressed in floating white linen, her bare arms toned and tanned, with leather bangles round her wrists and delicate silver rings on every finger. When she saw Cecily, her face lit up.

'You must be Cecily,' she said, coming out from behind the table. As soon as she was close enough she wrapped her arms around Cecily and pulled her into a strong hug. 'I'm so pleased to meet you. I'm Sofia.' She paused as if waiting for some form of recognition, but Cecily was none the wiser.

'Are you in charge?' she ventured.

Sofia smiled, seeming to sense how very little information Cecily had to go on. 'Sorry, yes. This is my retreat and I lead the yoga, too, so if you come along to the classes then you'll be with me. I'll get you a timetable after dinner and fill you in on everything. Here, have one of these.'

She led Cecily back to the drinks table and passed her a glass. 'It's a virgin tequila sunrise,' she explained. 'We don't serve alcohol but we're not puritanical about it. If you fancy a glass of something then there's nothing stopping you from wandering into a bar in the town. Have a taste.' Sofia smiled widely and nodded at the cocktail.

Cecily put the glass to her mouth and took a sip. It wasn't bad; very orangey and fresh with a kick of something sharp, but she couldn't help thinking that it would be better with tequila and grenadine.

'We meet for cocktails at seven-thirty each evening so that we can chat over our day before dinner. People tend to take them outside.' Sofia gestured towards an open French window that led out towards a pool.

40

'How lovely,' said Cecily, although going out and standing amongst a group of women she didn't know felt less than appealing at that moment.

As if realising her reluctance, Sofia pressed on. 'I know you're here by yourself but really, that's no problem. Ladies often come alone. There's such a friendly vibe and we've all got so much in common that it's easy to find people to chat to. Come. Let me introduce you.'

Sofia took Cecily by the arm and guided her towards the open door. Outside the air felt balmy on her skin and in her nostrils as she breathed in the heady scent of jasmine. Cicadas chirped noisily nearby.

'Everyone!' said Sofia, loudly enough that people stopped talking and turned towards her. 'This is Cecily from Yorkshire. She has just arrived and is here on her own so please could you all make her feel welcome.'

Cecily was impressed that Sofia knew this detail even though they hadn't discussed it. She was either particularly professional or she had taken a special interest in her. From the warmth of her greeting Cecily suspected that Sofia knew about the letter that had summoned her. Just what else did she know? Cecily wondered.

A murmur of welcomes rippled around the terrace and Cecily saw faces glowing in the golden light of evening, all turned to her expectantly. She felt suddenly shy. There were maybe a dozen women there, sitting in groups looking relaxed and happy. Most of them had the same vivid drink as she did but others cupped steaming mugs in their hands, which seemed odd on a hotel terrace in Greece, but she supposed wasn't, really.

'Hello,' she said to the collected mass, shrugging apologetically. 'Isn't it a beautiful evening?'

The small group nearest to her pulled their chairs back and made a space for Cecily to sit.

'Right,' said Sofia. 'Enjoy your drinks and I'll see you all for dinner at eight.'

Cecily turned her attention back to the group that she was now with. There were five around her table: two young women in their twenties whose skin and hair shone with health and who appeared to be friends already, judging by the way they were sitting, and then three older women who she suspected were also travelling solo. None were as old as she was, not that that mattered.

They smiled at her warmly but then returned to the conversations that they had been having before her arrival. Cecily tried to tune in. The younger two were discussing where to buy the best yoga wear and complaining about the cost. It wasn't a topic that Cecily could add much to so she turned her attention to the others. They were discussing diets that they had tried and failed with. Cecily didn't feel excluded, but at the same time there was no need to contribute to the discussion. It seemed to be enough just to sit and smile benignly and she was grateful that the group didn't appear to be at all cliquey.

Could any of them be her, she wondered? Cecily drank in their faces as they spoke, searching for anything familiar but finding nothing. Was this how the week was going to be, with her staring at strangers and chasing shadows?

'Whereabouts in Yorkshire do you live?' asked the woman nearest to her, making her jump. She was plump with a blonde, frizzy halo of hair that looked like it needed a good cut.

'Harrogate,' said Cecily. 'Do you know it?'

'My husband's brother lives in Doncaster, but we don't speak to him any more,' the woman replied, as if this explained her entire understanding of the county.

'Where are you from?' asked Cecily. God, she hated small talk.

'Milton Keynes,' came the reply.

All Cecily knew about Milton Keynes was that it had been a new town and there were concrete cows. Or at least there had been.

She had no idea if they were still there and worried that mentioning them might make her sound out of date.

'How lovely,' she said instead. 'And how long have you been here?'

'I arrived on Friday. I'm here for two weeks. I'm juicing,' she added with significance.

Cecily had no idea what that meant and it must have shown on her face.

'Instead of eating,' the woman clarified. 'Which is a shame, because the food is fantastic here. But needs must . . .' She patted her stomach, which wobbled like jelly and made Cecily feel slightly nauseous.

'Oh, I see,' she said. 'Is that hard? Not eating, I mean.' Cecily couldn't imagine existing solely on juice; surely it couldn't be good for you.

'It's not so bad,' the woman said. 'You get used to it. And no pain, no gain. Or loss, as the case would have it.' She chuckled to herself in a cheerful kind of way. 'I'm Sue,' she added.

'Cecily,' said Cecily.

After that Cecily followed the conversation as it flitted backwards and forwards, smiling and trying to look engaged and interested but without contributing much. The sun was dropping fast in the sky now, a fiery ball against a backdrop of orange and pink. From this terrace you would be able to see when it reached the water and there was already a golden triangle of light resting on the rippling waves. When her girls were little, Cecily had told them that if they listened hard they might hear the sun hiss as it hit the water. Her children were never far from her mind, she realised, even though they were grown up with children of their own.

Then Cecily thought about Norman, alone in their house in Harrogate, and worried about how he was getting along. No doubt he would be working on his jigsaw and would settle down later with whatever drama was on the television at nine o'clock. She would be on his mind too, she knew. She would call tomorrow, when she had something to report.

At eight o'clock and without any prompting the women all stood and began to move towards the dining room, as if pre-programmed. Cecily, now so hungry that her stomach was almost painful, was happy to follow them.

The high-ceilinged dining room was set with four large tables, each with appetising bowls of food placed in the centre. Cecily drifted from the group that she'd been with and found a seat with a different one, just in case there was a face she might recognise amongst the women there. No one seemed to object and soon she was tucking into a huge plate of food. It was very fresh and absolutely delicious, just as the woman on the bus had said.

Cecily was serving herself a second helping when Sofia appeared at her elbow. She was holding various pieces of paper.

'I have to pop out, Cecily, so we'll catch up properly tomorrow, but these are for you. There's a health screening form and the programme for the week. All the classes are out on the covered terrace next to the pool, so just take yourself there five minutes beforehand. There's no pressure. You can do as little or as much as you like.'

Cecily took the papers. 'Thanks, Sofia,' she said.

'And there's this, too,' said Sofia, and handed her a sealed envelope. *Mrs C. Nightingale* was typed on the front. Sofia held her gaze for a moment, as if trying to convey the significance of this third document. Cecily felt her stomach lurch and all the delicious food that she had just consumed seemed to turn to stone inside her.

'Thank you,' she managed to say.

'No worries. So I'll see you in the morning. Enjoy your evening and sleep well.'

Cecily nodded, but if this letter was from Marnie then she couldn't imagine that she would sleep at all.

9

Somehow Cecily got through the rest of dinner with the envelope burning a hole in her handbag. Part of her was desperate to run back to her room and tear it open, but instead she stayed where she was, dying to know yet fearful of the knowledge.

It was more than she could manage to make conversation, though, so she just sat and appeared to be listening as the chat continued around her, nodding from time to time and smiling but contributing nothing. Her mind was full of the envelope and the knowing look on Sofia's face as she handed it over. What had it meant?

It had to be another message from Marnie. There was no other explanation that made any sense, but the idea made Cecily feel lightheaded and distanced from what was going on around her, as if someone had turned the volume down. Again, Cecily cast her eyes around the collected group. Was Marnie amongst them? Most of them were too young, a couple too old, and the remainder? Well, she had no idea, but there was no spark of connection to any of them. And surely there would be. She felt sure there would.

So she just sat there until she felt strong enough to move.

After the dishes had been cleared, the other women began to drift away from the tables in little groups, some outside to go and enjoy the warmth of the evening and others cupping mugs of steaming herbal tea in their hands and heading towards the comfy chairs in the lounge. There was a real camaraderie, a sense of belonging, even though most of them appeared to be strangers to one another. Laughter rang out from various tables across the terrace and out into the darkening night beyond and, for a moment, Cecily thought that if she just tried a little harder, spoke to someone new, she could easily be absorbed into the heart of the group. She could make the most of this impromptu trip, putting aside whatever else may come from it.

But actually, she didn't have it in her. She was here for one thing, and one alone. The rest was just background noise. She made excuses about being tired from her journey, which wasn't a total untruth, and slipped quietly away.

Back in her room she opened the windows wide, letting the warm night air flood in. The sky was dark now and the ocean beyond the grounds was like a vast black hole consuming everything before her. It was odd to see so much space with no twinkling streetlights to break it up. In one or two places tiny pinpricks of yellow, fishing boats she presumed, seemed to pierce the blanket of water as if revealing something brighter beneath, but otherwise there was nothing. She thought she should probably close the windows again to protect against night insects but she found the dark expanse of nothingness strangely calming.

She sat on the edge of the bed and took the envelope from her bag. Her heart was beating so fast that it crossed her mind that she might have a heart attack here in Greece, so far from home. She shook the thought away as silly, but she wished that Norman was with her. He would hold her hands until they stopped shaking, would wait with her, silent and strong at her side, until she was ready to open the envelope and read its contents. But he wasn't here. She had chosen to make this journey on her own, and so now she had to face this moment without him. It was only fitting really, she supposed. She had been very much alone when it had all begun fifty years before.

She ran her fingers around the envelope, feeling for clues. It was bigger than its contents and the centre felt stiffer than mere paper. Was it a card of some sort? Unable to wait any longer, she carefully prised open the flap and slipped her fingers inside. She touched the glossy sheen of photograph paper, but that was all. There appeared to be no accompanying letter. Just the photo. Cecily felt a dart of disappointment. Had she been hoping for something else? She hadn't been aware of any hopes, but now it appeared that she had harboured them anyhow.

She pulled the photograph out. It was upside-down, so she turned it over. The image made her start and she let out a little gasp. It was a simple, uncluttered picture: a single bed covered with a white cotton counterpane and, sitting on that, a box about the size of a shoe box. It was decorated all over with pictures of yellow roses cut from wallpaper, faded now and curling in places near the edges, but otherwise looking well cared for, considering its age. Cecily would have known it anywhere.

'Oh,' she whispered as tears gathered in her eyes and then dripped down her cheeks. And then a sound that was more moan than word. Her shoulders heaved and she began to sob so hard that soon her muscles were aching from the effort. And all the time she clutched the photograph tightly, as if by holding it she could somehow summon the actual box to her.

Cecily had no idea how long she cried for, but eventually the tears subsided and she curled up on her side, pulling the sheet over her even though she had not yet undressed.

It must be her. There hadn't really been any doubt in Cecily's mind after she received the letter, but the photograph proved it. It was the self-same box that she had prepared fifty years ago. She recalled the time she had spent deciding how to decorate it, selecting the pictures that she thought would be perfect and cutting them out as carefully as she could before sticking them in place with tacky glue. The memory, long forgotten, was now delivered back to her whole and in startling detail, as if she had been keeping it safe somewhere for exactly this moment.

She had wished, of course, that the box would be treated with as much care and love as she had poured into the creation of it, although she had no way of knowing its fate. For all she knew, it might have been thrown away almost at once. But now she knew that it had been kept, preserved; dare she hope, cherished?

And today, all those decades later, Marnie still had it.

◆ ◆ ◆

The windows were still open when she awoke, the light bouncing off the white surfaces and making sleep impossible. Outside she could hear a man and a woman talking efficiently to one another in Greek, exchanging their orders for the day ahead. Pans clattered and someone tipped a collection of glass bottles into a recycling bin. The day had begun.

Having fallen asleep in last night's clothes, Cecily was now sticky and uncomfortable. She had also rendered her outfit unwearable again, which was a shame, as she was very fond of the skirt. Maybe there was a laundry facility here, or an iron at least.

The photograph lay on the white tiled floor several feet from the bed. It must have slipped from her fingers during the night. Cecily focused on it but was relieved to discover that it appeared to have lost its power it had had the night before. She could gaze upon it now and still maintain her composure.

She untangled herself from the sheet and headed to the shower. Her eyes felt tight and swollen and when she considered her reflection in the mirror she was unsurprised to see how small they appeared, narrowed by the swelling of her eyelids. Still, no one here knew what she usually looked like and her sunglasses could disguise things until they calmed down. She ran the cold tap and balled up some tissues to make into little pads that she pressed into her eye sockets, and enjoyed the cooling sensation they provided.

Breakfast was served outside on the terrace. She helped herself to some juice and a boiled egg and found a place at a table on her own. She still wasn't feeling ready for small talk.

Within seconds of sitting, a chair to her left was being drawn out and she looked up to see Sofia, dressed today in black Lycra, her hair tied casually into an unruly top knot.

'Good morning, Cecily. Did you sleep well?'

'Like a log,' replied Cecily, which was at least true.

'Great. It's lovely to have you here and, as I said yesterday, please feel free to join in with anything that takes your fancy.'

'Actually, I think I might just treat myself to an easy start. Life has been a little' – she searched for the right word – 'unusual over the last few days, and I think I need to give myself chance to take stock.'

Sofia was nodding, a tendril of escaped hair bouncing gently against her cheek. 'Well, we are a retreat,' she said with a smile. 'That's exactly what we're here for. There is absolutely no pressure to do anything. You just listen to your body and respect what it's telling you.'

This all sounded like a lot of mumbo-jumbo to Cecily, but she smiled politely. She was desperate to quiz Sofia about the envelope that she had delivered and about Marnie, but it was clear that now was not the time. Sofia was already moving away.

After breakfast, there was a little flurry of activity as women prepared themselves for the day. Cecily sat and watched, all the time keeping an eye out for anyone acting oddly who might be Marnie, but no one caught her eye.

Once the class had started and peace was restored, she wandered back to her room, collected her book, a tattered paperback that she'd been trying to finish for weeks, and went for an exploratory walk around the site. It didn't take long, and she managed to identify places to go both when she wanted company and when she didn't. Now she took herself to one of the quieter corners and settled in a wicker armchair. The cushions were warm and faded from the sun. How lovely it must be, she thought, to leave the cushions out from spring until autumn without having to constantly watch the sky for darkening clouds.

Cecily had always fancied retiring abroad. For many years, and after the trauma of what had happened, she had craved stability and routine. Norman had been perfect for that. He was her port in a storm, her lighthouse, there to keep her safe through all those difficult years at the beginning. Then they'd had the girls and she had begun to feel more grounded, the aching hole in her heart shrinking just a little. But since the girls had grown up, a yearning to break free from their life in lovely, leafy Harrogate and go find some adventure had been steadily growing deep inside her. She didn't want much, but she would love to watch the seasons change in a country that wasn't her own.

She wasn't aware of her eyes growing heavy but when her book slipped to the floor, the slap of paper on tile woke her with a start. She was still entirely alone. That was good. She wanted to be alone with her thoughts, her memories, the creeping guilt that was never that far away.

It was easy enough to stay in the shadows, so Cecily did just that for the rest of the day and the evening, joining the others only when food was served and then slinking back into her hiding place. Nobody bothered her. Nobody even gave her a second glance; not the women, not the staff, and no one who might be Marnie. And then it grew dark. Her first full day was over and she was no further forward.

10

ENGLAND

Felicity looked at her watch. Again. It was less than half a minute since she'd last looked. Where was he? He'd promised that he would be here. He had sworn to it, in fact, and yet it was time to leave and her husband was still conspicuous by his absence.

She checked her phone for a text, hoping to see something along the lines of *Running late. See you there* or *I've got us seats right at the front*, but of course there was nothing. She looked at her watch one last time. Well, it was no good. She was going to have to go without him. He could join her there and hopefully before Hugo noticed that his daddy was missing.

Grabbing her suit jacket and handbag, Felicity flew from the house and out to the waiting car. It was a ten-minute drive to the school and the concert didn't start for fifteen. She had time, although she would have to settle for a seat towards the back. She cursed Richard under her breath. If she'd known he was going to be so late she would have arranged to meet him in the hall. But of course, in her heart she had known. She had just hoped that once, just this once, he wouldn't let her down.

The car park was full but she found a spot in the grassy over-flow area. Cursing Richard yet again, she picked her way across the soft ground, trying not to let her spike heels sink too far into the soil. The door into the nursery part of the school was at the opposite end of the site, so Felicity moved as fast as her narrow skirt and heels would allow whilst retaining some dignity. She could feel the sun hot on her back through the fabric of her suit and wet patches were forming under her arms, although this might have been more from the stress of being late than from the exertion.

The hall was already full of parents, all waiting eagerly for their protégés to appear. As predicted, the only chairs left were at the edges and towards the rear. Felicity selected one that had a second next to it, although part of her thought that Richard should have to stand at the back for the duration. She tried to settle herself so that she didn't appear flustered to anyone who happened to be watching, straightening her spine and pulling her shoulders back to give the impression, or at least so she hoped, of someone who was so well organised that they could just slide into place at the very last moment. She knew that her position in the hall belied this, though. Anyone who knew her would know that she would never have arrived so tardily on purpose. She ran through some plausible excuses in her mind: a very important meeting that overran, a phone call from the CEO at the very moment she was leaving, being caught behind a tractor on the road so that her zippy little car couldn't get her there on time.

Basically, she thought, she could tell them anything except the truth: my husband was so busy screwing his PA that he missed his only child's school concert. Imagine their faces. In fact, if it wouldn't have reflected so badly on her, and Hugo, she would just have told the truth – or at least what she had imagined to be true as she had no proof of his infidelity. But she could feel it. She could feel it deep in the pit of her stomach. Oh, but the shame of it. It was so very, very clichéd. His PA, for God's sake! At least it wasn't the nanny, although Felicity had wondered if he'd left his grubby little paw prints there as well. She'd rather not think about that, not in her house, in her bed.

'Is that seat taken?'

Felicity glanced up and saw a woman with flushed cheeks and flyaway hair who definitely looked worse than she did.

'Sorry, yes. It's for my . . .' Then she recalibrated her thoughts. 'Actually, no. Please take it,' she replied.

Served him right. She was sick of covering for him. And, when he eventually did show up, he could explain to Hugo why he'd had to loiter near the fire escape.

But the minute the woman sat down, Felicity felt guilty. Poor darling Hugo. It wasn't his fault that his father was a waste of space, and she could hardly enlighten him. She realised that she should have saved the seat for Hugo's sake.

A hush fell over the hall as the children began to file in and take their places on the stage. Each made their way to their allocated chair and sat down quietly with no fuss. It was clear that they had practised this part, too. This was what you got at a fee-paying school. Nothing was overlooked or left to chance here. It was important that the parents could see that their money was being put to good use.

The children all looked alike in their little blue and white striped blazers and it was hard to spot Hugo in the throng. Then she saw him, his dark hair and earnest little face. She felt a little fissure open in her heart. It was so unfair that this crap was happening to him.

The headmaster followed the last child on to the stage and stood in the centre, waiting until he had perfect silence in which to speak.

'Welcome parents, grandparents, family and friends. It's so gratifying to see so many of you here this evening.'

Felicity felt her anger rise like a bubble in a lava lamp. She breathed out through her mouth slowly and calmly and tried to recentre herself. She wasn't going to let Richard ruin this for her when he wasn't even in the room.

'I hope you'll agree from looking at the programme that we're in for a treat tonight.'

Felicity had no programme. She must have missed them in her haste to sit down. She would have to remember to pick one up on the way out so that she could keep it safe in Hugo's treasures box.

'So, with no further ado, I will sit down and let us get under way. Please put your hands together for the Acreview Academy Acorns' Preschool summer soirée.'

The alliteration always made Felicity wince. She wondered how often the headmaster had to practise it out loud so that it didn't trip him up. The choir sang first, their little voices filling the hall. There were actions and even some rudimentary harmonising. It was suitably impressive for such young children. Next a girl from Hugo's class played the piano. She was remarkably good, Felicity had to admit, even though praising another child who was effectively in competition with her own didn't come naturally to her. She looked over the sea of heads to find the child's mother so that she could nod and smile her insincere praise in her direction, but she couldn't find her. She was no doubt sitting in the front row, where Felicity would have been if . . .

After that there was a percussion piece, which Felicity thought was a little bit scrappy, and then a medley of nursery songs sung by the youngest children, a couple of whom just stared, open-mouthed, at the audience. A tiny girl with blonde plaits located her parents and then spent the entire time waving at them enthusiastically, which elicited a ripple of warm laughter from the audience, resulting in her waving even harder.

Felicity was growing increasingly anxious as she waited for Hugo's turn to perform. If only she had a programme to see when he would be on; then she would be better able to manage her nerves. She looked furtively to either side to see if her neighbours had one that she could borrow, but the woman who had arrived later than her was empty-handed and the man to her other side was holding on to his so tightly that his thumb was moulding the paper to its own shape. She would just have to wait.

She didn't have to wait long.

'And next we have Hugo and his violin,' announced the headmaster.

Felicity sat a little forward in her seat, her heart pounding in her chest. Come on Hugo darling, she wanted to shout out. Remember everything that we practised.

Hugo stood up and came to the front of the stage. He had his music in one hand and the violin and bow in the other and he didn't seem to know how to settle himself at the music stand without putting one or the other down. He shot an uncertain look to his left where his teacher was sitting. She gave him an encouraging little nod but didn't come out to help him. It was all Felicity could do not to push her way to the front and assist. Why were they letting him struggle like this? Could they not see that he needed some support? The poor child would be totally thrown, which was bound to manifest itself in his performance. Felicity fought against every urge in her body and stayed in her seat.

Hugo, holding his violin and bow in his right hand, tried to use his left to place the music on the stand but it flapped uncooperatively and he couldn't get the thin paper to sit up straight. In his anxiety, he knocked the stand with his bow and the whole thing wobbled ominously and then clattered to the stage. The man next to her sniggered and his wife elbowed him in the ribs. The anger that had been building since Richard had failed to appear was now so close to the surface that Felicity had to clench her fists to disperse it. Her nails dug into her palms painfully and her biceps started to ache from the effort.

Finally, Hugo's teacher got up to help him arrange everything so he could begin. A hush fell across the hall. Felicity held her breath as she sent every positive vibe that she could muster over the many heads in front of her to Hugo. She willed him to play well, for his natural talent to shine out. He was a much better musician than any of the others on the stage, with the possible exception of that piano-playing child who, Felicity had to grudgingly admit, was quite good.

Huge raised his violin to his chin and Felicity bit her lip. His hands seemed to be shaking because the bow scuttered a little across the stings. Come on Hugo, she thought. Don't let me down. And then he began.

The piece was a polka, something he'd been working on for his Grade 1 exam, and Felicity had worried a little when she'd selected it for him to play. It was possibly the most challenging of the three he had to choose from, with its fast tempo and slightly unusual rhythms, but if he could pull it off then it was the one that would best demonstrate what a gifted child he truly was. Felicity worried now that the mishap with the music stand might have put him off his stride. She willed him to shine. If ever there was a moment for him to be his absolute best it was here, in front of all these parents. Her husband might be a cheating rat but her child could show them all that she was a force to be reckoned with.

Hugo began to play. His first few notes were shaky and his tuning was a little off. Why hadn't he tested that before he began, the way she'd shown him?

The man sitting next to her tensed his shoulders and whispered to his wife. 'They shouldn't let kids under ten anywhere near a violin.'

56

'Shhh,' his wife whispered back.

Felicity wanted to jab him in the ribs, tell him that there were any number of extremely talented violin players who were under ten and that, whilst Hugo wasn't having his best day, he too was on a trajectory to greatness. But instead she turned her body slightly away from him and focused all her attention on Hugo.

Her baby seemed to be getting into his stride now. His fingers moved quickly to negotiate the semiquavers and his bow danced lightly over the strings. This was more like it. See, she wanted to say to the man. See!

Hugo got to the end of his piece to polite applause. Felicity clapped enthusiastically and Hugo turned to face his crowd and gave a distinguished little bow, just as she had shown him; then he took his music and went to sit back down. Beat that! she thought.

She hoped that Richard was sitting behind her somewhere. But somehow she knew that he wasn't.

11

GREECE

The next day, Wednesday, Cecily was feeling more settled. A period of self-imposed exile had been what she needed when she arrived, but now she thought she wanted to join in a little. She was there, after all, and who was to say that she wouldn't spend the entire trip just waiting for something to happen. At least if she busied herself it would help to pass the time.

Showered, dressed and feeling decidedly peckish, she picked up the timetable of events and considered it. The first activity that morning was a walk out to see the sunrise. Well, she had clearly missed that. The sun was already up and burning brightly. Breakfast was apparently followed by beginners' hatha yoga on the terrace. That might be good.

Not really owning any sportswear, she had packed a couple of old T-shirts and some tracksuit bottoms, which were the closest thing she had. Now she slipped into the least scruffy of what she'd brought and headed to find out what the day held in store for her.

Sofia found her at the breakfast table.

'How was your day yesterday?' she asked her. 'You look better this morning, rejuvenated.'

Cecily thought that this was probably a kindly meant lie, but at least her swollen eyes had returned to normal after the upset of the first night.

'It was perfect, thank you,' she said. 'Just what the doctor ordered.'

'And today?' asked Sofia, but there was no judgement in her expression. Cecily could have suggested another day retreating in solitude and that would have been fine with Sofia, she could tell.

'Actually, I was thinking of going to the class at ten o' clock?' she said instead, her mouth turning down at the corners doubtfully. 'What do you think? A good idea?'

Sofia's expression broadened into a wide smile. There! She obviously did want her guests to join in, after all. She really was very pretty, Cecily thought, and then briefly and a little treacherously, oh to be young again.

'The hatha?' Sofia asked. 'That would be perfect. Have you done any yoga before?'

Cecily shook her head. Ridiculously, she felt like she had somehow let Sofia down by never having tried.

'No problem,' said Sofia. 'You'll love it, and I'll make sure that I explain it all so you know exactly what's happening. I'll see you over there shortly.'

Sofia made to stand up but Cecily put a hand on her arm to stop her. 'Thank you for passing on the envelope,' she said, trying to meet Sofia's eyes and convey some meaning beyond mere words.

Sofia sat back down. 'You're welcome. It's a peculiar situation, but hopefully it will resolve itself soon.'

Cecily's heart lifted. 'Do you know about it then?' she asked, cryptically, not wanting to give too much away in case Sofia was just the messenger.

Sofia gave a little shrug. 'Some,' she said noncommittally.

'And you know Marnie Stone?' Cecily pushed, and Sofia nodded.

'Is she here?' Cecily's heart was pumping so hard that she could hear it in her own ears.

'Not right now,' said Sofia. 'But she will be. You know, I can't tell you anything else, Cecily. I would love to. I really would. But Marnie has to do this her own way and we just have to go with it until she's ready.'

Cecily nodded. 'I'm sorry,' she said. 'It's unfair of me to push. It's just . . .'

Sofa nodded sympathetically. 'I know. I understand, I really do, but we are where we are. My best advice would be to make the most of your time here and see what happens.' Her smile slipped a little. 'You know she might decide not to introduce herself, don't you?'

Cecily nodded again. 'That's what is so hard,' she said. 'It feels like I'm on trial.'

Sofia pulled a face that suggested that Cecily was exactly right.

'I mean, I know it's entirely up to Marnie what she chooses to do, but I worry that I'll fail the test before I've had the chance to even meet her.'

'Like I said,' Sofia replied, getting to her feet for a second time, 'it's up to Marnie.'

And then she was gone.

There were five women already on their mats when Cecily showed up to her first-ever yoga class. She hovered on the edge of the terrace, unsure what to do, although surely she just had to choose a mat and sit down.

'Morning, Cecily,' called Sue from Milton Keynes. She patted the mat next to hers and Cecily picked her away across the floor to join her. 'Nice bit of yoga to get the day started. I never seem to get any better at it but I keep trying. At least I'm not getting worse!'

She laughed and her Lycra-coated stomach jiggled a little. Part of Cecily thought there should be a maximum age limit for wearing leggings and part of her respected Sue for having the confidence to wear them, knowing, as she must, that they were doing her no favours at all.

'I've never tried,' confessed Cecily. 'This is my first-ever class.'

Yoga, it seemed, was about getting your breathing under control and holding positions that felt very odd but were at the same time quite grounding, for relatively long periods of time. In the shapes where she was able to maintain her balance, she had a quick glimpse at her fellow students and noticed that none of them were markedly better or worse than her. Even the young ones didn't seem to have much more give in their muscles and ligaments than she did, and by the end of the class she realised that she had enjoyed it more than she had expected to, although the relaxation part at the end felt a little alien to her. Lying down in a room full of strangers in the middle of the morning wasn't something that she had ever done in the past.

Afterwards they wiped their mats clean, rolled them up and stacked them at the side of the terrace, and then Cecily followed the others to enjoy a little spell in the sunshine. Her eyes darted about as she walked, searching for anyone watching her from a distance. For a moment in the yoga class, Marnie had slipped from the front of her mind, but now she sprang straight back in. There was no one, though. It seemed that the waiting was to continue.

Those who hadn't been in the class were relaxing on loungers around the pool, chatting or reading. It was a little too hot in the sun for Cecily, though; she thought she might go back to her room to collect her paperback and then find a shady nook in which to enjoy it.

'Fancy a cup of tea?' asked Sue from behind her.

Cecily's initial reaction was disappointment that her few moments of solitude had been snatched away from her before they had even begun, but then she changed her mind. It was hard enough, all this waiting. She might as well try to pass the time of day with the others, and Sue was nice enough.

'That would be lovely,' she heard herself say.

'It's not real tea,' Sue continued wryly. 'What I'd give for a proper strong brew and a nice sticky bun.' She smirked, and her eyes twinkled with naughtiness. 'We drink Yorkshire tea in our house. I bet you do too, coming from there yourself.'

'They make it in Harrogate, not far from my house,' said Cecily. 'Well, I mean they don't grow the tea, obviously, but the teabag factory is there and they do the blending.'

'Isn't that interesting? You know, I never thought about where it came from. I just drink it.' Sue winked. 'But not here, sadly.' She ran her eye over the basket of various bags, her top lip curling a little in disgust. 'Fennel, peppermint, ginger, hibiscus, echinacea, rooibos, sage or lemon balm. Pick your poison.'

'Lemon balm,' replied Cecily doubtfully.

'Good choice,' said Sue, snatching a bag up from the basket, dropping it in a mug and passing it to Cecily. 'Best of a bad bunch. Take my advice, Cecily. Never go for the sage. It's undrinkable.'

'I'll bear that in mind,' said Cecily.

They took their tea out to the terrace and found a shady table under a fig tree.

'So,' said Sue, once she'd taken her first mouthful of tea and pulled a face. 'Do you have any kids?'

'Yes. Three daughters . . .' Three daughters. Every time Cecily said that her heart ached, and yet she had never answered the question differently. 'And six grandsons,' she added.

'All boys?' asked Sue, her eyes wide. 'Christmas must be loud at your house. I've got one of each. No grandkids yet – thank

God. I'm feeling old enough as it is . . .' A shadow of awkwardness crossed her face. 'Not that I'm saying you're old or anything,' she added. 'It's just that my eldest is only nineteen. It's a bit too soon to be having babies. And I've only just got over my fiftieth. That was a big enough shock to the system without adding grandkids into the mix.'

So she was just fifty. The same age as Marnie, Cecily thought. For a fleeting second Cecily scanned her face, but there was nothing to see. This was just Sue from Milton Keynes. Still, this was what a fifty-year-old woman looked like. That was useful, at least.

'My girls are all in their thirties now,' said Cecily. 'So I don't mind that they have children. And yes, Christmas is very noisy.'

Sue's eyes scanned down to Cecily's left hand and took in her plain gold band. 'And you're married?'

'Yes. To Norman. It's been forty years now. I've been very lucky.'

'My bloke ran off with his best mate, Rob,' said Sue. 'I had no idea. I don't think he did, either, to be fair, but they're still together, got a lovely little flat in the centre of town. Can't blame him really, but it left me high and dry. Between you and me that's why I'm here. Now I'm fifty I'm going for a bit of a reinvention. Lose the weight, have my hair done, new clothes. I'll be like a new woman!'

Cecily wanted to tell her that in her experience it was what was on the inside that counted, but she kept her wisdom to herself. 'Good for you,' she said instead.

'What do you fancy doing after lunch? I'm going to the rebounding.'

Cecily hardly dared ask.

'It's like little trampolines. You basically bounce for half an hour.'

'I think I might be a bit old for that,' said Cecily. 'I might go for a little walk down by the sea. Or a swim maybe?'

'Ooh, you're brave. I'm scared of the sea. Always have been since I was a kiddie. Can't trust it, that's what my dad said.'

Cecily smiled. 'Well, I can go and paddle at least,' she said, knowing full well that she would swim.

'You can follow that path all the way down to the cove,' Sue said, pointing to a little iron gate beyond the patio. 'It's a bit steep in parts and it's a drag to get back up, but it's worth it. And there's a little bar down there that serves delicious sangria.' She put a plump finger to her lips. 'I won't tell anyone if you don't!'

'My lips are sealed,' replied Cecily with a smile.

She nipped back to her room to put on her swimming costume. Maybe she wouldn't go in the water after all, but she liked to be prepared. There was no sign of Sue when she went back – gone to the rebounding class, no doubt. Nobody noticed as Cecily slipped through the little iron gate and headed down the path to the sea.

The path was rocky and steep, and she worried that she would lose her footing as tiny stones slid away from under her and pattered down the slope. There were rough gorse bushes on either side and at one point she feared that she had overreached herself in setting off; but then she calculated that it was probably as far to continue as it was to return, so she pressed on and shortly the path widened out and she could see the beach.

It was deserted.

Cecily picked her way across the pebbles to the water's edge. The waves were lapping gently, the tiny pebbles being pulled backwards and forwards by the current. They made a quiet shushing sound as they moved; the kind of sound that they piped in at a spa to make you relax. The sea was crystal clear and the brightest turquoise, growing deeper in hue the further out she looked. The beach was tiny, half-covered by gnarled old trees that cast shadows across much of it. Not much use for sunbathing unless you went really close to the shoreline. Rocks and cedars sprouted up from either side, so it seemed that the only way to get there was via the path that she had taken, or from the sea. But hadn't Sue said there was a bar? Cecily turned and saw that there was indeed a little wooden shack with a corrugated roof; a few tables and chairs were scattered outside with faded umbrellas offering a little shade. A pick-up was parked to one side, so there must be a road. She felt mildly disappointed that she had not been quite as off the beaten path as she had thought. Still, there was no one here now. She was totally alone.

She moved back to the shade of the tree and took off her sun-dress. Her swimming costume was a modest one but still revealed far more flesh than she would have liked; still, if she wanted to swim she would just have to deal with that. And she did want to swim, she realised now, more than anything. She picked her way across the pebbles. It was very inelegant and she was glad that there was no one there to see her. Then she stepped into the sea. It was warmer than she'd imagined but hardly tropical, and she braced herself as the water crept up her legs. When it reached her waist she took a deep breath and plunged the rest of her body under. The shock of the cooler water disappeared quickly and she picked up her feet and began to swim in a strong, steady breaststroke out to sea.

As she swam she thought about her family back home. Felicity would be furious if she knew that she had just taken off into the water without telling anyone where she was going. 'What if you got into difficulties?' she could hear her say. 'Who would know to come and find you?'

Sometimes she thought that her daughters underestimated her. They had never discovered what their mother was capable of because they had never looked. To them, she was just Mum, but they had no idea how strong she could be. No idea at all. What were they going to say when they found out? she wondered. Well, there was no point worrying about that now. She could cross that bridge when it appeared.

The cove began to open out and she swam alongside the various fancy yachts that were anchored there, their mooring ropes criss-crossing the bay like telephone wires. There looked to be a cave to her right and she altered her direction slightly to go and investigate. As she approached she could hear voices floating out across the water towards her. There were some boys in there already, their little boat pulled up on to the shingle so it didn't float away. They were chattering away to each other in a language that she couldn't quite identify.

She thought about turning back, but now she had come this far she wanted to explore the cave properly. Who cared if her white thighs jiggled as she walked? She swam in as far as the water would allow, and then stood up and wobbled her way across the pebbles and into the dark space. The boys turned to see what had made the noise but then immediately turned away. An elderly lady was of no interest to them.

The cave went a long way back and Cecily, feeling intrepid, followed the path inside. The floor was strewn with pebbles, all white as snow, bleached by the sea and the sun over thousands of years. It made the space look a little like a film set; it was hard to believe that they were quite natural, although obviously they were.

Cecily was further in than the boys had been now. Was that stupid? Did they know something she didn't? Then she heard them getting into their boat, recognised the chug of the outboard motor, their voices becoming more faint and then disappearing completely. They were gone, and she was entirely alone in a cave in Kefalonia with not a living soul knowing where to find her. Her feelings ricocheted between freedom and fear, but freedom won out.

She walked in a little deeper, her eyes adjusting to the darkness. The cavern was a lot bigger than it appeared from the mouth and went considerably further back than she had first imagined, but without a torch she couldn't safely venture much further. She felt both frustrated at her lack of equipment but also relieved that her mission had been thwarted by something outside her control, the thrill of excitement tinged with foreboding. What if she couldn't get back? What if her legs gave out? Or her heart? What if she fell here, couldn't swim to the beach and was trapped by the water? How long would it take for Sue to raise the alarm, or even notice that she was missing? Was there a tide, or could she just sleep in here if needs be?

Cecily shook her head and laughed at herself. She had gone into full risk-assessment mother mode, even though none of her children were here with her to be in danger. In any event, she should be heading back. She would start to get cold if she wasn't careful and it was a fair old swim to the beach. She bent down and picked up a single white stone. It was smooth and reminded her of a mint imperial. She held it tight in her palm, a souvenir of her adventure, and then she walked back into the water.

The swim back seemed quicker, and soon enough she was on the beach. She had no towel so she perched herself on a flat rock to dry off, feeling self-conscious but also a little decadent, like a fifties film star. The sun was high in the sky now; a tiny lizard skittered across the rock by her feet and disappeared into the undergrowth. She should have brought some money and then she could have had a glass of the famed sangria to celebrate surviving. She would come back the next day, she decided, and would be better prepared.

When she was pretty much dry, she slipped her dress over her head and pushed her feet into her sandals. As she looked up to relocate the path back up the hillside to the retreat, she saw that there was now someone sitting at one of the tables outside the bar. It was a woman with shoulder-length dark hair and skin tanned to a rich mahogany. She had sunglasses on, but Cecily had the impression that she was watching her.

She gave her a quick smile and raised her hand in acknowledgement. 'Hello,' she said. 'Isn't this a lovely place?'

The woman didn't reply, just shrugged. Normally Cecily would have left her to it, but nothing about being here on this quiet beach in Kefalonia, miles away from her friends and family and entirely alone, was normal. She felt herself being drawn in further. When she got closer, the woman lifted her sunglasses and pushed them back into her hair. She considered Cecily with coffee-coloured eyes, looking her up and down unapologetically.

'Cecily Nightingale?' she asked.

'Yes,' said Cecily uncertainly.

The woman nodded, moving her head slowly, contemplatively as she took Cecily in.

Then she spoke. 'I'm Marnie Stone,' she said.

PART TWO

1

ENGLAND

Cecily had been gone for two nights and Norman was feeling pleased with how things were going so far. As promised, he had cleared out the shed, and its former contents were now sitting in a little pile on the back lawn. The shed looked great, the lawn less so, but he could tackle that later that day, or maybe tomorrow. And his beef noodle meal had been relatively successful. Granted, it hadn't been quite as easy as Mr Oliver had made it look and he had struggled getting all the constituent parts ready at the same time, but overall it hadn't been a bad first effort. Cecily would be surprised when she got back and discovered that he had not only survived without having the meals that she usually prepared for him, but had thrived. It wasn't that he objected to being in the kitchen. It just wasn't how labour had been distributed over the years – but that could change. He wasn't averse to a bit of change, which was probably a good thing given what he assumed was happening in Kefalonia. He could see that there was likely to be a fair bit of change in the offing.

He made himself a cup of tea and took it, along with three custard creams because no one was counting, to consume outside whilst he decided on his next move in Operation Shed. But his mind was venturing further afield. Where was Cecily? he wondered. How was she getting on? She would be fine, he knew. Cecily was the most competent woman he'd ever known, but even she might be feeling a little unseated by the revelations of the last few days. In many ways, Norman wished that he had been more forthright when the letter arrived and insisted that he make the trip to Greece with her, but he knew that his protestations would have fallen on stony ground. This was something that Cecily had to do by herself. His place was here at home, holding the fort until she returned, and then helping her pick up whichever pieces needed to be picked up afterwards. He hoped that it wouldn't come to that, though. He really did.

The latch on the side gate clicked and Lily appeared with the baby on her hip.

'Morning, Dad,' she called cheerfully, and then, 'Oh my goodness! What did you do to the shed?'

'I told you. I'm having a bit of a reorganise whilst your mother's away.'

'I think you're going to have to reorganise a little bit harder,' said Lily as she stood and looked at the pile, her head cocked to one side. 'Would you like some help?'

'No, thank you,' replied Norman tightly. 'It might look a little messy but I assure you that there is a method in the madness. I know precisely what's there and what I need to do with it next.'

This wasn't strictly true, and judging by the smile that Lily gave him, she knew this as well as he did; but she let it go and came to join him at the table, sitting the baby on her lap facing outwards so that he could see what was going on. He banged his plump little palms on the table top until Lily gently took his hands in hers to stop him.

'We're on my way back from our music group,' she explained, 'and I just thought we'd pop in.'

'Isn't he a bit young for that?' Norman asked, eyeing the baby, who now had his fist stuffed so far into his mouth that it was hard to see how he was still managing to breathe.

'Of course he is,' replied Lily with a smile. 'Far too young really, but it gets me out of the house and talking to other humans. And it's fun.'

'We don't have another musical prodigy in the family just yet, then?' Norman asked wryly.

Lily gave him one of her disapproving looks. She had never liked family members to be unkind to each other, even in jest. 'Hugo is really good on his violin and you shouldn't tease Fliss about it. She takes it so much to heart.'

Norman was tempted to say that Felicity set herself up for a fall by going on about how talented Hugo was without, to Norman's ear at least, there being much to base such a claim on, but he bit his tongue.

'The three of us are going out tonight,' Lily continued. 'Third Wednesday of the month and all that.' And then, as an afterthought, 'You could come too if you like. We're just going for a curry.'

'That's very kind of you, Lily darling, but I have to be in to record your mother's programme tonight.' He had never entirely mastered the scheduling process. 'And I have another recipe that I'd like to try.'

'Okay,' Lily said. 'It's probably best if you don't come anyway. I need a quiet word with Julia. I'm sure she's up to something but she hasn't told me what it is yet.'

'That's not like you. I thought you could divine her every thought by some kind of twin telepathy!' He was teasing her now, but she didn't rise to it.

'Well, this time it's let me down,' she said. 'But I know there's something going on.'

73

'And how about Felicity?' Norman asked. His firstborn worried him the most. To the world at large, she presented a woman who was completely in control of every aspect of her life, but he knew that this was sometimes a facade and she was far too concerned about preserving that image. If you sat yourself at the top of the tree, then there was far further to fall when the wind blew. Little Hugo was a case in point. It would have been better had she had more than one child to withstand the glare of her spotlight, but sadly that hadn't been on the cards.

And there was that husband of hers . . .

'Is Richard still working in London?' he asked. His question was a loaded one, but Lily didn't seem to notice.

'As far as I know,' she answered simply. 'He's back at the week-ends though, so that's good.'

Norman made a noise that might have been a yes, but was intended as more of a grunt.

The baby started to grizzle, his cheeks pink and his fist slick with glistening dribble.

'Here,' Norman said, reaching out to his grandson. 'Come and say hello to your old grandad.'

Lily passed him over. The boy was fair like Lily, with wide blue eyes and a chubby face. He stopped grizzling for a second as Norman bounced him up and down, his stocky little legs kicking out against Norman's thighs, but then the grizzle turned into a cry and soon he was howling.

'Sorry, Dad,' said Lily, taking him back and pressing him into her chest, rocking gently. 'He's teething and I'll bet he's pooped from music class too. I should probably put him down for a nap.'

'And the others are all okay?' Norman asked. 'And Marco?'

Lily smiled. 'All great, thank you. Come on then, young man. Let's get you home. I'll call in again tomorrow,' she added.

'There really is no need, Lily. I'm perfectly all right.'

Lily pushed her long blonde hair away from her face and out of reach of the baby, who was grasping for it with his little hands. 'I know that, but I need to keep an eye on things just to make sure that you sort that shed out. Mum will go mad if she gets back and it's still like that.' They both looked over to the pile of unwanted items. 'Do you want that swing seat?' she added.

'I was going to take it the tip. The ropes are all rotten.'

'Can I have it, please? Marco can get some new rope and it could go in the tree at the back.'

Norman thought that his daughter's garden already contained more than enough play equipment, but then again, what would one more swing hurt?

'Of course,' he said. 'But make sure that Marco attaches it properly. Your mother will never forgive me if there are any accidents.'

'Don't worry,' Lily replied as she crossed the lawn to the pile and extracted the wooden swing seat. 'Thanks. Right. We'll be off. Ring me if you need anything, won't you?'

'Yes, Lily,' said Norman, saluting her. 'But honestly, I'm completely fine, and your mother will be back before we know it.'

'Well, if you're sure . . .' Lily walked back to him and planted a kiss on his head. 'See you soon, Dad.'

And then they were gone. Norman hadn't even offered her a cup of tea, although she probably wouldn't have wanted one. His own had gone a little cold now, but he drank it anyway and polished off the biscuits one after another as if someone might snatch them from him. Maybe he could ring Cecily at the retreat place? He had a phone number. But then again, if she needed him, wouldn't she ring home? It would probably be better if he just left her to it and waited until there was real news. Besides, he thought as he looked at the pile, he had things to be getting on with.

2

Julia arrived at the restaurant first. The man on the front desk welcomed her enthusiastically and she felt embarrassed, yet again, that she did not know his name. The three Nightingale sisters had been coming here every month for years and the time to confess that they had forgotten what he was called had long passed, so when he greeted them warmly they had to just smile. To be fair to them, he referred to each of them as Miss Nightingale, which was only actually correct for her, although Felicity still used her maiden name at work for complicated reasons that Julia had never quite understood.

The front-of-house no-name man showed her to their usual spot, a round table towards the back of the restaurant far from the toilets and out of sight of the windows so they wouldn't be spotted from the street. It wasn't as if they were famous or anything, but they had lived in the town for most of their lives and between them they knew a lot of people who might interrupt their precious time together.

Julia sat down in the seat that she usually chose and the man took her jacket.

'Can I get you a drink whilst you wait?' another man, their waiter this time, asked mere seconds later. They prided themselves on their service here.

Julia was about to order a large glass of Merlot, but then she remembered. 'Just a tonic water, please,' she said. 'With plenty of ice and lemon.'

She could pretend that it had gin in it if necessary. She hadn't yet decided whether she was going to tell her sisters her news. Keeping all her options open was the way forward at this stage.

The waiter arrived with her drink and looked as if he wanted to chat, but she put him off by focusing on her phone. She wasn't in the mood to hear about the rest of his family, not tonight.

'Thank you,' she said without looking up when he placed her drink in front of her. She felt a little guilty – but not enough to actually speak to him.

A message popped up on her screen. *Running late. There in ten.*

Lily. It didn't matter where they were going; Lily was always late. It was like being ten minutes behind everyone else was hard-wired into her personality. In fact, they often joked that the only thing that she had ever been early for was her birth.

Felicity was generally prompt but not always for her sisters, who clearly weren't important enough to impress with punctuality. Julia could hear her sister's voice now, though. Loud and strident, it carried across the restaurant as she said her hellos to the staff. Moments later, Felicity appeared at the table. She was, as ever, exquisitely turned out, in a fuchsia-pink suit and a pair of cream heels. Julia dreaded to think how much the ensemble had cost. Far more than her own rather well-worn outfit, that was for sure.

'Hi Ju,' Felicity said as she settled herself in the seat opposite.

For all her beautiful clothes, though, Julia thought her sister looked tired, and every one of her thirty-seven years. Her skin lacked its usual glow and there were plum-coloured patches under her eyes.

'Busy day?' Julia asked, and Felicity shrugged.

'No worse than usual. No Lily?'

'She's on her way,' Julia replied, and Felicity rolled her eyes.

The waiter arrived to take her drinks order and Felicity nodded towards Julia's glass. 'What are you on?' she asked.

'Gin and tonic,' lied Julia.

'That's a good idea. I'll have one too.'

Julia made sure that she didn't make eye contact with the waiter, not wanting to give him a chance to blow her cover.

'In fact, make it a double. It's been a pig of a day,' Felicity added.

The waiter retreated. Felicity picked up the menu and started flicking through it – a pointless exercise as they always ordered exactly the same food. When she got to the end she put it back down.

'How are you, anyway?' she asked, clearly an afterthought.

Julia wasn't offended. It generally took Felicity a good half-hour to unwind when she first arrived anywhere. Julia wasn't sure how she managed to function at such a high level of stress at all times. It couldn't be good for her.

'Busy,' she replied. 'You know. Same old, same old.'

Felicity nodded. If she had been talking to anyone else, Julia knew that she would then have complained about how busy she was, but that wasn't how things rolled between the three of them. They had given up doing competitive busyness a good decade ago; it just led to unnecessary sniping and always made Lily feel bad about herself, even though she was probably the busiest of all of them. It was just that nobody paid her to do her job.

'I'm hoping that we might get away for a couple of weeks in the holidays,' Felicity said. 'I could really use some time in the sun, but Richard's project in London just keeps dragging on so he probably won't be able to leave it.'

'You could always go away without him,' Julia suggested controversially.

Felicity looked as if she was contemplating this for a moment, but then she shook her head. 'I can't cope with Hugo on my own. You have no idea how exhausting a child can be. And who would I talk to at mealtimes?'

Julia delicately stepped around all the barbs in this comment, knowing that Felicity did genuinely believe herself to be the most hard-put-upon person on the entire planet. Being single, she had been on plenty of breaks by herself and she would kill to have a child to share them with, but nothing would be gained by making either point.

Instead she said, 'Are you okay, Fliss? You look tired.'

Just for a second, Felicity seemed to deflate a little, but then she gathered herself. 'I'm fine,' she said. 'It's just a bit hard being a single parent when Richard is away all the time.'

Julia's stomach turned over. How did she think she was going to cope on her own when her uber-efficient big sister was struggling?

'Will it be for much longer?' she asked, and Felicity shrugged.

'It should have been over already, but they just keep extending things.'

'And how's Richard coping?' Julia asked. 'He must be exhausted, too.'

Felicity's mouth tightened just a little and a few faint but distinguishable lines appeared above her top lip, like score marks in paper. 'He seems to be doing just fine,' she said shortly.

Julia waited to see if she would say anything else, but she didn't. There was trouble there, Julia guessed, which Felicity may or may not choose to share with her and Lily. It was always a hard one to call, although her sister's expression suggested that that was all she was going to give for now. Maybe when Lily arrived, she might . . .

And then Lily was there, her hair flyaway and her eyes wild.

'I'm so sorry,' she said breathily as if she had run every step of the way. 'I was about to leave the house and then the blessed twins tipped rice all over the kitchen floor and I had to stay to help Marco clean it all up.'

'Why didn't the twins clear it up?' asked Julia.

Lily looked sheepish. 'I know, I know. I'm making a rod for my own back.'

'And for their future wives,' chipped in Felicity archly.

'But they're so young yet,' said Lily. 'It's far quicker to do things for them, but I will get them to pull their weight when they're bigger, I promise.' She squeezed into the chair between them and Julia saw her relax, the responsibilities of motherhood lifted from her shoulders, if only for an hour or two. 'I called in on Dad this morning,' she added.

'How's he doing?' asked Julia.

'He was remarkably chipper. He seems to be coping really well without Mum.'

'And did you get anything more out of him? About what's going on, I mean,' Felicity said, but Lily shook her head.

'I didn't ask, to be honest. I just thought that they'll tell us when they're good and ready.'

Julia sighed. That was so like Lily. She was the one that their father was most likely to open up to, but also the one least likely to pry.

'Did you see them last week at all?' Felicity asked. 'I meant to pop round but I just ran out of time. Did Mum say anything then? Did she seem different?'

Lily shook her head.

'I got the impression that this was a very spur-of-the moment-thing,' said Julia. 'I'm not sure they even knew last week.'

'It's bloody weird, that's what it is,' said Felicity just as the waiter arrived to take their order, which Julia delivered without looking at the menu. 'Does she know anyone in Greece? Is there a school friend or something that she's never mentioned?'

But they drew a blank. It didn't matter how much they speculated. There were no answers.

'Hugo played beautifully in his school concert yesterday,' Felicity said, changing the subject.

Julia kept her mouth firmly closed. She had been to one of Hugo's concerts before, being the single aunt who clearly had enough time on her hands to sacrifice some of it to such a venture. She had spent the entire time with her fingernails jammed into her thighs to stop herself giggling at the awfulness of it. It had been truly excruciating, all those tiger mothers hovering over their little darlings as they performed, and then doing competitive praising afterwards; although Julia hadn't understood what there was to get so aerated about. They were just little kids banging out 'Clair de lune' on the piano or the recorder. Their efforts had hardly merited such glowing accolades. When Julia had described it to Lily, unable to keep the sneer out of her voice, Lily had pulled a face and told her off for being ungracious, and Julia had been left feeling inadequate because clearly she, being childless, couldn't possibly understand the joy of seeing your offspring succeed. Julia felt sure that if Lily had seen the display for herself she would have totally understood what she'd found so amusing, but as it was she wouldn't hear a word said against Hugo or Felicity.

'How lovely,' Lily said now. 'What did he play?'

Felicity's cheeks flushed with pleasure at the chance to relive Hugo's triumph. 'A polka from his Grade 1 pieces. It was a brave choice actually, pretty tricky. I was very proud.'

'Well done, Hugo,' said Lily, clapping her hands together just as the starters arrived, which made it look like she was trumpeting

81

the food. The waiter beamed, soaking up the presumed praise as if he had prepared the food personally.

'Richard didn't make it, though,' added Felicity, her voice darker and with a rare trace of bitterness. It was very seldom that Felicity spoke ill of her husband.

Here we go, thought Julia. She's going to finally tell us what he's been up to.

'Oh, poor Richard,' said Lily, either oblivious to the undercurrent or, more likely, giving Felicity an alternative conversational path through the mire. 'What a shame. Still, I'm sure he would have been there if he could. It must be so hard for him, missing out on milestones while he's away.'

'Oh, come off it,' snapped Felicity. 'He was working in Leeds that day. He had absolutely no reason to miss it. He just couldn't be bothered to make the effort.'

Lily closed her mouth. She would defend her brother-in-law because it was in her nature to see the best in people, but only up to a point. When the chips were down, the three of them would fight to the death for one another.

'I've had just about enough of it, to be honest with you,' Felicity continued. 'But I don't want to talk about him. He makes me cross and I don't want to feel cross when I'm with you two. I'm not having him spoil this too.' She lifted her head defiantly and tossed her hair as if shrugging all thoughts of her husband away. 'So, what's new in your worlds?'

'I was looking at courses yesterday,' began Lily. 'Online ones to do when I have a few minutes.'

How Lily ever found a few minutes to even clean her teeth was a mystery to Julia. 'Find anything good?' she asked.

'Well, I was quite tempted by upholstery.'

Julia shook her head. 'Where on earth will you fit that in on top of everything else?' she asked, incredulous.

'Oh, I've got plenty of time. It's not like I've got a job,' said Lily, and her cheeks flushed a delicate pink, making her look even more pretty.

'Lily!' replied Julia, aghast. 'Do I need to remind you that you have five children under nine? Of course you've got a job!'

Lily shrugged. 'Well, not really. Not like you two. And besides, I like to keep busy. And this will be useful. Those sofas of Mum's could definitely do with a bit of a facelift.'

'Well, I think you're mad!' chipped in Felicity. 'But whatever flies your flag, I suppose.' She shook her head fondly at Lily.

'Thank you, Fliss,' Lily said, looking pointedly at Julia. 'At least one of you understands what I mean. And anyway, I think it'll be fun.'

She winked at Julia who grinned back at her.

'I don't doubt it,' she said. 'And you'll do a brilliant job, I'm sure.'

The wine flowed, although Julia made a good job of avoiding drinking much of it, and so did the conversation, the three of them laughing or being outraged at the same stories, but soon Felicity was yawning and looking at her watch.

'I'm sorry, girls, but I'm going to have to love you and leave you. Early start tomorrow.' She got to her feet, arching her back and stretching. 'Let me know if you hear anything more about Mum. I assume she's not taken that mobile we bought her.'

Lily shook her head. 'It's on the kitchen table,' she said, and they tutted and shook their heads as one.

'Also, could you keep your ear to the ground for me, please, Lils? I might be in the market for a new nanny so if you hear of anyone, could you let me know?'

'Will do,' replied Lily lightly.

'Same time next month?'

'Same time next month.'

Julia and Lily watched as Felicity made her way to the door, waving her goodbyes to the staff as she went, and then turned to face each other.

'Do you think . . .' asked Julia, and Lily nodded.

'The rat. Poor Felicity. Why doesn't she ever tell us?'

Julia considered for a moment. 'Pride, I guess.'

'She should kick him out. Or at least mark his card.'

'I don't suppose she'll do that either.'

The pair sat in contemplative silence for a moment as they finished their drinks.

'Lily?' said Julia.

'Mmm?'

This was her moment, Julia thought. She should just tell her about Sam and what they'd decided to do. Lily would totally understand. And with her on board it would be easier to talk to Felicity and her parents. And yet . . .

'Oh, nothing.'

3

GREECE

For a moment it felt like Cecily's heart had stopped beating.

And then it was beating so fast that she was suddenly light-headed and unable to catch her breath. She put her hand out to grab the back of a chair to steady herself. She needed some water, some oxygen, Norman.

The woman, Marnie Stone, stood up and came towards her, offering a hand in support, and Cecily felt herself being guided down to the chair. Whilst she focused on stopping the world from spinning, the woman disappeared inside the bar and returned moments later with a glass and a bottle of water, which she placed on the table in front of Cecily. Cecily tried to open it but her hands seemed to have lost all their strength, and after a couple of failed attempts to remove the lid the woman took it back from her, opened it and poured some water out. Cecily took the glass grate-fully, her hand trembling as she lifted it to her mouth. Some of the water spilled over the lip of the glass and she felt it land on her chest and trickle down until it was absorbed by her damp swimsuit.

'Are you okay?' Marnie asked her. Her tone was short and prac-tical, as if her only concern was that Cecily might collapse and that she would need to deal with her.

'Yes. Thank you,' Cecily managed by way of reply. 'I'll be fine in a moment. It was just such a shock, you popping up like that. I wasn't expecting you.'

In fact, Cecily had been expecting her ever since she had arrived in Greece; maybe even since she first handed her over and walked away all those years before, and yet it was clear that she was still totally unprepared for this moment.

Marnie shrugged. 'Sorry. Should have given you more warning. But it was just you and me here. Felt like a good opportunity. Sorry,' she said again.

'Don't worry,' Cecily replied. 'I'm fine, honestly.'

The world was beginning to right itself again now, her ears tuning back into the noise of the cicadas and the waves pulling back and forth across the shingle. In the distance she could hear the goats' bells' constant jangle.

'Oh, just look at me,' she continued, suddenly aware of the wet patches that were blooming across her breasts from the damp costume beneath her dress. 'I look such a mess. I've been in the sea, you see. I swam out to that cave. Have you been in there? It's amazing. Anyway, I was just going to go back to the hotel to get changed and then you . . . And . . .' Her sentence dried up as if someone had taken away her power of speech, and yet it felt very important to fill the space between the two of them with words, to stop Marnie from just evaporating into thin air.

'I haven't been out there, as it happens,' said Marnie. Her voice was cool, in direct contrast with Cecily's prattle. 'I can't swim. No one ever taught me.'

'Oh,' said Cecily. And then, 'I see.' Her heart was still beating faster than usual and she put a hand to her chest as if she could slow it down by pressing on it. Marnie couldn't swim. What did that mean? Surely every parent knew how important a life-skill swimming was? Cecily pushed these thoughts away. There would be time to understand more about Marnie's life later. 'How did you know where I was?' she asked instead.

Marnie cocked her head towards the path leading back to the retreat.

'Saw you leave the hotel and followed you down here,' she said simply.

Had she been watching her the whole time? Cecily wondered. She hadn't noticed anyone at the bar when she had arrived at the beach, but she'd been out swimming for quite a while. Maybe Marnie had just been waiting for her? She tried to remember whether there had been anyone sitting here when she came out of the water but her mind drew a blank.

It was disconcerting, the way that Marnie was just sitting there. She seemed so calm, whilst Cecily's insides were in turmoil. Cecily was dying to look at her properly but that felt rude, so instead her eyes fluttered backwards and forwards between her face and the space just behind her. There seemed to be no question of them touching one another.

'And are you well?' Cecily asked.

Marnie looked at her the way a teenager might look at someone who has just asked them if they know how to use the Internet.

'Well enough,' she said. There was no accompanying smile.

'And you work here, you said,' Cecily pressed on.

'Yep. At the retreat.'

'Do you live here, then? In Kefalonia?'

'No. Sofia just takes the hotel for June. After that we go back home.'

Cecily grabbed at the snippets of information as if they were clues in a puzzle. 'And where's home?' she asked, but Marnie shook her head.

'You ask a lot of questions,' she said.

'I'm sorry. I don't mean to pry. I'm just not sure what to say. It's all very strange, meeting like this. I mean, I've thought about it over the years, of course I have. Dreamt about it, even, but suddenly I'm all flustered and, well, I don't know what to say.'

For the first time, Marnie's mouth softened. She didn't exactly smile, but Cecily felt rather than saw a lightening about her features.

'I live in London,' Marnie said. 'Me and Sofia. We live in London.'

Cecily smiled. 'How lovely. I live in Harrogate. In North Yorkshire.' But of course Marnie knew this; she had sent the letter there. Cecily felt even more flustered and foolish as she realised this. 'I live with my husband Norman,' she added.

Marnie shrugged as if this information couldn't be of less interest to her.

'Are you married?' Cecily asked, and then could have kicked herself. She was going to drive her away if she wasn't very careful.

Marnie shook her head, a single shake from left to right, as if protecting the information she didn't intend to share was using up too much energy. Then she looked at her watch and stood up. Cecily's heart lurched. She couldn't be leaving, not so soon.

'Better get back,' she said. 'Nice to meet you.'

Cecily stood up so quickly that she felt her head swim, and for a moment the world went black around her.

'But will I see you again?' she asked, aware of the tone of desperation in her voice but unable to do anything to prevent it.

'I expect so,' replied Marnie. She turned and strode towards the bar, then cut out on to the road beyond and disappeared from view.

Cecily just sat there. Marnie Stone. Her daughter, her first-born, given away and now reunited with her fifty years later. She had thought of this moment so often over those years but nothing, she realised now, had prepared her for the shock of the reality. She sat, slack-jawed, and watched the waves pull backwards and forwards, her mind unable to settle on one train of thought. Was Marnie all right? What had she thought of her, the mother who had let her go when she was a tiny baby and at her most vulnerable? When would they meet again and be able to talk properly? Would she be able to make Marnie understand?

The goats must have moved closer in their constant search for fresh fodder and the sound of their clanging bells now filled the air to the exclusion of everything else. She wasn't sure which was louder, the bells or the cacophony of thoughts that was playing in her head. She was tempted to put her hands over her ears to muffle the sound. The heat, which until now had embraced her, comforting as a favourite eiderdown, now felt stifling, as if it could prevent her from filling her lungs. She lifted the glass to her lips and drank greedily, then regretted it as the cold water made her suddenly nauseous. Instead, she closed her eyes and focused on her breathing, taking deep swallows of air until she felt a little calmer.

Gradually her equilibrium established itself and she felt able to stand and make her way back. She took the path at a steady pace, carefully placing her feet so she didn't slip. Well, she thought as she climbed, that hadn't been the emotional reunion that she had imagined, but it was, at least, a start. The main thing was that the two of them had now met. She had to assume that Marnie had more to give her. Why else would she have invited her to come all this way? Cecily would just have to be patient and wait until she was ready to talk.

4

When she finally reached the little iron gate at the top of the path, puffing from the heat and the exertion, and stepped out on to the hotel terrace, Cecily was relieved to see that Sue from Milton Keynes wasn't there. She didn't want to get caught up in a banal conversation about her trip to the beach, wasn't even sure that she could speak at all. She tiptoed past the women who lay, eyes closed, on sun loungers, and headed for the sanctuary of her room. As she moved her eyes scanned the place for Marnie, but there was no sign of her. Their encounter at the bar now felt a little other-worldly, as if Marnie might have been an apparition of some sort or something that Cecily had dreamed up through heat exhaustion. In her heart, though, she knew that it had really happened. Now all she wanted was to get back and ring Norman.

Once in the corridor she could see the maid's trolley, laden high with fluffy white towels, and prayed that it wasn't on its way to her room; but when she unlocked her door she was relieved to see that her bed was freshly made and the water on the bedside table replenished. She clicked the lock on the door so that she wouldn't be disturbed, and made for the desk, where she sat down heavily, her breath rushing out of her lungs in a little huff. She had no idea how to get a line to England or how much such a call might cost. She would have to get Norman to call her back.

A card by the phone told her how to reach England and she did as it said, tapping out their home number with sharp, decisive stabs of her finger. The line was silent and then the familiar ring tone began. Cecily checked her watch. It would be mid-afternoon there now. Norman was bound to be in, although he might be having a little nap without her there to prod him awake. And then it was answered.

'Nightingale speaking,' Norman said brusquely. The children had always teased him about his telephone manner, informing him that most people just answered the telephone with 'Hello' these days, or even 'Hi', but Norman insisted on preserving the old formalities.

'Norman. It's me. She's here.'

There was a slight pause.

'Oh. Well, that's good.' Another pause. 'Isn't it?'

'Yes. Yes. It's good. She spoke to me. I was at the beach. I'd been for a swim.'

'And . . . ? What did she say?'

What had she said? As Cecily thought back over their conversation she realised that it had consisted of nothing but pleasantries. 'Well, not much, really. I was a bit surprised to see her there, to be honest. Just out of the blue like that.'

'Of course. A surprise. I can imagine.'

'I think I rather made a bit of a fool of myself, Norman. I almost fainted.'

'Well, that would be the shock.'

'Yes. I suppose so.'

'Bit irresponsible of her to jump out at you like that.'

'Well, she didn't jump out. Not really. I just wasn't expecting her.'

'And? What's she like?'

Cecily paused. What was she like? 'I don't really know. We didn't really talk about anything. She seemed nice. A bit distant, maybe. Coolish.'

There was a pause and Cecily could visualise Norman nodding at the receiver, weighing up what she had said.

'And are you all right? You said you nearly fainted. Do you need to see a doctor?'

Cecily could hear the concern in his voice now.

'No, no. I'm fine. It was just the shock.'

'Because I can come, you know, if you need me. You just have to say the word.'

Cecily would give anything for Norman to be there right now, to hold her in his arms whilst she told him of her encounter in minute detail, but she knew that was silly. She would be home again in a few days. It made no sense for him to race all the way out here.

'No. I'm fine. Honestly. She looks like Ralph, you know. She's got his colouring.'

Norman was quiet for a moment. 'I wondered about that,' he said thoughtfully.

'I'm hoping that now we've met we'll be able to talk a bit more, get to know each other. She sent me a photograph, last night. Of the box I made for her things. The things I gave her . . . before she . . . before they took her away.' Thinking of the box made Cecily's throat start to tighten.

'She kept it. For all those years.'

A sob escaped.

'Now, Cecily. Don't go upsetting yourself. Everything is going to be fine. Have you made a plan to meet her again?'

'No. I'll just wait and see. She's here, at the hotel somewhere, she said.'

'Well, I'm sure she'll find you when she's good and ready. It was probably a bit of a shock for her, too.'

'I looked such a mess, Norman. I'd been swimming and my hair was dripping wet. Lord only knows what she made of me.'

'Don't worry about that.'

'I'd better go. This call will be costing a fortune.'

'All right.'

'Are you okay?'

'I'm fine. Don't worry about me.'

'Okay. I'll go now. I'll ring again when I can.'

'Look after yourself.'

'And you. I love you, Norman.'

'I love you too.'

The line clicked as Norman replaced the handset back in their hall in Harrogate, but Cecily sat with the receiver in her hand until it began to beep loudly at her.

She picked up the photograph of the baby box and stared at it again. Marnie had kept it for all those years. And she had arranged for Cecily to come to Kefalonia and now she had introduced herself. It must all bode well, surely? She had passed Marnie's first test. They had connected. Cecily gathered up these tiny threads of hope as if there might be enough to knit them together into a whole blanket.

Marnie still looked so much like Ralph, dear, dear Ralph. Cecily closed her eyes and pictured him as she remembered him: dark and stocky, brooding and handsome. How differently her life would have turned out if only she had been a little older when she fell pregnant. It was an imaginary game that she had indulged in many, many times over the years. They might have let her keep the baby, and she and Ralph would have married. She would have worked in an office just like she'd hoped and he would have done something terribly important in the Civil Service. Dear Ralph had had such aspirations, even when they were teenagers.

But then, if it had been a different egg that had been waiting inside her to be transformed, the resulting baby wouldn't have been Marnie, and if she had married Ralph then she would never have had her beautiful girls. And what about Norman; lovely, steady, loyal Norman?

Yet maybe there was a chance to recover something of what had been lost. She and Marnie had reconnected. It wasn't much yet, but it was at least a beginning. Yes, there had been a lifetime of water under the bridge since they last met, but that didn't mean that they couldn't look to the future and build something new, starting from now.

Cecily lay back on the bed and hugged a pillow tightly to her. She imagined Marnie in the home that she and Norman had created, absorbed into their busy, noisy family life. She saw her laughing as she bounced Lily's baby on her knee, the boys all tearing in and out, and Felicity recounting some anecdote in outraged tones whilst the others all teased her gently. She and Marnie might have lost fifty precious years, but that didn't mean that they couldn't build a relationship from this point on. And Cecily would finally be able to tell anyone who asked that she had four daughters, not just three, and she would do it with her head held high.

All she had to do was wait for Marnie to be ready to talk, and then Cecily would tell her everything, and Marnie would understand.

5

ENGLAND

Mornings ran like clockwork in Felicity's house. The alarm went off at 6.30 and she got up, dressed and was ready for her day before she woke Hugo at 7.15. They ate breakfast at 7.30, either in the kitchen at the breakfast bar or sometimes in the conservatory if it was warm enough. Being in there meant that she could admire her garden as she ate her avocado on toast, and also keep an eye on what the gardeners had (or hadn't) done.

Today was a conservatory day. Even though it was early, the promise of the warmth to come was already tangible in the clear, fresh air that poured in through the open doors. It was going to be a quintessential English summer's morning – which unfortunately she would be forced to enjoy from the comfort of her fully air-conditioned office with its hermetically sealed windows in the centre of Leeds.

Richard was a little late coming downstairs. Felicity wondered if this might be on purpose to avoid another confrontation, but she was all argued out. She didn't have the heart for another round. She had expressed her extreme displeasure at his failure to make it to Hugo's recital the night before. He had no reasonable excuse – just a meeting that ran over. Not his fault. Couldn't be helped. One of those regrettable things. Felicity had pointed out that she too had work responsibilities and yet had managed to plan her time efficiently so that she could be there for their son. On top of that, Richard's failure had meant that she had been forced to sit at the back, which had made it nigh-on impossible for her to support Hugo when he needed her most. For this Richard also had to shoulder the blame.

This discussion, fractious and fraught, had been carried out sotto voce, as Hugo was already in bed by the time Richard got home. His evils had therefore been compounded by his missing the chance to explain his absence to their son before he fell asleep. Felicity had taken pleasure in pointing out how upset Hugo had been by this, although Hugo being upset was actually the very last thing that she wanted.

Anyway, it was water, if not exactly under the bridge, then at least well on its way this morning. There was no point churning it all up again. Felicity was bigger than that. She poured some muesli into Hugo's bowl and then tipped the milk on top. Hugo immediately began to pick out the raisins one by one, lining them up carefully on his side plate.

'Hugo darling, don't do that. You should eat each spoonful just as it comes, not pick out all the best bits at the start.'

'But I only like the raisins,' Hugo complained. 'Can't I have Rice Krispies?'

Felicity ignored him. He had Rice Krispies on a Friday. Today was Thursday, ergo it was muesli.

Finally Richard appeared at the door. He was wearing his lightweight navy suit trousers and her favourite lilac shirt. His dark hair, still damp from the shower, was pushed away from his face and his lightly tanned skin glowed. His mouth, however, was fixed in a scowl.

'Is there any coffee?' he asked, and Felicity bit down her irritation. Of course there was coffee. There was always fresh coffee at breakfast, or was that something else that he failed to notice these days? She set her face in a smile, however, and cocked her head in the direction of the cafetière.

'I can get it for you, Daddy,' said Hugo, and before either of them could stop him Hugo had slipped down from his place and was lifting the full cafetière.

'Put it down, darling. It's hot!' Felicity said shrilly, standing to take it from him, but Hugo, anxious to show how very capable and grown up he was, turned quickly away from her and sent the cafetière knocking into Richard's leg. The coffee splashed up and over his shirt.

'Oh, for God's sake,' Richard said, crossly pulling the shirt away from his skin to prevent it scalding him. A brown splodge stained the lilac fabric like rot on a rose petal.

Hugo looked mortified, but before he could burst into tears Felicity was at his side. 'Don't worry, precious. It was just an accident. We know you were trying to be helpful and Daddy can just nip and change his shirt. No harm done.' She threw a warning glance up at Richard.

'That's right, mate. Don't worry,' he said through gritted teeth.

Richard ruffled the top of Hugo's head as if he were a puppy, but his face was black as thunder. Then he turned and stalked back out to get changed. Felicity found a cloth to wipe away the spilt coffee and Hugo returned, reluctantly, to his muesli.

There was a buzzing, and Felicity saw that in all the confusion Richard had left his mobile phone on the table. She didn't recognise it. He seemed to have upgraded to the latest iPhone without telling her. Then again, his phone never left his person, so he might have had this new one for months for all she knew.

She picked it up and looked at the screen. It was an unidenti-fied Leeds number calling.

She answered. 'Hello. Richard Rowland's phone.'

'Oh, hello. This is Mercurio here. The restaurant?'

'Ah, yes,' replied Felicity. Mercurio was a new and very expen-sive restaurant in Leeds. She hadn't yet been, as it seemed it was easier to find a leprechaun spinning golden shredded wheat than it was to get a table.

'I'm so terribly sorry, but we've had a flood overnight. The restaurant will have to close today so that we can get everything dried out.' The woman sounded like she might actually cry at this devastating turn of events. 'I'm afraid that we cannot honour Mr Rowland's booking for 7.30 this evening. We will, of course, offer an alternative date. If you could just pass this message on and ask him to ring us at his earliest convenience.'

'Will do,' said Felicity, and ended the call.

A booking for Mercurio? How on earth had he swung that? And why hadn't he mentioned it? It wasn't her birthday or their anniver-sary and there was no other reason to go out midweek, not when they'd need to get a babysitter or bribe Marie-Claude to stay late.

Richard walked back in, his shirt changed to a crisp white one. He must have decided not to be cross with Hugo whilst he was gone as he was smiling unnaturally, but when he saw his phone in Felicity's hand the smile faltered.

'Mercurio rang. There's been a flood. They've had to cancel your booking.'

She handed the phone back to him and in that moment she knew. Anger, panic, relief: they all left their tell-tale signs on his face in less than a second. And then she saw guilt.

'You didn't tell me you'd made a booking for us,' she said, and set her jaw to stop her own emotions from displaying themselves. 'Did you clear it with Marie-Claude to babysit?'

'Sorry, darling, but it wasn't for you and me. It was a work thing, a colleague up from London for the night. I wanted to show them that we have decent restaurants here in the Frozen North. I'll just have to get Shawna to book us somewhere else. What a shame.'

It was slick. She had to give him that. He slipped so deftly from panic to reason. Then he shrugged in a 'what can you do' kind of way and even chanced a little half-smile.

He thinks he's got away with it, Felicity thought. He thinks he's had a narrow escape but that he's safe. Just how stupid did he think she was? To be fair, it had taken her a while to spot the signs, and to begin with she had thought that her rival was Marie-Claude. In fact it probably had been, at one time. But with all this work in London, all these nights away, it didn't take a genius to work out what was going on. No doubt he'd been planning to take whoever it was out for dinner and then he'd have rung later to say that he might as well stay over in town rather than wake her and Hugo by clattering in in the small hours. The sly bastard.

Felicity lifted her coffee cup to her lips and thought. Now was not the moment. Not with Hugo there. In fact, she would be much better keeping it all to herself whilst she decided what was best to do next. If this was going to implode, then she needed to get herself in exactly the best position to minimise the impact.

'Yes,' she said sweetly. 'A real shame. But I'm sure the indefatigable Shawna will save the day.'

He'd been there too, she thought. There had been a period the year before when their life had been peppered with unsatisfactorily explained late nights, showers taken before he slipped into bed next to her, whispered phone calls. But then normality had been restored and Felicity had assumed that whatever, or whoever, it had been had run its course. She would be lying if she said that it did not hurt, but these things happened, she knew, and she was nothing if not pragmatic. As long as Richard was discreet and her lifestyle remained unaffected, she could allow him his little dalliances.

Or so she had thought. But if he was straying again now, so soon, then she might have to alter her position. There was only so much a wife, even one as prepared to turn a blind eye as she, could tolerate. For now, though, she would merely observe.

Richard nodded, his full smile restored as his confidence returned. 'And as it'll be a late one I'll probably just grab myself a room in town and stay over, save me waking you. Is that okay?'

Felicity fixed her smile. 'Of course it is, darling,' she said.

6

GREECE

It was already Thursday and time was running out. Cecily's flight home was booked for Friday and she had still not had a meaningful conversation with Marnie. It was going to have to happen soon or it would be too late. Cecily supposed that she could always change her flight, extend her stay, assuming that the hotel had a free room. If not, maybe she could move out, go and stay somewhere else. There must be another hotel nearby with vacancies. She could feel panic rising in her like a flood, and she had to swallow it back down as she tracked the alternative plans in her head.

Then she reassessed. It was Marnie herself who had initiated this whole trip. Surely she wouldn't let her leave without taking the chance to talk properly? Cecily leaving Greece without a real conversation made no sense at all, until she remembered how Sofia had suggested that she was there on trial. Perhaps she had failed the test? She couldn't imagine what she might have done wrong, but that made no difference. If Marnie had decided that she didn't want anything to do with her then that was Marnie's prerogative, and there was nothing Cecily could do to change her mind. She would just have to hope that she'd said or done the right things. However, the thought of having come so close to getting her daughter back and then losing her again made Cecily feel sick. How would she ever bear that, knowing that somehow she had proved herself inadequate?

Still, looking on the bright side, there was a good chance that today would be the day, so she had better be ready. She dressed carefully in her favourite raspberry-pink sundress and applied a lick of matching lipstick before heading down for breakfast.

Sue from Milton Keynes was standing in reception with her suitcase packed. She gave a little wave to Cecily as she walked by.

'That's me all done for another year,' she said, shrugging her shoulders woefully. 'It's been lovely to meet you, Cecily. Next time I'm in Yorkshire we'll have to get together.'

Cecily smiled and made the necessary pleasantries, but neither woman made any effort to swap contact details.

In the dining room the usual suspects were all gathered, chatting animatedly about what they hoped the day ahead held in store for them. Sue had been the only person that Cecily had really spoken to, and now she was too nervous to be bothered with starting again with someone else. She cast a quick glance around, but when there was no sign of Marnie she settled herself at an unoccupied table away from the others. What did it matter if they thought her a little standoffish? She wasn't here to please them.

Cecily collected some freshly chopped fruit and Greek yoghurt in a bowl and drizzled them with sticky golden honey. Even the honey had sunshine in it, she thought as it caught the light. She would have to adapt her breakfasts at home to something similar. This combination was so delicious and so simple.

She had just taken her first mouthful when Sofia appeared at her elbow. Her mouth too full to speak, Cecily nodded her greeting.

'Hi, Cecily,' said Sofia. She was dressed in varying shades of purple Lycra today, her slim toned body and smooth brown skin radiating health. 'I have a message for you from Marnie.'

Cecily's heart began to bang and her scalp prickled. This was it. It was going to happen.

'She wondered if you'd like to join her for a walk? If you're free, that is.'

Cecily tried to swallow the food in her mouth before she spoke, her words coming out in a rush. 'Yes. Of course. When? Where?' She was aware of how desperate she sounded, but she didn't care. She was desperate.

'Outside the main door in fifteen minutes. She can make it later if . . .'

'No, no. Fifteen minutes is fine. I'll be there.'

Sofia smiled and then floated away. Cecily looked down at her bowl, suddenly no longer hungry. She forced herself to take another couple of mouthfuls but then abandoned it, drank a glass of orange juice and rushed back to her room to collect her bag. Her mind was racing. What time had it been when Sofia spoke to her? She should have checked. Now she had no way of knowing when the clock had started ticking on the fifteen minutes. It couldn't have been more than five so far, she was sure. She would clean her teeth and then go and wait by the door so that there was no danger of missing Marnie.

She virtually ran down the corridor on her way back, but when she got to the front of the hotel there was no sign of her. Cecily could feel sweat gathering across her back; her armpits were damp and her hands clammy. Would Marnie ever see her looking her best?

'Cecily.'

She heard a voice behind her and turned to see Marnie emerging from the kitchen door and strolling towards her. She didn't appear the slightest bit nervous.

'Hello,' Cecily said, suddenly, and ridiculously, shy. 'I got your message.'

'So I see,' said Marnie, raising a sardonic eyebrow, and Cecily felt foolish.

'Shall we go?' said Marnie, cocking her head towards the road beyond the hotel.

Cecily nodded and they set off, she tripping along behind Marnie like a child until the pavement was wide enough to accommodate them both.

Even though it was still early, the air was already warm and sultry and the cicadas were singing merrily in the bushes that lined the road.

'So,' said Marnie when the path widened and they were shoulder to shoulder. 'Why don't you tell me something about yourself?'

She didn't look at Cecily as she spoke, keeping her gaze fixed firmly on the road ahead. Maybe that was why she'd chosen a walk, Cecily thought, so they could talk without actually looking into one another's eyes?

'Oh,' replied Cecily, slightly taken aback by having the attention thrust on to her so soon. 'All right. Well, I'm Cecily Nightingale. You know that, of course. I'm married to Norman. We've been married since 1977. We have three daughters. Felicity is the eldest. She's thirty-seven and she's married with a little boy, Hugo. Then there's the twins. They're thirty-five. Well, actually Julia is still thirty-four. It's her birthday in a few weeks.'

'But you said they were twins,' said Marnie.

'Yes. It's a bit peculiar really.' Cecily was used to explaining the oddness of the twins' birth but now it felt as if Marnie was accusing her of lying, and she could feel herself becoming flustered. 'Lily, she's the elder, she was born prematurely, but the doctors managed to keep Julia inside me until I reached full term. So they are twins really, but Lily is older than Julia by seven weeks.'

'That's weird. But kind of cool,' said Marnie.

Cecily nodded and relaxed a little. It was kind of cool. 'And now Lily has five boys and Julia . . . Well, she's been busy with her career. She's a doctor, but there's no husband or children. Not that that's an issue, of course,' she added quickly. 'And you said that you weren't married, I think.'

Marnie laughed. It was a dark, bitter sound, as if the mere idea of marriage was preposterous. 'Me? No.'

'Any children?'

'Definitely not. Not sure I'd have made the best mother.'

Cecily wasn't clear what she meant by this, but now wasn't the time to ask.

They walked on in silence, Cecily taking her lead from Marnie. They were leaving the town behind now and the few sandy-coloured houses that punctuated the rocky fields had a shabby, unkempt look about them, although there were smart cars parked in drive-ways and washing hanging out to dry.

'And how about you?' Cecily asked, trying to inject meaning into the trivial question with her tone of voice. 'How have you been, Marnie?' She knew that it was ridiculous to ask about an entire life as one might enquire about a holiday, but where else could she start?

Marnie didn't answer at once. Her silence hung between them accusingly.

'What do you want me to say, Cecily?' she said eventually. 'What do you want to hear? That my childhood was idyllic, that my parents showered me with love and affection and I grew into a healthy and fulfilled woman?'

Well, yes, thought Cecily. That was exactly what she wanted to hear.

'I'm okay,' Marnie said instead. 'I get by. My parents did their best. It wasn't that great but we got through it and I'm still here. I didn't think I would be once or twice, but I did what I had to to get through. I'm happy enough now.'

She didn't sound it, though. She sounded as if little could be further from the truth. Cecily longed to sit her down and have her daughter tell everything that had happened from the moment she had said goodbye to her. She wanted to throw her arms around Marnie's neck and reassure her that everything would be all right from this point forward.

But that was not her place, and anyway, how could she possibly say that? She knew nothing about this woman; not really. She was stymied until Marnie gave her permission to approach. She had sacrificed any rights that she might have had a long time ago.

Cecily changed tack, trying to keep the conversation light between them. 'And you said that you worked with Sofia, is that right?'

Marnie nodded.

'Do you teach yoga too?' asked Cecily brightly, but Marnie made a scoffing noise at the back of her throat.

'God, no. I'm a cook. I do the food.'

Cecily was delighted. 'Oh, the food is just fabulous,' she said. 'The woman who arrived with me said that the food was the reason she kept coming back.'

Marnie mouth twitched into a suggestion of a smile, and she shrugged.

'Have you always been a cook?' Cecily asked, latching on to this flicker of positivity as if it were a beacon.

Marnie nodded. 'Studied at catering college after I left school. I'd like my own place one day but . . .' she shrugged again. 'Well, you know what it's like. Things never quite work out the way you planned, do they?'

In fact, they had a tendency to do exactly that in Cecily's world. 'No,' she said, shaking her head. 'They don't.'

A little further along the road, Marnie stepped away from the tarmac and they began to follow more of a track up a bank.

'There's a deserted village up here,' she said. 'Been empty since the fifties.'

'What happened?' asked Cecily, although she had no interest in why the village had been abandoned.

'Apparently they were building a new road but the villagers didn't want it to go through their village. Thought it would spoil the place, bring strangers etcetera and so they refused permission. The road went through the next village instead; all the trade went there and so this place died. Be careful what you wish for, eh?' She turned to look at Cecily, eyebrows raised.

What did she mean? thought Cecily. What had Marnie wished for? Was Cecily somehow a disappointment to her? 'What a sad story,' she said.

The houses were all dilapidated, their walls collapsed and roofs long fallen in. Trees grew where furniture should be and briars and bindweed strung with bright blue flowers scrambled over everything. It was actually very pretty, if you didn't think about it too hard.

Marnie swept her hand over a low wall to remove the worst of the debris and sat down. She reached into her backpack and took out two bottles of water, handing one to Cecily, who accepted it gratefully. The sun was hot on her head now and a drink would be very welcome. Cecily sat on the wall, too, taking care not to sit too close to Marnie and crowd her. Marnie took a packet of cigarettes and a lighter from a pocket and lit one. She offered the packet to Cecily who shook her head, hoping that she didn't look too judgemental.

They sat there in silence for a moment with just the noise of the insects buzzing around them. A scrawny-looking cat with patchy fur approached them cautiously, obviously hoping for a snack. It rubbed itself against Marnie's outstretched hand and Cecily tried hard not to recoil. Who knew what diseases such a mangy-looking creature might carry? Marnie seemed unconcerned.

'Did you think about me at all, Cecily? After, I mean.'

The question hit Cecily like a punch and tears sprang to her eyes. She blinked rapidly to disperse them. 'Oh yes,' she said, her voice breaking a little. 'I have thought about you every day for fifty years.'

Marnie nodded slowly, her face impassive, giving nothing away. 'So you were, what? Eighteen?'

'I was fifteen. Sixteen when you were born. Just a child myself, really.'

'Were you raped?'

The question was so stark, so very unexpected that for a moment Cecily couldn't respond. Whilst she gathered herself Marnie sat and continued to pull on her cigarette nonchalantly, her eyes narrowing with each drag.

'No. It wasn't like that at all,' said Cecily, anxious to get things straight so that Marnie could understand. 'I was young and it wasn't planned but I loved your father very much. We would have kept you if it had been up to us, but it wasn't. Decisions were made for us. We had no say in any of it.'

'Bit like me then?' replied Marnie steadily.

She was so cold, Cecily thought, so hurt. Questions banged against each other in her head. Was this hurt my fault? Did I do this to her? To my own child?

Marnie dropped the cigarette on the sandy ground, stubbing it out with the toe of her trainer, and then immediately lit another.

'It was 1968,' Cecily said, as if the date alone could go some way to explaining how it had been. 'Things were very different back then for unmarried mothers, especially ones as young as I was.'

Marnie made a triangle of her fingers and tapped them against her lips thoughtfully. 'Then tell me,' she said. 'Tell me what happened, Cecily, so that I can understand.'

PART THREE

1

WALES

Despite everything that happened to me that spring, it's the rabbit that I always think of first. Somehow, the memory of it became etched into my mind so clearly that I can still picture it now, fifty years on. I suppose the little creature stuck with me because it was smaller and even more vulnerable than I was, and yet it wasn't frightened. That tiny rabbit made me feel brave when I was at my most scared.

I remember standing on the gravel drive in front of the main house, my newly made friend Peggy at my side. I felt Peggy's hand searching for mine, her palm uncomfortably clammy against my cool skin. I shrugged her off dismissively. I wasn't feeling ready to be comforted just yet and certainly not by a stranger.

I watched as my parents' red Humber drove down the sweeping drive and away to the road beyond. To start with, I could just make out my mother waving goodbye through the back windscreen, but as they got further away all I could see were reflections in the glass. I concentrated hard on not crying. I didn't want Peggy to spot any chink in my armour. She might seem nice now but I knew enough about teenage girls to be wary. I clenched my jaw tight and blinked hard to disperse the tears before they had a chance to escape down my cheeks.

And then, as the red car became a dot and finally disappeared entirely, the baby rabbit hopped across the drive in front of me. It was tiny, no bigger than my fist, and it was completely black. I stared at it, puzzled by its random appearance. I thought it must be an escaped pet, but the house was so isolated with fields on either side that it was hard to see where it might have come from. It seemed not to understand that we might be a threat to it as it hopped nonchalantly by. It was so small and defenceless and yet it had a cockiness about it, as if it would happily take on all comers. That was how I was going to be, I decided. I might be far from home and with no idea of what was about to happen to me, but I could be fearless too. I nodded to myself in recognition of a decision made.

Peggy had set off back towards the house, but when she realised that I wasn't at her side she turned back and saw me staring at the creature.

'Them's lucky,' she said, nodding sagely at the rabbit. 'Black rabbits. Rare as hen's teeth, me dad says. We should make a wish on 'im.'

She screwed her eyes tight shut and crossed her fingers on both hands. I wanted to tell her that it was bad luck to make a cross with each hand, but instead I closed my own eyes and wished that when all this was over I could go back home and find Ralph still waiting for me as he'd promised.

When I opened my eyes again the rabbit was gone.

'Come on,' said Peggy, setting off again. 'We'd best get back or we'll miss tea and then there'll be nowt else 'til breakfast.' She was walking at quite a pace despite her size, and I had to run a little to catch up with her. 'There's scones on Saturdays,' she added, which presumably explained her haste.

'What did you wish for, then?' she asked me when I'd caught her up and we could talk more naturally. It appeared that Peggy had a very shaky understanding of the rules of wish-making.

'I can't tell you that,' I replied indignantly, 'or it won't come true.'

She threw me a look that told me she thought I was one step short of an idiot.

'Don't be stupid,' she said, her voice rich with disdain. 'Wishes don't ever come true. Do you think I'd be here if they did?'

I supposed she had a point. Off the top of my head I couldn't think of a single wish that had worked out recently. That said, I was only just sixteen and still an innocent in many ways. I might be too old for Father Christmas but I was still hedging my bets as far as magic was concerned.

'Well, I'm still not telling you,' I said, my chin raised defiantly.

We walked in chilly silence for a moment or two but then I remembered what my mother had told me. It was important that I did my best to get along with people and make some friends. After all, we were all in the same boat.

'How long have you been here?' I asked in an attempt to dispel the coolness that seemed to have settled between us.

Peggy, it seemed, was no sulker, and she immediately warmed back up.

'Two weeks,' she said. 'It's not so bad really. The grub's good and it's warm indoors. And they're mostly kind to us. Got me own bed here too. Have to top and tail with me sister at home.'

She grinned at me, her dark eyes mischievous, and I decided that whatever happened to me whilst I was here I would stick close to Peggy.

When we reached the house I made to go in through the front door, but Peggy pulled me back.

'We're not allowed in that way,' she said. 'That's for visitors. We can't use the main staircase either, so don't let Matron catch you. She's nice enough, but she's a stickler for the rules.'

Peggy led me round to a side door, which presumably had been the tradesman's entrance at some point. It struck me as funny that things had come to this, me skulking around the edges of society, and I made a note to tell Ralph in the letter that I planned to start that evening.

I followed Peggy into the house and down a dark corridor. The sounds of teaspoons on china and chattering voices became louder as we reached a dining room. Peggy went straight in but I hovered on the threshold and took stock. I had no idea who else would be here, hadn't given it any thought, but now I suddenly felt very shy. At home no one had known about me, bar my parents and Ralph's. Now it was no longer a secret and I would have to deal with the responses of strangers. I was young, but not too young to know that I was disgraced.

I took a deep breath and stepped into the room. It was a similar size to our dining room at home, but all the space was taken by two long trestle tables that ran parallel from one end to the other. Girls sat in long rows, chatting and laughing amongst themselves. Each had a plate and a cup and saucer in front of them.

My eyes darted, trying to locate Peggy. I didn't feel ready to meet anyone new just yet.

'Cecily. Over 'ere,' I heard her call and, grateful to have been rescued, I started across to where she had taken a seat.

She tapped the bench next to her. 'This is Cecily,' Peggy announced to the collected group. 'She's new.'

'Hello, Cecily,' a few voices called out. I smiled at no one in particular and then rushed to take my place next to Peggy, keeping my eyes low, my freshly made resolution to be fearless falling flat at the first hurdle.

Food was served. It was simple but tasty with plenty of bread for those who were still hungry. The promised scones followed, still warm from the oven, but served with margarine instead of butter.

When I felt a little braver I risked a glance at the others. I was probably the youngest, I decided. Some of them looked almost as old as my own mother. I hadn't imagined that, but I supposed it might make sense. It looked like several of them would be due any day and their bumps made the gentle swell of my own stomach seem inconsequential. I knew it wasn't, though. I would reach where they were soon enough.

There seemed to be some flat-stomached women, too, who I imagined must be the staff. I recognised Matron from the meeting with my parents before they left. She nodded at me when she caught my eye, and I nodded back and risked a little smile.

When the food had been demolished the girls all stood and took their own plates and cutlery into the kitchen. I followed and found a team already washing, drying and putting away the dishes.

'We work on a rota,' said a shrill voice to my left. 'As you're new you are given today to settle in, but then you should check the lists on the noticeboard daily to make sure you don't miss your turn.'

The speaker was a tall, dark-haired woman with horn-rimmed glasses that she peered over as she spoke. She was carrying a notebook and a pen which she jabbed into the air aggressively to emphasise her points.

'Each girl is allocated a number of chores, which must be completed to a satisfactory standard. If you are unsure what is expected then you should ask, and you will be trained accordingly. No excuses are tolerated.' She stared pointedly at my stomach. 'You should report here after morning prayers tomorrow and I will take you through what needs to be done. Do you understand?'

I nodded. As I looked up I caught sight of Peggy standing just behind her and mimicking her silently. She had the woman off to a T but I didn't want to get caught laughing, so I pulled my eyes away from her and back to the floor where I hoped they would not betray me.

'Good,' said the woman and then turned and stalked away, Peggy dropping her arms back to her sides just in time.

As the woman left the kitchen, Peggy and one or two of the others burst into laughter so loud that I feared the woman would immediately reappear and catch them, but she didn't.

'That's Mrs Croft,' said Peggy. 'She likes stuff done just so, and woe betide you if don't get it right. Her bark's worse than her bite though. Just do as she says and stay out of her way and you'll be all right.'

I was beginning to feel overwhelmed by so many new things. The clock on the wall said that there were still hours to go until bedtime, but suddenly I was bone tired. What I wanted more than anything was to be left on my own, but it was hard to see how I would ever get any time to myself whilst I was here.

Later that day I discovered the only place where I would have any private time. My bed was in a dorm with three other girls, Peggy included, but it was my only refuge. As I tried to settle myself under the unfamiliar flannel sheets and coarse woollen blankets, I could hear quiet but distinct sobbing coming from one of the other beds. No one got up to comfort whoever it was. It seemed as if this tiny display of despair was just accepted as part of life here.

I peeked out to see who was upset. The room was dark, save for a chink of light under the closed door. I couldn't make out any faces, but I thought the sound was coming from Peggy's corner.

2

The next day I was woken by the clanging of a brass school bell being rung in the corridor outside our room. I didn't remember falling asleep, but I seemed to have slept soundly enough and felt quite rested. I lay in bed as the others all came to with much groaning and complaining about the earliness of the hour, and ran a quick check of my emotional state. As far as I could tell, everything seemed to be all right in that department. I was well aware that the fitting response to the unholy mess that I found myself in, and the consequential banishment from the only home I had ever known, was distress. Obviously, I was supposed to feel sad and ashamed of myself and probably a little bit lonely, too, but what I was actually experiencing was a low-level hum of excitement. My mind kept flitting back to the Malory Towers books that I had propped up in the bookcase in my bedroom at home. If you closed your eyes to the obvious differences between us, I felt a little like Darrell Rivers, the heroine of the Enid Blyton stories.

This wasn't so far-fetched. The Home was a boarding school of sorts. I had a dorm to sleep in, a matron to enforce the rules, meals served at giant tables and girlfriends with whom to consume midnight feasts – well, I had Peggy at least, and whilst she was a little older than me, she already had the makings of a pal. I couldn't help but feel that this whole thing was more of an adventure than a punishment. And what was so wrong with that? My parents had always drilled into me that I should strive to make the best of any situation, and I couldn't do that if I was constantly on the brink of tears.

As a result, I was more curious than worried about how the day ahead might pan out. It was a Saturday, so I assumed we would be spared school, although even that didn't seem so bad here. Peggy had told me that although she had already left school back in Oldham, she was happy to go to classes at the Home and that the teacher was content to have her.

'Gets me out of doing the chores,' she'd said with a wink. 'I messed up me O levels. Never really saw the point of 'em at the time. I wanted to get out of school as soon as I could and start grafting, but then this happened' – she rubbed her bump affectionately – 'and me plans changed.'

I had wanted to ask her what her plans had changed into, but I didn't want her to think I was nosy. No doubt she would tell me in time. Peggy was 'one of those girls who opens her mouth before she engages her brain' – this being a favourite expression of my grandmother's, and used in such a disparaging way that I had always thought, until now, that it was a bad thing. However, I rather liked the way Peggy just said the first thing that came into her head. It was refreshing, and you knew exactly where you stood in her eyes. There were definitely worse faults.

I was aware that I was going to be away from school when the rest of my classmates were taking their exams. My father had made some off-colour joke about how he had spent a fortune on my education only to have me miss the vital part, and my mother had hissed at him to be quiet. He'd been smiling when he spoke though, joking and making light of my terrible predicament. I was lucky, I knew, that my parents had been so understanding. Some story or other would need to be concocted to explain my absence and subsequent need to resit the fifth year. There had been talk of home tutoring, too, but I thought that if I worked hard at my books whilst I was at the Home, then maybe I could minimise how far behind I fell and redeem myself more completely on my return. My dream had been to go to secretarial college. I saw myself trotting along to an office each day wearing a smart pencil skirt and a pair of kitten heels, with my lunch neatly wrapped in greaseproof paper. My parents had said that they saw no reason to change my plans, and so I assumed that that would be what happened to me next. I was sixteen and my life was still being done to me, rather than something in which I was making any active decisions.

I sat up in bed and looked around the room. The girl in the bed next to mine, Julie, was still nothing more than a lump under the blankets, but Peggy and Susan were up and getting dressed. My eyes were drawn to their silhouettes; both were further along in their pregnancies than I was. I was fascinated. I had never seen a pregnant woman before, other than ladies I'd passed and ignored in the street and whose shapes were hidden by voluminous smocks in any event. Even though I'd had several months to get used to the idea, I still could not connect what I saw of their bodies with my own. And so, as they pulled their undergarments on, I marvelled at their heavy breasts and the swell of their stomachs. Each was a different shape. Susan seemed to be large all over, with the tops of her arms and her thick thighs all wobbling gently as she moved. Peggy's bump was small and neat and confined to the space beneath her ribcage. It reminded me of a picture I had once seen of a python that had swallowed an egg whole. Susan also had savage-looking red welts over her skin as if someone had taken a belt to her. I later learned that these were stretch marks, but it didn't occur to me at the time that such vicious marks might have occurred naturally.

Susan caught me staring at them and she scowled at me as she pulled her petticoat over her head. I averted my eyes, but I could feel my cheeks and the tips of my ears burning.

'Prayers then breakfast,' said Peggy, before Susan could say anything to me about my wandering eyes. 'Then we do our chores and then we get the afternoon off.'

I nodded, keeping my eyes low, and hopped off my bed. Even though I had watched the others, I now felt shy having to change my own clothes in front of them. However, no one gave me a second glance. The pregnant female form was clearly of no interest to them, not like it was to me.

I pulled my clothes on as I'd seen the others do. None of them seemed to have bothered with a wash, so I didn't either. No one I'd met so far smelled bad, so there must be the application of basic hygiene at some point. I wondered about the prayers as I hadn't seen a church on my tour of the facilities. The memory of being shown around the Home with my parents the day before sent a sharp stab to my heart, which took me by surprise. Maybe I wasn't quite as together as I'd thought.

Prayers, it turned out, were held by Matron in the day room, a large sunny space that must have been some kind of drawing room when the house was occupied by a family. It was filled now with utilitarian tables, each with four chairs tucked neatly underneath. There were no soft furnishings of any kind other than the woebegone velvet drapes that had faded to an ugly russet colour over the decades that they must have been hanging there.

Most of the tables had filled up, so Peggy and I took one right at the front where there were still two adjacent chairs. I glanced around for a celebrant of some kind, but then Matron began to speak.

'Let us pray,' she said, and I bowed my head and closed my eyes. 'Have mercy on me, O God. Wash away all my iniquity and cleanse me from my sin. For I know my transgressions, and my sin is always before me.'

'You can say that again,' whispered Peggy, thrusting her stomach forward so that it hit the table in front. I bit back a giggle.

'Create in me a pure heart, O God, and renew a steadfast spirit in me. Do not cast me from Your presence or take Your Holy Spirit from me.'

I was starting to feel that the prayer was an attack on me personally. I didn't feel like a sinner, although I had been told that what Ralph and I had done was sinful by our local vicar when he came to explain our options to my parents and me. Matron was clearly thinking along similar lines.

'Amen,' she finished, and those around me responded in kind. I didn't say 'Amen'. I resolved that I wouldn't join in with any prayers that cast me in that unfavourable light.

There was a general stirring around me as heads were lifted and comments whispered to neighbours.

'Now, ladies,' Matron continued. 'Breakfast is ready in the dining room and then please can we all get on with the business of the day.'

'The business of unpaid skivvy,' muttered Peggy, and I nudged her in the ribs. Maybe I would be better off not hitching my wagon to Peggy. I had a feeling that she was going to get me into more trouble than I might manage on my own. But that, like being here in this slightly down-at-heel place, was all part of the adventure. I knew I shouldn't think of my stay this way but at that stage, when I had just arrived and it was all still ahead of me, I couldn't help it.

Breakfast was pretty much as tea had been the night before, and I noticed that most people were sitting in the same places. I followed suit. Ralph would say that I was being institutionalised. If he'd been there, he would have sat in someone else's seat just to see what would happen next. I might have done that too if he'd been with me, but on my own I never felt quite as brave. I supposed that there would be an element of churn as people arrived, had their babies and then left. My eyes did a quick scan of the room to see if I could guess who would be next, but under their checked smocks one bump looked pretty much like another. I would ask Peggy when we had a quiet moment.

After we'd eaten and cleared everything away, Peggy and I consulted the list of chores. I found my name.

'Hall and main stairs,' I read. 'Well, that doesn't sound too bad.'

Peggy ran a grubby finger down the list until it settled on her name. 'Me too,' she said. 'They must've kept us together so I can show you the ropes. Come on.'

She led me down a dark corridor to a scullery where we located a galvanised steel bucket and rag-headed mop apiece. We drew some hot water from the tap and set off to our work station. It was hard to stop the water from sloshing out of the bucket and all over the wooden floors; Peggy was better at it than I was, having got the knack of counterbalancing the weight of the bucket in her right hand by leaning hard to her left. She looked ridiculous, but she managed to walk without spilling a drop. I began by waddling along with the bucket held out in front of me, which left a trail of puddles in my wake so big that I had to return to the tap and refill the bucket. All the time I could hear Peggy guffawing.

''Ave you never carried a full bucket?' she managed to cough out between fits of laughter.

I hadn't, it was true, but honestly, how hard could it be? The second time I adopted Peggy's style, although I still spilled a little. By the time we got to the bottom of the stairs I had already cleaned much of the scullery corridor as well.

We set to, mopping the stairs, which looked perfectly clean already to me. When we reached the halfway point, Peggy was puffing. She stopped, leaned the mop against the wall and pressed her hands into the small of her back, pushing her hips forward so that her bump threatened to alter her centre of gravity.

'God, I'll be glad when the baby's out,' she said. 'It just makes everything twice as 'ard as it used to be.'

I hadn't really noticed this happening to me yet. It was true that Peggy's bump was larger and far more cumbersome than mine, but also, as housework was something that I'd never had to do before, I had no point of comparison.

'When are you due?' I asked.

Peggy shrugged. 'End of May, so what's that? About two months?' Her shoulders slumped and she blew out her lips in a huge sigh.

My baby was due mid-June and although I didn't know much about these things, I thought she looked far more than three weeks ahead of me.

'Could it be twins?' I asked tentatively. I didn't know whether there was any offence to be accidentally given or taken here. Might she think I was saying she was fat?

'Fuck me, I hope not,' said Peggy, her eyes wide.

I had never heard anyone swear like this before and it felt deliciously bad. Ralph and his brother sometimes swore at each other for effect, but only when they were certain that no one would hear them, and certainly never the 'f' word.

'Can you imagine having to push two of the little blighters out of you?' Peggy continued.

I hadn't even considered how it might be to push out just the one. My levels of naivety horrify me when I think about it now. I was led like a lamb to the slaughter, but Peggy certainly seemed to have more of a clue about the process of giving birth than I did and had given her situation more thought.

'Me mam says there's room for me and the baby at me gran's, but she won't take kindly to three of us turning up,' she said.

'So, are you going to keep your baby?' I asked. It was definitely too personal a question for so early in our acquaintance, but the idea of taking the baby home with me had not been something that had ever been discussed, so my curiosity was riding roughshod over my manners.

'Maybe,' Peggy said, picking the mop back up and starting to flick it across the landing. 'Depends.' And then, after a moment, 'Probably not.'

She fell quiet for a moment and I, picking up her mood, got on with my mopping. We didn't talk about the babies again that morning. I was desperate to build on the snippet of knowledge that I had gleaned, but Peggy seemed reluctant. It didn't matter, I decided. There would be plenty of time for more discussions along that line. I still had three months to go and hopefully I'd understand much more by the time my baby finally arrived.

3

Despite the apparent unlikelihood of such a thing, I grew to enjoy my Saturday afternoons at the Home. With the chores all done and no lessons or medical appointments to attend, our time was our own. Sometimes we would walk down to the town to pick up a yard of ribbon to finish off some booties or to buy some talc or other little luxury for us or our unborn babies. There was a cinema, and that was a favourite treat for those that had the money, because once you were inside the dark auditorium you couldn't see if anyone was staring at you. That was the thing that I found hardest of all: the way people reacted to us all, the great disgraced.

I'm not sure I had fully appreciated the impact of the position in which I found myself until I moved into the Home. Of course, it had been a shock when my period had failed to come, not once but twice. Ralph and I thought we had been careful, but apparently not quite careful enough. After that, I decided to confess what had happened to my parents. Ralph thought that this was a mistake, although I have no idea what he thought we should do instead. We had our first ever argument about it, in the old abandoned cottage behind our house – the very place, in fact, where the baby had begun – but in the end he had to accept that we needed some help. He even offered to marry me, although I wasn't sure that he meant it. We both had plans, and being married didn't fit well with them.

Anyway, then we had a family conference and it was decided that we were too young to be married with a baby. I remember the relief when this decision was taken out of my hands, and when I cast a sidelong look at Ralph, who was sitting, hair combed and tidy, on the very edge of his chair in our best room, I thought I saw the same in his expression.

Mummy was marvellous about it all. She kept stroking my hair and hugging me so tightly that I thought she was trying to squeeze the baby out of me. Daddy said that he didn't give two hoots for what other people thought and that I should stay at home and have the baby there, but Mummy was more pragmatic.

'That's all very noble of you, Peter darling, but we have to think practically,' she said. 'It's lovely that Ralph has offered to do the right thing by Cecily – you're such a treasure.' She had reached out and patted him on the hand and a blush swept across his cheeks as he accepted her praise. 'But we don't exist in a vacuum,' she continued. 'We have to think of Cecily's future. What we want is neither here nor there. It's what everyone else will think that's the issue. I know we are progressive and forward-thinking in this house – this is 1968, after all . . .' Her hair was cut in a boyish bob and she pushed it away from her eyes and tucked it behind her ear, as if the shortness of her hairstyle underlined her point. 'But not everyone thinks like us. So, I think Cecily should go away to have the baby and then some lovely couple who can't have children of their own will adopt it.'

My father opened his mouth to object, but my mother put her hand up to silence him. 'We can't have a baby here, Peter. It's impossible. Cecily has to finish school and I have my work. I think this is the best solution for everyone.'

There were tears glistening in her eyes. I wondered if she was sad for the baby or for me. I didn't feel sad, not really. It was a bit like being in a radio drama. I had lines that I had to repeat, but after the broadcast was over I would go back to being Cecily and not much would have changed.

Ralph was nodding. I knew that he loved me, but I could tell from the tension ebbing from his shoulders that he was relieved that such an easy solution had been presented to him. Only my father seemed openly upset by what we appeared to have agreed. He shook his head and pulled at his bottom lip as if we were all making a terrible mistake. My mother gave him a look that said 'we can talk this through later' and he raised his eyebrows and shrugged, but he didn't raise any further objections to the plan out loud.

So things were arranged through the church that my parents never attended, and I moved to the Home for the duration of my 'confinement', as the vicar had called it, with very little fuss. It came as a huge shock to me, the first time I saw the disdain in the eyes of people on the street and heard the mocking calls that the local boys shouted after us as we walked by. It wasn't pity that I saw, but something closer to disgust, and I learned that I was expected to feel ashamed of my condition.

I adapted quickly, not making eye contact with anyone nor passing the time of day, as I had been taught was polite. When I was with Peggy she never stopped talking, which made it easier not to notice the scornful looks and comments made not quite under the breath. Some of the other women from the Home were defiant, walking with their heads held high as if to challenge the locals to pass comment. Peggy and I weren't that brave, but I sometimes wished that we were.

As the Home was run by the Church of England, we were made to go to St Michael's on a Sunday morning, but we had to sit in the pews reserved for us at the back. I would keep my eyes low as I filed into my seat, but I could feel the contempt of the congregation as if it were a hot brand. We were the tarts from the Home, the fallen women, those girls who were no better than they ought

127

to be. Our disgrace was there in front of their eyes, writ large in the shape of our growing bellies. But, as with all things, I got used to it.

However, when we were safe in the grounds of the Home, we could forget the scorn of the world outside. We were teenage girls, after all, and it wasn't in our natures to dwell on things. My favourite Saturday afternoons were the ones that we spent outside on the lawn. As spring pressed on and the days became warmer we'd put blankets down on the grass and lie on our backs staring up at the clouds, spotting shapes in their ever-changing forms. We watched magpies and squirrels and even a shy deer that we saw in the distance once or twice. I told a couple of the girls about the little black rabbit that I'd seen on my first day, but we never saw a black one again, just the run-of-the-mill brown ones.

Peggy had been knitting a little matinee jacket for her baby in a pale primrose. The front and back were fashioned in an intricate lacy stitch and she had somehow crafted little flower buds into it as well. It was a work of art, and made the rudimentary hat that I was hacking my way through look even more shaming.

'Oh, look at that! I've dropped another stitch. Two rows ago too. I can't be bothered to pull the whole thing back. Do you think anyone will notice?' I lifted the forlorn little rag up for Peggy to see, and she laughed and shook her head.

'Maybe if the baby has three ears it can poke one out of each of the holes.'

I'd noticed that those who were giving their babies up for adoption never used a personal pronoun.

'Oh, be quiet,' I laughed, leaning over and poking her with a knitting needle. 'I'm learning here. I haven't done knitting since' – I thought about this. I hadn't knitted anything since we had been shown the basics in junior school – 'well, not for years, anyway. I'm doing my best.'

'Well, heaven help the poor little sod if they put that in its baby box. It'll grow up thinking its real mother was a cretin.'

'Yours is just gorgeous,' I said, partly to stop me thinking about the baby box and partly because it really was. 'Where did you learn to knit like that?'

'Me nan taught me,' said Peggy without looking up from her work.

It was clear that I was going to get no further explanation. I'd noticed that most of the others were happy to talk about their lives away from the Home, but Peggy always seemed a little more reticent to share. All I really knew was that she came from Oldham and that she shared a bed with her sister. It wasn't much to go on. She didn't ask me about my life, either. I would have been happy to tell her about Ralph and our plans for when we were older, but if ever I began a conversation along those lines she would suddenly think of something she had to do and wander away.

When I think about it now, I realise that whilst Peggy was my closest friend in those months, we didn't really know each other. Our conversations were about silly abstract things. Did we think it would be easier to live with no sight or no hearing, would it be better to be a ladybird or a moth, how long could you hold your hand in a bowl of iced water before you got chilblains? It was as if she was purposefully trying not to create any memories or leave any part of herself there. Looking back now, she was probably very wise.

4

I don't think I had fully grasped the implications of my situation until the first time I knew for sure that one of the babies had been taken away. Before that it just didn't feel real. My intellect knew that there was a baby growing inside me, but somehow I was shielding myself from the truth of that. After all, it was easy enough to push uncomfortable thoughts from my mind, and they kept us so busy with school and chores that there was very little time to just think. So I simply avoided doing it.

The day that all changed for me, I was sweeping the corridor near the nursery. I knew that this was where the babies lived, and to start with I'd been happy enough to go up there; but as my time wore on, my feelings began to change. Even though it should have been a joyful place by rights, filled as it was with all those healthy young lives, the atmosphere was gloomy and cheerless. The women who were there seemed totally focused on their child, each committing to memory as much as they could as the time ticked on. It was a thin line, I was starting to understand, between providing warmth and comfort but not becoming too attached, for they all knew how things would end.

I was humming a tune to myself as I swept the dust into a neat little pile, happily in a world of my own, when I heard the sound.

It was more of a howl than a cry, and there was more anguish in that uttered noise than I had ever heard before or since.

I dropped the dustpan and brush and hurried along to where the sound had come from. It was clear that someone needed help at once, and I was on hand to at least see what the problem was.

Slumped on the floor by the door to the nursery was Kathy, one of the older women. I hadn't really spoken to her much but I knew her name. To start with I thought she had fainted, and I could feel panic rising in my chest as I tried to decide what I should do, but then she shuddered and began to sob. The pain in each utterance was so tangible that it was almost as if she was being beaten.

I started to reach out to her but then I stopped myself. How would that help? I didn't know her and I was just a child, and so I backed away. I don't think she even registered that I had been there. I collected my dustpan and brush and then hurried downstairs to find someone better placed to help than me. The first person I ran into was Mrs Croft, the domineering woman who coordinated the rotas. Generally I had tried to stay out of her way on the advice of Peggy, but now I needed her.

'There can be no cause to run, Miss Hardcastle,' she said. 'Please try and show some decorum.'

'I'm sorry,' I muttered, 'but it's Kathy . . .' I pointed back the way I'd come.

Mrs Croft looked at where I was pointing, then back at me, and then her face softened. I saw that behind her severe spectacles there was a real sorrow in her pale eyes.

'Where is she?' she asked gently.

'By the nursery,' I replied simply.

Mrs Croft nodded her thanks and then set off towards the nursery.

Later, when I mentioned what had happened to Peggy, she just twisted her mouth into a grimace and shrugged. The clear message

131

that I received was that there was nothing to be done about it, and certainly nothing that would be achieved by discussing it. We would have our babies and then they would be taken away. That was just the rhythm of life there.

I never saw Kathy again, although the sound of that anguished cry as it ricocheted off the walls has never left me.

After that, my immediate future became more real for me. Up until then I hadn't really given so much thought to it, living mainly day by day and barely allowing myself to acknowledge the changes in my body. Now, I caught myself touching my stomach more often, rubbing the bump reassuringly and even whispering to it when I was sure that no one would hear me. They hadn't said that this was something I shouldn't do, but I was starting to feel instinctively that it would be frowned upon.

I tried to imagine what my baby would look like, who he or she would take after. Should I picture him or her with the cool, northern European genes of my family or the darker, more brooding look that was Ralph's? I even started wondering about the couple that might adopt my child. Would they really give my baby more than I could? Many of the women in the Home were giving up their children to what they hoped would be a better life, but I was from an affluent family. Who was to say that my baby wouldn't be better off with me?

And as I began to think like this my days became a little darker, even though summer was just around the corner. The reality of what I was about to do hung over me until I could no longer escape the shadow it cast.

I started to notice that some of the other girls would huddle together for hushed conversations when they thought there was no one to overhear. When I was newly arrived there, my teenage mind assumed that they were all talking about me and laughing at me behind my back, although I couldn't imagine what they found to say as we were all in the same boat in the social disgrace stakes, and I hadn't done anything to attract unwelcome attention. Now, though, I started to wonder whether they were actually talking about their babies and their hopes and dreams for both their own futures and those of their unborn children.

After my unsuccessful attempt at a conversation about all this with Peggy, I tried to befriend a couple of the other girls, smiling at them at mealtimes and offering them the water jug if I saw their glasses empty. However, as if sensing my ulterior motive, they didn't reciprocate, sending me tight little half-smiles in return and then turning back to their companions. It was clear that I wasn't going to be accepted into their inner sanctum.

Sometimes, the older women who had been pregnant before would talk a little about the actual experience of giving birth. Conversations like this were a double-edged sword for me. We were provided with almost no information by the Home and I grasped at every snippet, although the whole business sounded little short of barbaric and it frightened me greatly. I was missing my parents and my friends and Ralph dreadfully by then, and I longed for them to visit. I felt sure that if I had been at home, my mother would have helped me plug some of the gaps in my meagre knowledge. Then again, at least whilst I was away I didn't have to witness her disappointment. I knew that she tried to hide this from me, but I had seen it flit across her face and settle in her snatched glances at my father.

One thing was clear, though. There was nothing I could do to change any of it. I was going to have a baby very soon and it had been decided that it would be best for everyone if I gave it up for adoption. My part in the whole sorry pantomime was to keep my chin up, get through it with the least amount of fuss and then return home and pick up where I left off. This had all seemed so simple when I first arrived; now I wasn't so sure.

5

As summer was starting to knock on spring's door, the atmosphere in the Home lightened a little and girlish laughter rang through the corridors more frequently. There seemed to be a synchronicity of sorts between what was happening to us and to the world beyond the windows. Lambs had appeared in the fields around the house, and I wasted time watching them playing together, never more than a stone's throw from their mothers' sides. The trees, so bleak when I'd arrived, were now lush and verdant and the birds set about their morning chorus with more vigour.

We continued to grow, too. My baby wasn't due until the middle of June, still over a month away, but Peggy's date was fast approaching, and the closer it got the more pensive she became. I tried to jolly the old Peggy out of her, sometimes with success, but often she preferred to work in a thoughtful silence with me tagging along at her side.

'Oh, bugger this for a game of soldiers,' she announced one day as we were dusting in the dining room. She flopped down in the nearest chair, her smock ballooning around her. 'I don't see why they can't give the chores to them that's still got a way to go,' she complained, running her palm across her forehead. 'Every bit of me is jiggered. Even my hair feels done in.'

Assuming this was a joke, I was about to laugh, but when I saw her expression I stopped it short. She really did look as if the mere act of standing up was more than she could manage. I had never seen her look so exhausted and pale, and it wasn't like her to complain about anything unless she thought she might get a smile out of someone as a result.

'Should I go and get someone?' I asked anxiously. 'Matron maybe, or Mrs Croft?'

Having witnessed how Mrs Croft had been with Kathy I felt better disposed towards her, although I hadn't seen her display that kind of compassion since.

Peggy pulled a face that suggested she thought this an unhelpful suggestion, and then shook her head. 'I'll be all right,' she said. 'I just need to get me breath.'

She closed her eyes and exhaled in and out through her mouth, her breath short and ragged as if even this simple act was a challenge.

'Give me that polish,' I said, taking the tin from her. 'I'll finish off here and you can take a breather.'

Peggy nodded at me gratefully without opening her eyes.

She was still there when I'd finished the cleaning, but I was relieved to see that she now had a bit more colour in her cheeks and her smile was back.

'I wonder if I might pop early,' she said as we wandered outside to enjoy a bit of fresh air before tea. 'Me sister's first came two weeks before its time. Gave us all a proper surprise, he did.'

Then she let out a big sigh and a melancholy expression flitted across her face like the shadow of a cloud passing overhead. It was easy to forget why we were there and what lay in wait for us, especially when they kept us so busy during the days, but from time to time reality would catch us unawares. We were aware that the clock would really start to tick for us once our babies were born. Adoptions could go ahead once the baby was six weeks old – it was

135

something to do with the law, I gathered, although no one seemed terribly sure of the ins and outs. So if Peggy's baby did come early, her stopwatch would start counting down sooner. Even though we hadn't met our babies yet, I felt sure that we were all savouring the precious time with them inside us, and anything that cut things short was bound to be unwelcome. Even though there were women there who made out that they couldn't wait to get back home after they had given birth, I struggled to believe that they meant it entirely.

'Oh, I should think baby's far too happy in there to want to put in an appearance just yet,' I replied as cheerfully as I could manage, but we didn't make eye contact. Neither of us could be sure of any such thing.

Peggy's baby came that night. I think it must have been all the strange noises that she was making that woke me, because as I struggled up from sleep to consciousness there seemed to be no other reason why I should be awake. The others in our dorm were all still sleeping soundly, judging by the heavy, regular breathing that hung in the darkness between us. Peggy seemed to be struggling to get comfortable and I could hear her puffing out in long, deep sighs. Then she let out a sharp little cry.

'Are you all right?' I called to her across the blackness.

There was another muffled cry, as if she had stuffed the sheets into her mouth. I swung my legs out of bed and crossed the room to hers as fast as I could manage.

'Me waters broke,' she said. 'The bed's all wet.'

'Don't worry about that now. Can you sit up? Just stay here and I'll go and get someone to help.'

Usually Peggy would have objected to that suggestion, but instead she just moaned more loudly. The sound frightened me a little and, grabbing my housecoat, I made for the shadowy outline of the door.

'I'll be right back,' I said. 'Don't worry.'

My heart was racing as I left our dorm. Matron's room was across the landing and down the corridor. It was very dark and I had to find my way by running my hand along the wall as my eyes adjusted to the gloom. I'd never wandered about at night before, so I had no idea where the light switches were and I stubbed my toes on the skirting board, but I tried to push the pain from my mind. It was nothing compared to what Peggy seemed to be going through, and anyway this wasn't about me. I had to get help.

Eventually I found what I thought was Matron's room and knocked sharply. I was surprised by how fast it opened. Matron stood there, her nightdress slightly askew. She was wearing a hairnet to keep her grey curls under control and her eyes appeared smaller and more insignificant than they did during the day. It felt as if I was seeing something that I shouldn't, like getting an illicit peek into the staffroom at school.

'What is it, Cecily?' she asked. Her voice was very calm, even though it must have been apparent that a crisis was unfurling somewhere.

'It's Peggy, Miss. I think she's started.'

'It's a little early,' said Matron, and for a moment I thought she meant the hour until I understood that she was referring to the baby. For a moment I worried that she might try to send me away with a flea in my ear, so I prepared to stand my ground. I might know next to nothing about labour, but it was clear to me that something very significant was happening to my only friend.

I was about to stress how real I thought the emergency was but Matron just set off towards our dormitory without requiring any further explanation. The darkness seemed to present no obstacle to her and I assumed that she must have done many nocturnal dashes through the corridors of the Home in her time.

By the time we got back, the others were awake. Susan was stroking Peggy's back, which seemed to be irritating rather than soothing Peggy. Julie was bouncing from one foot to the other and wringing her hands, but not doing anything helpful.

Peggy was sitting up now, her face a sheen of sweat, strands of dark hair clinging to her neck. A wave of panic hit me. Was this what it was like, having a baby? Was this what I should be preparing myself for? I pushed the thought aside. I couldn't waste time worrying about that now. Peggy needed me, and even though I had no idea what I could do to help her I wanted to give her my whole attention.

'When did it start, Peggy?' asked Matron.

'About midnight,' Peggy said through gritted teeth. 'The pains are about every five minutes now.'

'Then I think we need to get you downstairs. Can you walk, do you think?'

Peggy nodded, although I had my doubts.

'Cecily, can you get Peggy's housecoat and slippers, please?'

I did as I was asked and dropped to my knees to slip the slippers on to her feet. I felt completely useless, but this tiny gesture was something that I could do to help my friend.

Leaning heavily on Matron's arm, Peggy pushed herself up to standing and the pair of them shuffled towards the door.

'The rest of you go back to sleep,' said Matron firmly as she flicked off the light and closed the door behind them.

After a brief discussion, the three of us slunk back to our beds, and soon enough the regular breathing recommenced. Sleep didn't come to me, though. I lay in the dark, staring up at the ceiling, thinking about what I had seen and what could be happening to Peggy elsewhere in the building. Matron had seemed very calm, so I had to assume that this was how labour usually progressed. I didn't know whether this was something I should worry about, but as there was nothing I could do to change things I decided to be grateful that I had had a gruesome preview of what might be in store. In a little over a month, this would happen to me, too.

I turned over on to my side and stuffed a pillow between my knees, which made things a little more comfortable. As I rearranged myself, I felt a sharp kick to the wall of my womb and I stroked my stomach reassuringly. My baby, the baby that Ralph and I had lovingly but accidentally created, was lying safe and warm inside me. As I drifted off to sleep, I didn't let myself think about what would happen when it was time for him to emerge. It never crossed my mind that my baby might be a girl. After my months in the Home, I had formed a view that being a boy was most definitely preferable to being a girl. Wasn't Ralph at home, after all, just continuing with his life as if nothing had changed? There was, or so it appeared to me, no justice for girls.

6

Peggy wasn't at breakfast. I was disappointed, but I supposed that having the baby would mean that the normal pattern of our lives might be disrupted for a little while. Not having had anyone in my dorm give birth up until then, I hadn't really noticed what happened next or how long it was before the new mother reappeared.

'Peggy went down in the night,' announced Susan to no one in particular.

A few of the others nodded or raised their eyebrows.

'That's early, isn't it?' asked someone, and Susan nodded excitedly.

'Nearly four weeks early,' she said proudly, as if this had been her doing.

I felt disgruntled and a little cheated. Peggy was my friend and it was surely my job to impart her news to the collected company. However, no one seemed particularly interested in the information in any event.

Undeterred, Susan tried again. 'You should have seen her. Puffing like a steam train she was, poor thing.'

Again a nod but not much more greeted Susan's news, and so she gave up and turned her attention back to her neighbour.

Peggy wasn't there at lunch, nor at teatime either. By then I was starting to worry about her, so I decided to take my courage in my hands and go to find Matron. I had never had cause to have a direct conversation with her before the previous night, but I felt sure that she would tell me how Peggy was and the sex of the baby, at least.

After we had cleared up, I made my way to Matron's office. It had been a hot day, the kind you sometimes get in May and that takes you by surprise. The heat was fading now but the sunlight that flooded in was golden, casting everything in an almost ethereal light.

The door to Matron's office stood open and I could see her sitting at her huge desk, spears of sunlight falling on her back from the window behind her. I knocked tentatively on the door and she looked up impatiently. When she saw it was me, though, her face softened.

'Ah, Cecily,' she said kindly. 'I was going to come and find you. Please come in. Close the door behind you, would you?'

It was like being summoned to see the headmistress at school, and I felt my heart pump harder even though I had done nothing wrong.

'Sit down,' Matron said, gesturing to the chair opposite her.

I sat, perching on its edge to the extent that my increased size allowed me to perch at all. I found that I was biting my fingernail and I had to make a conscious effort to drop my hands to my lap.

'Thank you for your help last night,' she began. 'I was glad to see that you stayed so calm. Was that the first time you've seen anyone in labour?'

I nodded.

'It can be a little distressing to begin with, especially when it is happening to someone you are close to. You are close to Peggy, aren't you?'

I nodded again.

'How is she?' I asked. 'And the baby,' I added, although this was very much an afterthought.

Matron took off her reading glasses and placed them deliberately on the desk in front of her. I could see the dints above her nose where they had been resting.

'Peggy is fine,' she said.

I smiled and opened my mouth to ask when she would be back with us, but Matron put up a hand to silence me. 'However, I'm very sad to tell you that her baby was stillborn. It was a little boy.'

It took a moment for her words to settle in my mind and I stared at her dumbly as I processed them. Peggy's baby was dead. All those months of carrying it, him, and it had all been for nothing. She had been through it all: the pregnancy, the catcalls, the stigma, being banished to a place away from everyone who loved her, and finally the labour, and yet she had no baby to show for it. Poor, poor Peggy.

This wasn't where my mind settled, though. Another, stronger thought came to me then. She need never have moved here in the first place if the baby was going to die anyway. What a waste of all those months.

My sixteen-year-old self still had so much to learn about love and loss, about grief and pain. To me it seemed simple. Now Peggy would never have to go through the horrors of giving up her baby, because there was no baby to give up. That had to be a better solution than what I was going to have to deal with, so that made her luckier than me. And even if she was a bit sad just now, she had always known that she would only have the baby for such a short time so things surely weren't that bad.

My adult self struggles to recognise me in this callous thought process. When I think of all the hours that I spent over the following decades dreaming about, but also weeping over, the baby that I had and lost, it seems incredible that I could ever have thought in this unemotional way, but I suppose I was so very young and I understood nothing.

So, having established in my own mind that there was a bright side to what Peggy had just been through, my mind then turned to my friend.

'Can I see her?' I asked.

That was the answer to my conundrum, I thought. As soon as I had Peggy in my sight, I would be able to judge what the correct response to the death of her baby was. Peggy was so much better at explaining these things than me. When I saw her face, I would know exactly what she thought about everything, and I could take my lead from her.

And I did want to see her so much then, I realised. Even though she had been in the labour suite for less than a day, I missed her more than I could have imagined and I couldn't wait for her to breeze back in, all smiles and sarcastic comments. She could tell me what it was really like to have a baby, give me all the details that the midwives seemed so reluctant to share. We could cry over her loss and then get back on with our day-to-day life.

'I'm afraid Peggy has gone,' said Matron.

My jaw fell open. Gone? How could she have gone? I'd only seen her the day before. I shook my head. Matron must have got it wrong. Peggy would never just leave without even saying goodbye. She was my friend. She was my best friend.

'We don't usually recommend that a new mother travels so soon after giving birth,' Matron continued, ignoring my obvious shock, 'particularly not in circumstances like these, but Peggy was determined to get back to her family. She discharged herself this afternoon.'

That sounded so much like my friend Peggy, not allowing herself to be dictated to by others, ploughing her own furrow.

'But what about her things?' I asked desperately, although this was immaterial really.

'Mrs Croft collected them whilst you were in school,' Matron said simply.

'And she's really gone? Without saying goodbye?'

My eyes started to prick and before I could check them, big fat tears were rolling down my face. Peggy was the closest thing that I had to family at the Home, and yet she had deserted me without a second thought and gone back to her real life as if I meant nothing to her at all.

Matron tipped her head to one side and gave me a sympathetic look. 'There, there, Cecily. Don't let on so. I'm sure you'll miss Peggy very much, but you can't blame her for not wanting to come back and see you all with your babies when her little boy is with God.'

But I could blame her. I could blame her very much. How could she just have abandoned me without even saying goodbye? In that moment, I felt like I would never forgive her. And then I realised that not only would I probably never see her again to forgive, but that now I was entirely on my own.

I stood up and, without saying another word to Matron, I turned and fled.

7

The six weeks between Peggy leaving and my baby being born passed in something of a blur for me. I went through the days just as I always had, with chores and school each filling the space between dawn and dusk, but there was little joy to be found in any of it.

Once, when I had about a month to go, my parents came to visit. It was the first time that I had seen them since they had dropped me off all those weeks before. Visits were allowed, but hardly encouraged. No private space was made available for us and so we sat in the dining room and spoke in hushed tones for fear of being overheard.

I thought my mother looked thinner than I remembered, but perhaps that was because I was surrounded by pregnant women now. Despite this, though, she seemed determinedly cheerful, as if maintaining a stiff upper lip was her mission for the day. By contrast, my father seemed on the verge of tears, and each time I looked at him he dropped his gaze slightly so that our eyes did not have to meet.

'You look so well, darling,' said my mother as she settled herself into the threadbare dining chair opposite me. 'You are positively blooming.'

'Yes, I'm fine,' I replied flatly.

'How is the food?' asked my father. 'They're clearly not starving you.' As soon as he'd said this, he seemed to regret it, as if he was casting aspersions on my bulk, which was ridiculous bearing in mind the baby that I was carrying.

'The food is fine,' I said. 'We get decent enough portions and there are scones for tea on Saturdays.'

The moment I said this, it brought Peggy to mind, but I tried push the image of her away. I knew that if I told my parents about her it would make me cry, and then I might never stop. I hadn't managed to make any other friends since she had gone, and whilst I did have people to talk to, none of them seemed very interested in me or my ideas. But if I told my parents this, my mother would worry, so when she went on to ask about the other women, I made up some lie about my many and varied friendships. This seemed to satisfy her, and I felt relieved that I had saved her that pain at least. There was no point in making her miserable on top of everything else that I'd done to them.

'How's Ralph?' I asked.

I had been writing to him regularly each week, and he had always responded eventually. However, his letters had become more rushed and less heartfelt as the weeks dragged on. I couldn't decide whether he was growing less fond of me or if his daily life was now so busy without me in it that he wasn't sure which parts I would be interested in. Either way, the distance between us seemed to be growing ever greater.

'Well,' said my mother awkwardly, 'we don't see so much of him these days, now that you're here, but I understand that he's doing well and working hard for his A levels.'

Somehow I had forgotten that Ralph would sit his A levels that summer and then move on to university, leaving me behind. It had all felt so far away when we had discussed him leaving the previous autumn, but now I supposed he had only a couple of months before he went to begin his new adventure without me.

'Oh,' I said. I wasn't sure what else to say.

Suddenly my father sat forward in his chair, his head thrusting close to me and his grey eyes locking on mine.

'Are you sure about the adoption, Cecily?' he asked earnestly, grasping my hands and squeezing them tightly. His hands were cool and dry, and even though he hadn't held my hand for years, they felt so familiar to me. 'It's not too late to change your mind, you know.'

My mother reached out and tapped him on the knee.

'Hush, Peter,' she said. 'We've discussed this. You know that it's for the best if Cecily gives her baby to somebody who is longing for a child and can give it a loving home.'

'But we could give it a loving home,' said my father imploringly, turning his full attention on her instead of me. 'You know we could.'

My mother shot him a look and he dropped his head, focusing on a crust of bread that had been dropped at lunchtime and overlooked.

I said nothing. What was there to say? I knew that if we kept my baby, then my dreams of college and a job in an office would be destroyed forever. I didn't feel old enough to have a child, despite the obvious evidence to the contrary. The idea of bringing a baby home, explaining it to the world at large and living with the consequences of being an unmarried teenage mother, was more than I could contemplate at that time.

'I know. I'm sorry,' sighed my father, as he slumped back into his chair. 'I just wish that things could be different for you, my princess.'

Looking back, I don't think I had any appreciation of how very forward-thinking my parents were. But they were in the minority in 1960s Britain, and my dear mother was astute enough to realise that their love for me and my unborn child would not be enough to protect me.

I think I made a switch in my mindset that afternoon. It finally became obvious to me that having my baby and then giving it away was something that I was going to have to deal with for the rest of my life. As my parents drove away that second time, I walked back to the Home alone and dry-eyed.

I went into labour the day after my baby was due. I approached the whole experience with a resigned pragmatism. What else was there to be done? The birth was straightforward, as far as I understood, and the baby, a girl, was healthy. There were two midwives with me, one old enough to be my grandmother and more stern than anyone I had ever met. She barked orders as if I were a private in the army and I simply did as I was bid until the placenta was pulled from me and it was all over. The other midwife was younger and more sympathetic. When the baby had been cleaned and swaddled in a pale green blanket so that only her face was visible, she passed her to me with a kind smile.

'Here you are, lovely,' she said. 'Have a little cutch with her before we take her down to the nursery.'

I saw the other midwife shake her head, but I reached out and grabbed my baby before they could snatch her away. I will never forget the smell of her, so fresh and new and perfect. When each of my other children was born, I found that instead of being caught in the joy of the moment, my mind immediately whisked me back to that sterile room and the first time I ever held a child of mine. The fact that no one would take the new one from me seemed to offer very little comfort.

8

It's hard to explain now how it feels to hold your newborn baby in your arms, knowing that in six weeks' time someone will take her away. I certainly wasn't ready for the emotional tsunami that engulfed me. To be fair, I had tried to prepare myself beforehand. I'd told myself that it would be best to regard my child dispassionately, knowing as I did that she would be mine for such a short time. For those six short weeks I had a job to do, and it would be best for everyone concerned if I just got on with it and didn't dwell on anything. But when I gathered her tiny body into my chest and nuzzled the top of her downy head with my nose, the love that I felt for her seemed to come from a place so deep inside me that it was almost as if the child was an actual part of my own body.

She was the spitting image of Ralph, right down to her slightly flattened nose. She had thick dark hair, so much of it that it looked a little odd on such a tiny baby, and Oxford-blue eyes that appeared almost black in electric light. Someone once told me that nature makes sure that a baby looks like its father so that he is drawn to protect his own. Looking at the little life that Ralph and I had created, it was easy to believe that this was true. If I hadn't been there to see her emerge from my womb, I might have been forgiven for thinking that she was no child of mine. When I looked into her funny little wrinkly face I saw nothing familiar staring back at me.

I almost felt cheated. I had done all the work. I had incubated her for nine long months and endured the excruciating pain of childbirth. It seemed so unfair that nothing about her mirrored my own image. I remember thinking that maybe, in time, my side of the family would emerge in her features, and then I remembered that that would be something I would never witness.

I'd barely had time to unwrap her and count her tiny fingers and toes when the midwife lifted her out of my arms and took her to the nursery. I wept then, although I did not know whether this was in relief that the moment that I had been building up to for so long had now passed, or in fear of what was to come. The midwives left me alone, either from kindness or to avoid having to deal with another newly bereft mother, and I sobbed quietly until I had nothing left to give. Then, around half an hour after they took my baby away, the older woman came to tell me that a bath had been drawn for me. Gingerly I slipped down from the bed and followed her, every muscle in my body aching, including my heart.

After I was clean again, they brought me a cup of tea and two slices of buttered toast and I was allowed to go to my bed in the dormitory for the new mothers, which was to be my base for the remainder of my time at the Home. Even though I didn't believe that I would ever sleep again, I drifted off quickly and woke to the alarm bell the following morning as usual.

Nothing had changed, and yet everything was different.

Life as a new mother in the Home wasn't at all what I had been expecting. I had thought I'd be busy with my school work and chores, but now my main job was caring for my baby, and I was run off my feet. Who knew that such a little person could create so much work? Peggy had told me that in the home where a friend of hers had been sent, the mothers weren't allowed to touch or even see their own baby, and were made to care for another woman's child. Thankfully the regime was different where I was. I'm not sure now which was kinder – getting to nurture our own baby, albeit briefly, and then to feel the pain of their absence more keenly, or to make that break from the very start. It wasn't something that I thought about at the time, but I have contemplated it over the years since. I think, though, that despite the pain at losing my baby and how much that hurt, I was grateful for the little time that we did spend together. Then I could pretend that there was to be no adoption and that I would take her home to a perfect little cottage where Ralph and I could play house together.

The babies were all kept in a large airy nursery on the top floor of the house. I knew where it was, of course, but had only ever peered in through the door before. Now I was allocated a table on which to change my baby, a basket for her things and a cot where she would sleep. The new mothers slept in a room just next door, and we took it in turns to spend the night in the nursery and go to wake a mother when their baby needed feeding.

Some of the others complained about the broken sleep when their turn came around, but I loved my nights on duty. I would tiptoe from cot to cot and watch the babies sleeping. I liked to compare them all, noticing which was larger, which had rosy complexions and which were more olive-skinned. Even though I knew that I was biased, I felt certain that my baby was the most beautiful of them all. It seemed to me to be an objective fact. My child had more delicate features and a symmetry to her face that some of the others definitely lacked.

One day there was only me and one of the midwives in the nursery. The others had taken their babies out for a walk, but mine was a little snuffly and so it had been decided that we should stay indoors until her breathing improved. She was lying on a rug at my side whilst I endeavoured to set a sleeve in a jacket that I was knitting. Whilst my work would never come anywhere close to the standard of Peggy's, my skills had improved over the months and I could now make a passable stab at a more complicated garment.

The midwife, I think her name was Stella, was rearranging the blankets in the cots, smoothing each down and then turning back a corner so that the space looked cosy and inviting. When she came close to us, she leaned over my baby and stared at her hard, absorbing all the details of her face with focused intensity. Some of the older babies could smile, I'd noticed, or at least pull an expression that might be interpreted as a smile, but my little girl was endlessly solemn, rarely crying and never giving anything away about what might be going on inside her head.

'She's such serious little thing, this one,' said Stella, reaching down to run the pad of her finger over my baby's cheek. 'And that tiny face seems so wise. It's almost as if she's been here before.'

It was a silly thing to say; of course, as you couldn't possibly tell how intelligent the child was just from looking at her, but I could kind of see what she meant. There was something about my baby's eyes and the way she watched you that made you think that she was quietly getting the measure of you and storing her observations up for another time. I wonder now if she knew, at some instinctive level, what was going to happen to her. As I looked at her lying there staring up at us, I could feel my throat start to tighten and I breathed in steadily, as I was learning to do when this happened, to make the burden of impending loss easier to bear, and refocused my attention on my knitting.

'When is she next due a feed?' Stella asked me, and I was relieved to be back in the safety of more quotidian matters where I felt less emotionally exposed. I looked up at the big clock on the wall. We were supposed to feed our babies every four hours whether they seemed hungry or not, although some of them started to grizzle long before the time was up. When I heard them, my breasts would swell and ache as the milk strained to be released, and little damp circles would form on my vest and blouse even though it wasn't my baby that had cried. Just thinking about her could be enough to set me off as the four hours came round. The power of my body's response to the smallest provocation would have been fascinating to me had it not been so heartbreaking.

We were permitted to feed our babies for the first four weeks, and after that they were weaned on to the bottle in anticipation of them being taken to join their new families. Every part of me dreaded this transition. Once our baby was weaned, the midwives would bind our breasts tightly with long, butter-coloured bandages to stop our milk from flowing and trick our bodies into thinking that it was no longer required. Sometimes I had seen the damp patches of milk blooming on the blouses of bound women, the layers of fabric insufficient to disguise the flow that our instincts drove ever stronger. I had seen these women in the dorm at night, crying with the pain of their swollen breasts for which their babies were no longer allowed to provide any relief, and I thanked God for each day that I was able to lift my own child to my nipples.

'She'll feed again on the hour,' I replied as I struggled to unpick the stitches that I'd just done.

'And she seems to be breathing a little easier now,' Stella added. 'I think she's over the worst of that little cold.'

I wondered what would happen if my baby was below par on the day that they came to take her. Surely they wouldn't release her if she was unwell? It would be confusing enough for her to be taken by strangers without feeling poorly on top. But this thought had too many constituent parts that were painful to consider, and so I resolved to take just one day at a time and to make the most of every moment that I had left with her, however long that might turn out to be. I knew that some of the mothers managed to hold on to their babies for longer than the six weeks, no adoptive parents coming forward to claim them, but mine was so beautiful that I knew they would find someone for her as soon as they were allowed.

We weren't encouraged to name our children. This, we were informed, would result in an unhelpful attachment forming, as if the mere adding of a name was the thing that would create an unbreakable bond between mother and child. Therefore, each child was simply referred to as 'baby' or, where confusion might arise, our surnames were added. I assume this was designed to be as impersonal as they could make it without actually resorting to numbers, but in many ways calling her Baby Hardcastle did more to link her to my family and all the history that was caught up in that name than if I'd just given her a Christian name.

Despite the rule, however, many of us did choose a secret name that we used in our heads and whispered in their ears when no one else was listening, as if the memory of the sound of our voices might become lodged in their heads and sustain them once they were parted from us.

I named my baby Faye after Faye Dunaway. Ralph and I had sneaked into the pictures to see *Bonnie and Clyde*, me borrowing a pair of my mother's high heels and her reddest lipstick to convince the ticket seller that I was sixteen. I did not want my baby to turn out to be a bank robber, but I did hope that this moniker, even though it would be hers for such a short period of time, would imbue her with a spirit that would stand her in good stead when she faced adversity as her life progressed. Of course, I longed for her to live a charmed existence, but although I was young, I wasn't naive and I knew that she would have to face some hard times. Also, more practically, a neat, one-syllable name was easier to disguise as I whispered it into her tiny shell-like ear.

A chatter of voices outside signalled the arrival of the others back from their walk. My baby, Faye, turned her head towards the sound but she didn't seem alarmed by it. I was so proud of her then. It sounds silly now, to be proud of such a small, insignificant action, but that's how it was; we only had the small things to hang on to, and I was determined to hang on to as many as I could.

9

They didn't tell me exactly when it would happen, although I'm sure they must have had a date in their sights from the very beginning. Of course, I could tick the days off the calendar myself, but I chose not to for reasons of self-preservation. I simply took each day as it came, learning and becoming more confident with each one that passed.

In the long weeks before my baby was born I had imagined that when the day finally came to give her away, I would be prepared. After all, I reasoned to myself, I would have had six long weeks to say my goodbyes, and I really was desperate to get home and to slip back into the life that I had left behind. But as my six weeks anniversary approached, I could feel a desperate kind of panic settling over me. It felt like a balloon in my lungs, each day blown a little larger so that my breath shrank until all I had left were little snatches of oxygen to survive on. I would grasp any opportunity I could find just to stare at her as I tried to fix each of her features in my mind, like a photograph developing in a darkroom. I examined the way her tiny fingernails were set, how her hair grew from her forehead around the swirling cowlick that she would no doubt curse when she was older, the darkness of her eyes, no longer deep blue but a rich brown like roasted coffee beans, which matched the colour of her hair perfectly. Each of these details I clutched to my heart as if someone could steal them from me. I wanted to be able to describe her minutely to Ralph so that it would be as if he had seen our daughter for himself. I would be given a single photograph, I knew, but that could only show one side of her, one expression, one moment captured of her ever-changing face. The rest I would have to preserve for myself.

It was a Wednesday, the very last day of July, and the day dawned warm and bright when really it should have been dark and brooding to match the occasion. I knew as soon as Stella told me that I was required in Matron's office that my time had come. Fear grabbed me, fixing me to the spot, and I saw in her face that I was right.

She gave me a weak smile. 'It's all right, Cecily,' she said gently. 'They won't take her whilst you're gone. You'll have the chance to say goodbye.'

Taking her at her word, I made my way with heart pounding and legs trembling to Matron's office for what would be the final time, running my fingers through my hair as I walked. My young body had already shed the extra pounds that the pregnancy had created, and I remember feeling that it was vital that I looked my best so that Matron understood, if she had not done so before, that although I was young, I knew how to present myself and was the kind of mother that my baby could be proud of.

I was determined to be strong, but the moment I sat and looked into Matron's kindly face my resolve fell apart. Tears were running down my cheeks before she had even begun to speak. She commenced without introduction, as if to spare me having to wait any longer for the terrible news that she had to pass on.

'Today, the couple who will adopt your baby will come to collect her,' she began. 'As you know, there will be no opportunity for you to meet them personally, but they have been through a stringent vetting process and I can tell you that they are a highly suitable couple with no other children of their own.'

Was that it? Was that all I was permitted to know? I was just expected to give up my child, the most precious thing I had, to people judged suitable by some test that I knew nothing of.

But of course, that was exactly what I had agreed to, and now I had to trust the system and release my baby into it.

Unable to speak I simply nodded, wiping my tears away ineffectually with the back of my hand.

'They will arrive at 2 p.m., so you may spend the next hour with Baby to bath her, give her a bottle and get her prepared. Have you made her a baby box?'

I nodded again.

'Then get that ready also,' she added. 'Mrs Croft will come and collect Baby from you just before two. Do you understand, Cecily?'

I looked up then and our eyes met through the film of tears. Her eyes also had a glossy sheen. I wonder now how often she had done this thankless task and whether she responded like this each time, although perhaps I was a special case. I hoped that it was clear to her that in different circumstances I might have made an excellent mother. That, however, could never be. My child was to be given up and there was nothing either of us could do to make things different.

'Afterwards you may pack your things together. I have telephoned your parents and they will be here to collect you at four.'

At least I could be grateful for this. I would not have to sleep another night here. Then I thought of Peggy. I had been so angry with her for just leaving without saying goodbye, but now I could completely understand how she had felt. Without a baby I had no place here and I wanted to be as far away as I could get.

'Do you have any questions?' Matron asked.

My head was filled with questions but I knew that she wouldn't be able to answer any of them, so I just shook my head.

'In that case, go back upstairs to your baby.'

I stood up and crossed her office to the door. Suddenly, remembering the manners that I had been taught, I turned.

'Thank you for everything, Matron,' I managed to say.

'No. Thank you, Cecily, for the decorum and courage that you have shown us. You have been a delight to have and I truly hope that your future brings you everything you wish for.'

Except the one thing that I cannot have, I thought.

Upstairs my baby had been moved to a private room off the main nursery and a baby bath filled ready for me to use. I collected the little gingham dress that I had bought for her and the box that I had decorated with pictures of yellow roses, cut carefully from old rolls of wallpaper, from under my bed. Then I went to spend my last moments with my baby.

I have never shared my memories of that day. They are my private, cherished possessions. I have taken them out often over the years and polished them until they have shone like precious stones, admiring them one by one but also handling them with great care; for each is like a poisonous dart with the power to fell me if I drop my guard for even a second.

PART FOUR

1

GREECE

The sun had reached its zenith in the faultless blue sky and was making its slow traverse towards the west when Cecily finally got to the end of her story. The water that Marnie had brought with them had long since run out and her throat felt parched and rough as sandpaper. At some point the sun had rested on her bare arm and she knew that the skin was burned and would be sore later, although now it just glowed comfortingly, like an inner heat source.

When she had finished her tale the pair of them said nothing; shell-shocked, numb or just contemplative, Cecily had no idea which. Tears had trickled down her cheeks as she told of her days in the Home and she could feel the trails of salt still, pulling her skin taut where they had dried. Marnie, however, had remained impassive throughout, clearly listening but with no outward indication of what might be going on in her head.

Despite her tears, Cecily had almost enjoyed it. Telling her story, bringing the Home and Matron and Peggy, sweet, dear Peggy, back to life in her mind had not been as difficult as she had feared. She had only told it once before, to Norman when they lay in bed in those heady, grief-stricken weeks after Ralph's funeral. But after that, she had shut the memories of those few months away and only lifted the lid on them from time to time. She had thought about Marnie every day, but the rest of it she had pushed to the back of her mind on purpose. There had been no need to replay that in her head.

They were still sitting on the wall looking out at the dilapidated buildings and overgrown shrubland. Cecily's back was stiff and sore from staying in one position for so long, but she worried that if she gave any indication of her discomfort the gossamer thread, as fine as a spider's web, that now linked her to Marnie would be broken.

'You kept the box,' Cecily said now, searching for another point of connection between them. 'The box I made for you to put your little things in when your parents came to collect you. You kept it.'

Marnie shrugged. 'I only did that to piss them off,' she said, without making eye contact.

She was hurting; Cecily could see it in her every movement, hear it in each word that she spoke. Whatever had happened to her in the decades since Cecily had given her that final bath and dressed her so carefully in the pink gingham dress had clearly left its mark. She was like a sea urchin, wrapped in a carapace of spiked shell. Cecily assumed that this hard outer casing was protecting something softer inside, but so far she had seen no evidence of that. Her child, left under the auspices of someone else, had grown into a very different person from the one she had imagined, different from her half-sisters. Was this something else for which Cecily should now feel guilty, a new culpability to add to her list? If so, then she was willing to claim it, to take it on as one of her own. She knew that she could have fought harder to keep her baby. Her father had already been half-persuaded. It would have been like pushing at an open door to get him to change his mind. Or she could just have taken the child and run, saving them both a lifetime of regrets and recriminations. She hadn't done those things at the time, but she would do whatever she could now to make things better.

Marnie stood up, and something closed around her.

'I need to go,' she said baldly. 'I'll have missed lunch, but I have to be there to prep dinner. Can you find your own way back?'

Before Cecily had a chance to reply one way or another she was gone, her broad shoulders with their backpack moving swiftly away, retreating, escaping.

It was hot, surely more than thirty degrees now, and Cecily felt lightheaded both from the stress of the last few hours and from dehydration. Somewhere not far away she thought she could hear the odd car rumble past and the sounds of glassware clinking. Perhaps there was a bar nearby? She could go and get a drink, collect herself before she went back to the hotel.

Instead of retracing their steps, Cecily set off in the opposite direction towards the sounds of civilisation. The path here was narrower and in places brambles scratched at her ankles, but it soon become obvious that her instincts had been right and she found herself in a small village. There was a church, a shop with dusty inflatable pool toys on its forecourt, and a café. Cecily made for the café and sat down at a table near the edge of the terrace. When the waitress came, a girl barely old enough to hold a tray steady but who spoke remarkably good English, she ordered a large beer and a panini.

She had no idea how the morning had gone as far as Marnie was concerned, no clue as to what she thought or was feeling. She wasn't even sure what she felt herself, other than an overwhelming bone-tired weariness. She had imagined meeting her firstborn child endlessly over the years since she had let her go. She had supposed that laying eyes on her and explaining her actions would be cathartic, the catalyst for a great outpouring of emotion on both sides, which would release a dam of some kind and allow all the feelings that she had blocked to flood over her.

As it was, all she felt was numb.

She ate the sandwich without registering it and drank the beer greedily and too fast, so it left her feeling woozy and otherworldly. Then she paid the bill and began to walk back, choosing not to cut through the abandoned village but to follow the road – the one, she assumed, that the villagers had rejected – back down to the town. It was mid-afternoon by the time she finally got to the hotel, by which time the back of her neck and her face were also burnt by the sun, not that that was of much concern to her.

She avoided the main reception, slipping quietly down the little path to the side and approaching the staircase to her room that way instead. She wasn't sure who she was trying to evade – the other guests? Sofia? Marnie? What she knew was that she wanted to be alone, to shower and change, and then she would wait to see what happened next.

When dinnertime came, she made her way down to the dining hall. A long-sleeved blouse and a scarf disguised the worst of her sunburn but she could do nothing about her pink face, the skin stretched tight and shining over her forehead and cheeks. A couple of people let their gazes linger on her and she saw sympathy in their expressions, but no one was impolite enough to comment and so she ate her delicious dinner, made more delicious by the knowledge that her daughter had prepared it, in silence.

There was no sign of Marnie.

2

ENGLAND

Julia had peed on the little plastic stick and a smiley face emoji had appeared, as if it was totally delighted to have been dowsed in her urine. It appeared that she was ovulating. She had actually laughed out loud as she stood in the cubicle at work and peered at the damp stick. She wasn't sure if this was at the silliness of the emoji, excitement at what the test had revealed or nerves at what it meant. There was no time for analysis, however. She needed to contact Sam.

She put the stick on the toilet floor and pulled her mobile out of her handbag. If her patients could only see her now; she must be breaking no end of health and safety and hygiene rules. She pulled up messages and found Sam's name.

The eagle has landed!!! she typed.

Honestly. She should have come up with a better message, but she couldn't stay where she was for much longer and she was too excited to think creatively. She watched as little bubbles appeared on the screen. Sam was typing a reply.

OMG! Do you need me right now?!
No! Any time over the next couple of days is fine.
Tonight? Was going out but can cancel.

Julia felt a twinge of guilt. Sam was doing this for her out of the goodness of his heart, and already she was making demands of him. But before she had time to reply there was another message.

Will cancel. Yours at 8?

Perfect xxxx replied Julia.

She wrapped the stick in copious quantities of loo roll and popped it in the sanitary towel bin. She didn't want to get caught with it in her bag or for it to make her office smell. Then she flushed the loo again, washed her hands efficiently and went back to her office. A light on her screen told her that her next patient was already waiting for her, and as she buzzed them in she pushed everything else out of her mind.

She didn't think about the smiley face again until she was on her way home. What did she need to get in for the evening ahead? Snacks? Yes. No wine, of course, although maybe Sam might want some afterwards. Or maybe they would have another try tomorrow? Best not get any wine at all. She needed those little sperm swimming hard. What about Sam? Would he need some help? Her mind squirmed at the thought. Obviously he wouldn't want her there, but perhaps a DVD or some magazines? Ewww. Julia shuddered. She didn't want to know any of that. Sam could sort himself. All she needed was a little syringe full of his sperm and then she was good to go. At least the clinical part of the operation didn't worry her.

At home, she lit candles and put Norah Jones on the sound system, which immediately struck her as ridiculous. She wasn't trying to seduce Sam. Heaven forbid. Then again, there was bound to be a little bit of tension. Even though they knew each other inside out, this was always going to be slightly weird. She might as well do everything she could to create a relaxed atmosphere.

Despite knowing her own body well, she hadn't really thought about how quickly they would reach this moment. It was only a few days since she and Sam had agreed to go ahead, and the details of how the arrangement would work were still pretty sketchy. Julia had intended to have a full and frank discussion with him about his role in the baby's life but somehow, when the moment for that had arrived, she had shied away from it. She wasn't sure why. Maybe it was because it was embarrassing, although how much of a dad he was going to be was far too important to be overlooked for such a feeble reason. More likely, though, it was because Julia just knew in her heart that Sam would behave honourably, however she decided to play things. He would do as she asked, and content himself with whatever she wanted of him going forward. That was why he had been the obvious candidate in the first place. There was nothing about Sam that she did not trust.

All that said, she knew that she shouldn't just leave things to luck. Apart from anything else, Sam needed to know exactly where he stood in relation to this baby that they were trying to make together. That was only fair. It was vital, Julia thought, that Sam didn't feel trapped, and she was perfectly prepared to bring a baby up on her own if he decided that his contribution should be limited to his sperm alone. But she hoped that he would want to play a larger role, even if she wasn't quite sure what that would be just yet. Consequently, the sample sperm donor agreement that she'd pulled off the internet to formalise the arrangement was still lying on her kitchen table, unsigned.

And yet here they were, about to begin. She had thought about delaying until the next month when no doubt she would ovulate again, but then she had calculated how many more ovulations there might be. A worst-case scenario put it at less than fifty, and the older she got the less chance there was of a viable egg. No, every second counted now, and no opportunity could be wasted. The finer points of their arrangement would just have to wait.

The doorbell rang, making Julia jump, even though she was expecting it. Her insides squirmed as she rushed to let Sam in, and she hoped that it wasn't going to be too horribly awkward.

Sam stood on the doorstep with a bunch of sweet peas, their stems wrapped in silver foil. He thrust them at her and their delicious scent filled her nostrils.

'Freshly picked by my own fair hand,' he said with a grin, pushing past her and into her sitting room where the candles were flickering prettily even though it was still light outside.

'God, you're really going for it, Ju,' he said as he took in the scene. 'Can I give you a tip? I'm a sure thing!'

He was laughing at her, and this made her laugh too. 'I know that, but it's all just so weird that I didn't really know what to do.'

'So you went for the full-on seduction. Nice!' he mocked. 'Are there oysters in the fridge too?'

'Oh, shut up,' said Julia, thumping him gently on the arm. 'I just wanted to make things nice and relaxing.'

Sam stopped teasing now and put his arm around her, squeezing her tenderly. 'And you've done a very good job,' he said more gently. 'I think maybe I should just go and get on with the deed, then you can do' – he paused, his face twisted in mock horror – 'whatever it is that you're going to do, and we can enjoy our evening.'

Julia relaxed a little, relieved that he had made the suggestion so that she hadn't had to. She didn't want to rush him, but at the same time she didn't want to sit around watching the clock whilst he built himself up to his big moment. She handed him a clear plastic pot that she had taken from the surgery.

'Is that all?' he asked her with a smirk. 'What will I do with the rest?'

'Just stop it! Go and do what you have to do, give me the pot back and then it's over to me.'

Sam disappeared into her bathroom. Should she have put some clean towels out, a roll of kitchen paper? Oh God, this was awkward. She turned Norah off and put the television on. The *EastEnders* theme tune was just finishing and she turned the volume up. She was sure that Sam would execute his duties in silence, but she didn't want to risk overhearing anything. What would she tell their child about the night of its conception, she wondered? And then dismissed the thought. Had her parents ever told her anything about hers? No, of course not. These things were no business of the offspring. Jolly good thing too.

Sam seemed to have been gone no time at all when he reappeared, brandishing the little pot high above his head in triumph.

'Behold!' he said. 'My seed for the lady.'

Julia rolled her eyes and took the pot from him. It felt warm under her fingers. Life. She retired to her bedroom where she had already placed the new syringe ready.

Afterwards they ate tortillas and soured cream and watched whatever was on the television in a little huggle, Julia's legs in Sam's lap.

'Do you think that's mission accomplished?' Sam asked.

'I doubt it. Not first time. But you never know. People do get pregnant on a first attempt.'

'So, if we did,' Sam said thoughtfully – Julia noted the personal pronoun approvingly, 'when would he or she be born?'

'March,' said Julia simply. She had done the maths herself.

'A spring baby,' said Sam, nodding appreciatively. 'Not too old that they have to trail-blaze and not so young that they get behind at school. Perfect.'

'But we probably won't get pregnant this month, not first time,' said Julia. 'Well, the odds are against it, at any rate.'

'Ah, but the odds haven't taken my super-swimming champion sperm into account!' Sam laughed.

Julia nuzzled her head into his chest. And made a wish.

3

Cecily will be back tomorrow, Norman thought to himself as he washed up. After the promise he had shown earlier in the week, he had resorted to fish and chips for supper that night. Well, you could have too much of a good thing, and to be honest that Jamie Oliver chap could be a bit too perky day after day.

His meagre pile of crockery washed, dried and put away, Norman poured himself two fingers of whisky into a cut-glass tumbler and then took it to enjoy outside. It had been another glorious day. There seemed to be no end to this spot of wonderful weather. The position of the sun in the cloudless sky made the front of the house the best place to sit at this time. Being at the front had the added bonus that he didn't have to stare at the pile of shed contents that still lay accusingly on the lawn at the back. He would tackle it tomorrow before Cecily got home. If the worst came to the worst, he could always just put the whole lot back where it came from, or maybe transfer it to the garage where at least it couldn't be seen.

From his seat he could survey his little empire, a little ragged-looking these days to be truthful, but still all bought and paid for. Gardening had never really been a passion of his, but they had always kept on top of things horticultural after a fashion. Most of the planting had been done by Cecily in periods of wild enthusiasm. He could see the remains of her 'white and green' phase, and the 'zingy hot' border that had never really worked in their corner of North Yorkshire; and those ridiculous silver balls on sticks that she had bought years ago at Chelsea Flower Show. She had carried three of them on the train home, only for one of the three to be stolen within weeks of her plunging it into the flower bed. Two silver balls on sticks had always looked wrong, but she had never got round to replacing the missing one and so there they had stood for, he thought back, what must have been at least a decade.

The warm evening seemed to have brought his neighbours out too. There was the sound of a game of football coming from next door, and the appetising smells of a lit barbecue floated in the air. Somewhere someone was practising a saxophone, although Norman was tempted to tell them that they'd be better off doing that indoors until they improved a bit.

So Cecily had finally met Marnie. It was an unusual name, Marnie. Norman remembered that Cecily's secret name for her baby had been Faye, after some film that she and Ralph had been to see. Faye was a soft name, as light as thistledown. Marnie, by contrast, was full of hard edges to bump your tongue into. And from what Cecily had managed to tell him over the phone, the new name pretty much reflected the person. Norman had had no preconceived ideas about what he wanted his niece to be like. His only concern throughout this had been for the well-being of his wife, but of course in the back of his mind he had hoped for a joyous reunion, in which the child welcomed Cecily into her life with open arms and an open heart.

That wasn't quite how things had worked out as far as he could gather, but that was only to be expected at this early stage. Fifty years was a long time to be apart; a lifetime, in fact.

What would Ralph have made of all of it? he wondered. Norman had a sneaking suspicion that Ralph wouldn't have given a damn. Absorbed by his new life without Cecily in it, he had been less than interested in his progeny when the news of her arrival had been fresh. After fifty years of no contact, he would probably have forgotten that she ever existed.

The child did look like his brother though, Cecily had said. Dark and brooding. And it sounded as if she shared more than just looks with her birth father. Ralph hadn't been the easiest person to get on with either, despite the rose-tinted spectacles through which Cecily had always insisted on seeing him. Although he could charm the birds from the trees when it suited him, he could also be self-centred, challenging and downright argumentative. It was easy to forget the realities of his personality after holding him high on death's pedestal for so long. Norman remembered, though, how their parents had regularly lost patience with Ralph when they had been growing up, doling out punishments for his many and varied misdemeanours left and right, so maybe it wasn't surprising that his child also seemed to be restless and dissatisfied with life. That might have just been part of the hand that biology had dealt her at birth and nothing at all to do with what had happened since.

His mother and father might also hold some responsibility for Marnie's personality in the genealogical lottery game. They had been dour people, quick to judge and to blame; such a contrast to Cecily's easy-going, liberal-minded parents. When the Hardcastles had first telephoned to talk about 'the young people's issue', Norman and Ralph's parents had been totally at a loss; whereas Cecily had been open and honest about the pregnancy, Ralph had told no one, hoping, Norman assumed, that the whole problem would just disappear of its own accord.

However, there had been the inevitable summit of the two families, the Nightingales sitting in the Hardcastles' quirky drawing room, sipping sherry awkwardly whilst the issue of what to do next was discussed. Norman could picture the scene, even though he had been safely away at university when the drama had played out, and only learned of it when he had overheard Ralph boasting about his sexual prowess to some schoolfriends that summer. In his mind's eye he could visualise his parents sitting bolt upright and unsmiling as their son's disgrace was laid bare before them, and his heart ached for poor, beautiful Cecily, caught in the turmoil but unable to struggle free.

To be fair to Ralph, he had at least offered to do the right thing by Cecily at first, although his resolve had never been tested because the problem was taken out of their hands. Cecily had been smuggled out to a home in Wales and some excuse made to cover her absence. The Nightingales, disaster having been narrowly averted, never mentioned the baby or Cecily again. When Ralph had passed his A levels, he had been ushered off to university without being given the chance to reacquaint himself with his first love, and he hadn't looked back. The whole sorry episode was to be erased from memory like an unsatisfactory meal or a disappointing novel.

And it might have been, too, had Ralph not fallen ill. Norman had wondered whether his illness was a kind of kismet, the universe paying him back for his abandoning his beautiful girl to her fate. The treatment for leukaemia had come on in leaps and bounds in the 1970s, but still one half of all those diagnosed succumbed to the disease, Ralph amongst them. Cecily had come to the funeral, a young woman of twenty-three by then. She was elegant and poised in her black trouser suit, a bright red scarf at her throat, which had almost sent his mother into an attack of the vapours. When Norman spoke to Cecily at the wake, shyly at first and then buoyed by several glasses of beer, she had told him that the scarf represented Ralph and his vital joie de vivre as well as the red blood cells that had deserted him.

Norman knew straight away that he would fall in love with her, that there was nothing he could do to prevent it. Her double loss, first her child and then the boy she had loved, had given her a compelling inner strength that she gathered quietly about her like a mantle. She seemed equipped to bear this extra loss, the death of her first love, in a way that Norman admired. She had even borne the gentle snubbing by his parents at the funeral, their failure to engage or even acknowledge her. He had been ashamed of their treatment of her, but she seemed not to care. She was there, she told him later, simply to say goodbye to Ralph. The rest of it was of little importance to her.

The two of them had grown close after the funeral, leaning on one another for support when none was forthcoming from other sources. Cecily had told no one about her baby and so was limited as to what she could share about Ralph with those outside her family. He was simply a childhood friend to anyone who asked, and not the person with whom she had shared those most intimate moments at such a tender age. Only Norman knew the truth, and so she could talk to him openly about her grief, not only at Ralph's death but also the loss of their baby and her dreams. They had grieved together, over cups of tea and then dinner and then ultimately, inevitably, in his bed.

When he had proposed two years later, his parents had wanted nothing to do with the wedding, and so they had eloped with the full blessing of Cecily's family. Somewhere along the line, they had tacitly agreed that the story of her life before him, of Ralph and their baby, was best laid to rest. And so it had been, until the letter had arrived the week before.

Norman finished his whisky. It was almost ten o'clock, but the garden was still as bright as day. It was the summer solstice, he realised, the day when the year is perfectly balanced on a knife-edge between darkness and light. From now on, the world would slip inexorably towards winter. He hoped that this new development, the rediscovery of Marnie, wasn't also something that was going to pull them towards blackness and cold.

4

GREECE

After dinner Cecily was making herself a cup of peppermint tea to take back to her room when she felt someone at her elbow. She spun round, hoping that it was Marnie, and was then disappointed to see Sofia standing there.

'You caught the sun,' Sofia said, and Cecily pulled a regretful face.

'I'm usually so careful, but I was talking to Marnie and I didn't notice that I was burning. And then it was too late.'

'Yes,' Sofia said. 'She told me that things were pretty intense.'

'You've spoken to her?' Cecily asked. Her voice sounded anxious, the kind of tone she might have used if she was fearful of something happening to one of her daughters – one of her other daughters, that is. 'Is she all right? She just disappeared after I'd told her everything. I've been worried about her.'

'We have spoken, yes,' Sofia confirmed. 'She told me what happened. Don't worry. She's okay. She's just retreated to process it all. She does that,' she added with a little smile. 'She'll talk when she's ready.'

Cecily was grateful for this insight, at least.

'But I was worried about you,' Sofia continued. 'I was wondering whether you needed someone to talk to.' She laid a gentle hand on Cecily's forearm as she spoke.

Cecily had thought that she was dealing with everything so well, that she could handle the morning's events on her own, but now that the offer of a discussion was on the cards she grasped at it. 'That would be lovely,' she said.

'Let's go on to the terrace,' suggested Sofia. 'It's quieter out there.'

She led the way out towards the pool and then up to a table and chairs near the cliff path. It was just getting dark, but the Mediterranean air around them was still warm and sultry. There was a candle in a glass jar on the table and Sofia took a lighter out of a pocket and lit it. It cast a feeble glow over the table, not enough to see by, but comforting nonetheless. Cecily could hear the waves dragging the pebbles back and forth on the beach below them.

'Tell me,' said Cecily as soon as they were sitting. 'How has Marnie taken everything?'

'She's okay,' replied Sofia. 'She knew what she was letting herself in for when she contacted you. She's been thinking about doing it for a long time. I think it was turning fifty that finally decided her. A kind of now or never thing.'

'I just hope she understands what it was like back then,' said Cecily. She rubbed at the skin on the palm of her hand with her thumb, backwards and forwards, feeling the tiny bones shifting under the pressure. 'Girls these days have so many options, but it wasn't like that then. I was told what would happen and I just had to go along with it. There was no choice. I need her to understand that – that it wasn't my decision to give her up.'

Cecily instantly regretted her words. Her own needs were of the least importance here, and she didn't want Marnie or Sofia to think that she was making the situation about herself in any way.

But Sofia didn't seem to have noticed. 'Knowing that you had no option might make things easier for her,' she replied gently. She sat back in the chair, her hair wild around her shoulders. 'Marnie is a complicated person. What she wants and what it seems like she wants don't always marry up. You sometimes need to make allowances for her. I think that she gives out vibes that don't always . . .' Sofia paused, choosing her words, 'that aren't always that helpful for getting people on her side.'

Cecily thought about the interactions that she and Marnie had had so far, and could immediately see what Sofia meant. She nodded encouragingly, but was reluctant to agree for fear of seeming to criticise her daughter. That was the last thing she wanted. Marnie might be cold and difficult to approach, but she wasn't going to love her any less for that.

'I'm not sure how much to tell you about her,' Sofia continued, puffing her lips out in a sigh as she considered. 'In an ideal world, Marnie would tell you this herself, and maybe she will one day, but right now time is short and she is taking time out to process everything. And you're leaving tomorrow, right?'

'Yes,' said Cecily. She looked straight into Sofia's eyes.

'I don't want you to take this the wrong way, Cecily,' Sofia began slowly. 'No one is blaming you for anything here, but Marnie had a really hard start in life. Her adoptive parents . . .' She paused again, twisting a strand of hair round and round her finger. 'Well, put it this way. I'm not sure they were the kind of parents that she would have chosen for herself. They didn't mistreat her but they were . . .' Sofia seemed to struggle for a moment to come up with the right word,

'. . . inadequate. Marnie never felt cherished by them, or even loved. It's not that they were abusive in any way. Please don't take that away from this. But I'm not sure they knew how to love and they don't seem to have had even the most basic grasp of what a child needs to feel safe and secure. Especially not one like Marnie, who was already feeling like an outsider. They didn't even tell her she was adopted.'

Cecily was appalled. 'But I thought that was standard practice – that they were all advised to tell the children from the very beginning.'

Sofia shrugged. 'Well, Marnie found out because some kid at school read her file and told her. So she spent the first twelve years of her life knowing that she didn't fit in, but not understanding why. And then when she found out she was adopted it answered some questions but raised a whole load of others. I'm sure her parents had their own reasons for keeping it to themselves. Maybe they thought they were doing the right thing. I don't know. But whatever the rights and wrongs, Marnie found out that was she was adopted by accident.'

An unfamiliar but visceral anger began to bubble up inside Cecily as she considered the implications of this. She had pictured Marnie's adoptive parents reassuring her that she was so wanted, had been especially chosen by them rather than simply being the baby that nature had allocated. She had always imagined her being showered in the love that she had been prevented from giving her. This new version of events did not tally with that one iota, and it shook her to her core.

'I think her relationship with them went downhill from there,' said Sofia. 'She left home when she was sixteen and went to live with a man who was quite a lot older than her and who didn't . . . well, let's say he didn't have her best interests at heart. She struggles with trust now, and building relationships.'

'Thank goodness she has you,' said Cecily, and then added, more doubtfully, 'You're her friend, aren't you?'

Sofia cocked her head to one side. 'Yes,' she said with a wry smile, 'I suppose I am.'

A trio of women came out on to the terrace, their voices shrill and grating in the quiet of the night, and the moment was broken.

Sofia sat back in her chair and looked at her watch. 'Anyway,' she said, 'that's probably enough. I'm sure Marnie will tell you more when she's good and ready.'

'But I'm leaving in the morning,' Cecily interrupted, a note of desperation in her voice. 'I mean, I could stay on . . .'

She let the suggestion hang in the air, but Sofia shook her head. 'I'm sorry, but your room is booked next week and speaking entirely selfishly, I need a cook with her mind on her work. I think the pair of you have achieved as much as can be expected for now. We finish here at the end of the month and then we'll go back to London. I'll encourage her to get in touch with you again at that point. I can't guarantee that she will, but that's the best I can do.'

Cecily nodded. 'Could I have your address in London?' she asked. 'So that I can write?'

Sofia shook her head. 'I think that's up to Marnie. You can ask her by all means, but I suspect she'll want to keep control of this for now.'

Cecily could understand that. Marnie would no doubt work her way through it all in her own time and she just had to be there waiting when she was ready to speak.

'Will I see her again before I leave?' she asked. Her voice cracked as she spoke and she could feel tears pricking in her eyes, though she was trying to stay businesslike and keep her emotions in check.

'That I don't know,' said Sofia. 'We shall just have to wait and see what she does next.'

It was like dealing with a wild cat or a python, Cecily thought. Marnie was unpredictable and potentially dangerous, emotionally if not physically. She just had to keep calm and not make any sudden moves.

Sofia got to her feet. 'It's been lovely to meet you Cecily,' she said. 'I'm so glad you came. If I were Marnie, I'd be delighted that you were my birth mother.'

Cecily smiled her thanks. She hoped that Marnie was thinking along similar lines. The trouble was, it was beginning to look like she would never find out what Marnie thought.

5

Cecily had thought that she would toss and turn all night, but when she opened her eyes narrow stripes of daylight were already framing the curtains. It was morning. The minibus was arriving to take her back to the airport at eleven. She just had to have her breakfast and pack her case.

Would Marnie appear? Cecily longed to see her. The thought of returning home without at least getting to say goodbye was devastating. It was as if all the pain of the fifty years of separation was gathering in her heart at the thought of leaving without seeing her again.

On top of that, and on a more practical level, she desperately wanted a photograph of her to show to Norman. Was that too much to ask? She feared that perhaps it was. Marnie didn't, on first meeting at least, seem the type to want to pose for the camera. It was immaterial, in any event, as she had no means of taking one. She hadn't thought to bring a camera with her. The girls would just have taken a picture on their phones, but that was beyond her and anyway her phone was in the kitchen drawer at home. Maybe Marnie had a phone, or Sofia.

But even as Cecily tried to think through the logistics of this, she knew that it would never happen. She wouldn't ask and Marnie wouldn't offer, always supposing that she even saw her before she left. From what Sofia had said the night before, it didn't sound as if that was guaranteed.

Maybe Cecily could track her down herself, go to the kitchens and ask for her? But no. Her instincts held her back, told her that that would be a mistake. Marnie was in the driving seat here, and she just had to go where Marnie took her.

She repacked her case with a quiet efficiency: so many unworn clothes. The time spent here had just slipped away, and she hadn't done half the things she'd imagined she would. She had only taken one yoga class, but she had enjoyed it. Maybe she could find a class near home. Lily would know what was available.

Thinking of Lily made her suddenly and unexpectedly home-sick, and she wished more than anything that she could magic her-self back to their house in Harrogate at that very minute, just to see her family, to ground herself in the familiar and give her strength for what was to come that morning. Her girls had complicated, busy lives, much of which she didn't truly understand, but they were bright and positive in their outlooks, most of the time at least.

The contrast between them and what she had learned of Marnie thus far was so marked. Obviously, how someone was brought up would have a significant impact on how they turned out. Surely, though, there was some nature in and amongst the nurture, some-thing of the Nightingales that had always been buried deep in Marnie and perhaps made no sense to her until she'd found the missing pieces in the jigsaw of her life. But Cecily could see noth-ing of her other children in her firstborn. In fact, there was only the striking physical resemblance to Ralph to suggest that Marnie was connected to her at all. Nothing else about her was in any way familiar. Cecily wasn't sure how she felt about this, so she pushed it to the back of her mind. She would find a level with her daughter eventually, she was sure; it was just going to take time.

She ached for Norman, too. He would work through everything with her in his steady, measured way, making it all seem, if not straightforward, then at least achievable. Just now, though, as she stood in her hotel room and pulled the zip closed on the suitcase, she felt as if she had inadvertently wandered into quicksand and had no way of pulling herself free.

She would go down for breakfast, she decided. For all she knew, Marnie might be there and waiting for her. Marnie was well aware that she was leaving that morning. Hadn't she made the arrangements in the first place? And Sofia would surely have reminded her, if she was so engrossed in her work or her own thoughts to remember. There was no way that having brought Cecily all this way, she would let her leave again without reaching a conclusion of sorts, without making or at least hinting at a plan for what might happen next.

But Marnie didn't appear. Cecily ate her breakfast slowly. Other women sat down, ate and left whilst Cecily peeled an orange, laboriously removing every slither of pith before separating each segment and laying them in a semi-circle on her plate. By the time she'd finally put each piece into her mouth, the translucent skin had started to dry and pucker a little.

Yet there was still no Marnie. Cecily looked at her watch. It was ten-thirty. She needed to go back to her room, collect her things and check out; she still wasn't convinced that there wouldn't be a bill for her to pay. But one thing was certain, at least. She didn't have time to sit there any longer.

In her room she checked under the bed and in the wardrobe for stray items, plucked her toothbrush from the cup by the basin and slipped it into her case. Then she took one last, wistful look around. In other circumstances, she would have loved this little room with its fresh white walls and its spectacular views, but she felt like circumstances had not allowed her to fully appreciate its charms. I'll come back again, she whispered to herself. And I'll bring Norman. He'd love it here.

There was nothing to pay, the man on reception assured her. And still no Marnie. How was she supposed to say thank you for everything, let alone goodbye? Sofia had said that they would be at the hotel only until the end of the month. Was there enough time for her to write when she got home? Would the hotel forward any correspondence on to Sofia after she'd left? Would she send a letter on to Marnie?

Then it occurred to Cecily that she should have written a note setting down everything that she still had to say. Panic gripped her. Why hadn't she thought of that before? Of course, that was what she should do. She looked at her watch. She had just over ten minutes before the minibus was due to leave. There was time.

'Could I have a piece of paper and a pen, please?' she asked the man on reception anxiously.

He obliged, and she went to sit at a console table to write a note. She still had eight minutes.

Dear Marnie, she began.

What did she want to say? Thank you for finding me. Thank you for my stay here. Please keep in touch. It all felt so very mundane when there were so many much, much bigger and more important things that she needed to say.

Thank you so much . . . she wrote.

'Cecily.'

She looked up, and Marnie was standing there in her chef's whites.

'Oh, thank goodness,' Cecily said, the words slipping out of her mouth before she had time to decide if they were appropriate. 'I thought I was going to have to leave without seeing you and I so wanted to say thank you for getting in touch and well, everything, really. See, I'd just started writing you a . . .'

Her voice drifted off. Marnie was just staring at her, unsmiling.

'Well, anyway, it's been so good to meet you, Marnie,' Cecily pressed on, forcing her voice to sound calmer and more controlled. 'I would love for you to get in touch again. When you're ready, that is.'

It felt crucial not to scare her off by being too familiar, but at the same time Cecily needed Marnie to understand how very important it was to her to stay in contact now that they had found each other.

Marnie still didn't speak, but for the first time she allowed her eyes to properly lock with Cecily's. Cecily could feel her examining each of her features in turn. She did this without any self-consciousness, happy just to let her eyes roam Cecily's face as if it were a portrait in a gallery rather than a living person standing before her.

There was the sound of an engine outside and a heavy door opening and then being slammed shut. Someone came into reception and called a greeting to the receptionist in Greek. He acknowledged him and then spoke to Cecily.

'Mrs Nightingale. This is your transfer.'

Panic struck Cecily. She couldn't go, not now. There was so much still to say. How could her trip be over? And what would happen next?

The bus driver came across, nodded at her case and then trundled it back across the tiled floor towards the entrance.

'I'll be right there,' Cecily managed to say. 'So, it looks like I have to go,' she said to Marnie. 'I can't tell you how thrilled I am that you found me. Please consider contacting me again. Perhaps you could come and meet the rest of us. I would love . . .'

Had she gone too far? Marnie seemed to recoil a little at the mention of her family, or had she just imagined it?

And then Marnie held out her hand, her eyes never leaving Cecily's face. Cecily took it and squeezed it gently, trying to convey everything that she was so desperate to say in one touch.

185

Marnie nodded. Then she dropped her hand and headed back towards the kitchens. Their meeting was over.

Cecily's eyes brimmed with tears. She lowered her head and without speaking to the receptionist, walked straight towards the minibus.

As the bus beetled through the narrow streets to pick other passengers up, Cecily found her sunglasses in her bag and put them on. She held a clean tissue to her face but with a gargantuan effort she found that she was able to contain her emotion, not allowing it to overflow and impinge on those around her. This was something she was good at. After all, she had had plenty of practice.

6

ENGLAND

Lily had planned a big family Sunday lunch to mark her mother's return. She had mentioned it to the others. Julia was up for it immediately; Felicity was a little vague to start with, but then had come round to the idea. Her father had baulked at the suggestion.

'I'm not sure it's a good idea, Lily,' he said. 'Your mother will have only just got back. She might be tired.'

'She'll have been back two days by then, Dad. I'm sure she'll be fine. And you know how she always loves to see us all together. Don't worry about the food. Marco and I will bring it all with us. The weather is so fabulous. We can have a picnic on the lawn. Have you got rid of all that shed stuff?'

Her father had cleared his throat and muttered something unintelligible. If she knew him, it would all be back in a pile on the floor of the shed.

'And we want to hear all about Greece. It's the perfect chance for Mum to tell us what she got up to out there. So that's settled, then?' She had rung off before her father had had a chance to raise any more objections.

She and Marco had put together a menu: tomato focaccia and fresh herb frittata, cured meats, olives and a cheese board, a crisp green salad and some cold melanzane parmigiana served in thick, oozing slices. She had shopped for it all the following day and cooked the things that were to be eaten cold. She rang Julia and asked her to be in charge of getting the drinks. She could split the cost with Felicity but they both knew that there was no point asking Felicity to actually pick anything up herself unless you were prepared for a three-ring circus of excuses and complaints.

At the appointed hour they drove round to her parents' house, the food tucked neatly in several large picnic baskets that were balanced on the knees of the bigger boys. She had rugs and some large floor cushions too, even though her parents also had plenty of outdoor furniture, and all her melamine crockery and 'glassware'. There was no point risking the boys accidentally smashing any of her mother's china.

Lily wanted everything to be perfect.

Julia's car was already parked in the drive when they arrived. The boys tumbled out of the people carrier and straight into the back garden to climb the trees that she and Julia had climbed when they were small. Marco shambled off after them and Lily carried the baby out in his car seat to sit under the large copper beech at the front.

Julia appeared with some folding picnic chairs. When she saw Lily her face broke into a broad smile. 'Hi Lils. This is a great idea. Thanks for organising everything.'

'No worries,' replied Lily as she returned to the car to fetch the rugs and cushions from the boot.

'It's like a TARDIS, that car,' laughed Julia.

'Needs must,' replied Lily. 'I must pop in and tell them we're here. Have you seen Mum yet?'

'Briefly,' said Julia.

'Any clues?'

Julia shook her head. She was trying to open a folding chair but was having no luck; it remained resolutely closed. 'Bloody hell. How does this thing work?' she asked in frustrated tones, and then, 'Shit! That hurt,' as the chair bit her.

She dropped it on to the grass and put the damaged finger into her mouth to suck. Lily picked the chair up and opened it in one smooth movement, placing it down in the shade and moving on to the second one.

'How did you do that?' Julia asked in disgruntled tones.

'It's easy when you've got the knack,' replied Lily.

Richard's car was approaching. You would be able to hear it in the middle of a battlefield, Lily thought. Its engine had that expensive roar that signalled its cost to those who knew about such things, and was just irritating to everyone else. She thought it unnecessarily ostentatious, but she would never have said that out loud for fear of upsetting Felicity and because Marco and her father seemed to swoon over it every time Richard brought it round. The car thundered into the drive and the little family of three hopped out. They looked dressed for the races rather than an impromptu family picnic. Lily looked down at her own shabby cut-offs and faded printed blouse. They really did occupy different planets, she and her sister.

'Hi, Hugo. The boys are round the back. With Marco,' she added when she saw concern cross Felicity's face. Hugo looked to his mother for confirmation and then skipped happily down the path at the side of the house to find his cousins.

'Hi, Richard. How are you?' Julia asked.

Richard gave a tight little nod and Lily cast a discreet sideways glance at Julia, who rolled her eyes.

'I'll just go and . . .' said Richard, and then disappeared off down the path after his son.

'Everything okay?' Lily asked Felicity.

'Fine, thanks,' she replied curtly, as if holding her temper in check was taking every ounce of her energy. 'Where are Mum and Dad?'

As if on cue their parents appeared. Their father came down the steps to join them on the lawn, but their mother hovered near the house.

'Mum! Hi,' Lily called to her. 'Have you had a lovely time?' She thought her mother looked tired, and her face had the pinkish tinge of too much sun.

'You had nice weather then?' Felicity asked, touching her own forehead to draw attention to her mother's.

'Yes. I got a bit caught out,' her mother said, her expression sheepish. 'I made a proper mess of my face and my arm.' She rolled up her cotton sleeve to show a prawn-pink patch with a distinct white line where her watch had been.

'Ouch,' said Lily. 'That looks sore. Have you put some aloe vera on it? You know, that plant I gave you.'

Her mother shook her head sorrowfully. 'I'm sorry, darling. I didn't think. I'll do it later.'

'Come and sit down, Mum,' said Felicity, gesturing at the chairs. 'You too, Dad.'

'Yes,' Lily added. 'You two relax and I'll get all the food ready. You're not to lift a finger.'

Lily felt a reluctance in their mother. She seemed to dither where she was for a moment, not wanting to move forward but unable to go back inside, but then she came and sat down. Their father stood solemnly behind her like a Victorian gentleman in a photograph.

'So, are you going to tell us why you had to go rushing off like that?' Felicity asked. Lily could hear the irritation in her voice and hoped that she wasn't going to start a row. 'I mean, it must have been something pretty important, to leave us all in the lurch like you did.'

Julia threw her a look telling her to be quiet, and Felicity threw one back that said, 'What? It's a legitimate question.' However, this wasn't the time for sniping between the two of them and Lily raised a warning eyebrow at them both. Their mother, however, didn't seem to notice. Her eyes were focused on the grass in front of her, and then she looked towards their father rather than them. He reached out and patted a reassuring hand on her arm.

'Of course I'll tell you. It's just that now, what with everyone here and the children and everything . . . well, it might not be the best time . . .'

Lily's insides twisted. Was her mother ill? Was that it? But then, why go racing off to Greece? It made no sense.

Their father spoke now. 'Actually, Cecily, maybe now would be a good time, whilst the boys are all busy in the back garden.'

Their mother looked nervously down the path and then back at them. 'I suppose you're right. Sit down for a minute, girls.'

Their father settled himself on the other chair whilst the rest of them gathered on the rugs at their parents' feet. It looked like something out of *The Little House on the Prairie*, Lily thought.

'So?' asked Felicity impatiently. 'What's the big secret?'

Their father raised his eyebrows at her and she looked a little chastened. Their mother was playing with a button on her blouse, twisting it round and then back so that Lily feared she would pull it free and leave a hole in the cotton. Then she took a deep breath.

'Last week I received a letter,' she began. 'It was from someone that I haven't seen for a very long time.' She looked over to their father, who smiled at her reassuringly. 'In fact, I hadn't seen her, Marnie she's called, since she was a baby. She was my baby. I had her. She was adopted when she was six weeks old.'

The words came tumbling out in a rush, all on top of one another like water in a brook, and Lily wasn't sure that she'd heard right. Judging by the looks on her sisters' faces, she wasn't alone. Felicity opened her mouth to speak but their mother raised a hand to silence her, and pressed on.

'When I was fifteen, I fell pregnant. I had the baby, but because I was so young it was agreed that she should be adopted. I never heard from her again until I got the letter last week.'

As the words settled in Lily's brain, the full enormity of what they meant loomed up around her like a spectre. Giving up your child, your own flesh and blood, to a stranger? Lily could no more contemplate such a thing than run all the way to Timbuktu in flip-flops.

'Oh, Mum,' she said, her eyes already glossy with tears. 'That must have been so awful for you. To go through pregnancy and birth so young. And then to have to hand the baby over . . .' She ran out of words and just sat, open-mouthed, in horror.

'I can't believe you haven't told us that before now,' interrupted Felicity. 'She's our, what? Half-sister? Surely we had a right to know that we had a half-sister out there somewhere?'

Julia spoke now. 'Don't be ridiculous, Fliss. This was Mum's business. It's been up to her whether she told us or not. And how did it go in Greece, Mum? What was she like?'

Lily watched as her mother decided how to reply.

'She was nice,' she said after a moment. 'It was a shock for her, meeting me and hearing about you. But she seemed nice.'

'Nice,' repeated Julia.

Their mother, clearly appreciating the inadequacies of the word, shrugged. 'I didn't spend very much time with her, as it turned out. And I did most of the talking, telling her all about her father and how she was born, why she was adopted, that kind of thing. But she did seem to be . . . well, she's understandably a bit thrown by it all. It was a lot for her to take in. But yes . . she seems nice.'

'Are you still in touch with her father?' asked Felicity sharply, turning to look at Norman as if outraged on his behalf.

'Her father died a long time ago,' their mother said quietly.

'Oh, Mum,' whispered Lily. 'How awful. It must have been terrible.'

Their mother smiled fondly at Lily. 'It was, darling. Truly awful, but luckily for me I had your father to help me through.'

'Were you all friends then?' Felicity asked.

'Marnie's father was my younger brother Ralph,' said their father.

'And he died of leukaemia, didn't he?' clarified Lily.

'That's right. When he was twenty-five.'

Lily could just have let rip and howled there and then. It was so heart-wrenchingly sad. She could hardly bear the thought that her mother had had to go through childbirth so young and give up the baby and to lose the man she loved on top of that, and all before she was even twenty-five. It was too, too awful.

'Hang on,' said Julia, brow furrowed. 'So that makes this woman, Marnie did you say her name was? That makes Marnie our half-sister and our cousin at the same time?'

'Yes. That's right.'

'Well, that's a bit weird,' Julia said, a half-smile on her lips as she thought it all through. No one else was smiling.

'And how was she?' Lily asked. 'Has she had a good life so far? Was she pleased to have found you? When will we get to meet her?'

Their mother put her hands up to protect herself from the onslaught of so many questions. 'I'm not sure she had as nice a child-hood as you three. Her adoptive parents seem to have been a little . . .' She paused, seeming to choose her words carefully. '. . . unconventional in their approach. She was understandably reluctant to give too much away about them. But she did make the move to get in touch, so I'm hoping that we can move things forward from here. I'd like her to come and meet all of you, but that's obviously up to her. I've left things very much in her court for now.'

The baby let out a little cry in his sleep and they all turned to look at him in his car seat, relieved to have a distraction.

'And that's everything,' their mother added. 'I just wanted to let you know.'

'So, when is she coming?' asked Julia. 'Will you fix a date?'

'Nothing's agreed as yet. I need to wait for her to get back in touch with us. She knows where we are.'

'Well, it's not very considerate to leave you hanging on like that, Mum,' chipped in Felicity. 'Not knowing what's going on is hardly very satisfactory.'

'Maybe not,' said their mother. 'But it's the best we have for now.'

They sat quietly for a moment, each with their own thoughts.

And then the boys appeared together like a dust storm, arms and legs almost indistinguishable from one another, with Marco and Richard bringing up the rear.

'When's lunch, Granny?' said Frankie as he barged past Enzo to get to the adults first. 'We're starving.'

Lily got to her feet. 'You can all go inside and wash your hands and when you come back it will be time to eat.'

The big boys ran off again, Leo, Luca and Hugo trailing after them, barely able to keep up but determined not to be left behind.

'Is the food still in the car?' asked Marco. Lily thought he was going to complain that she wasn't taking the food hygiene seriously enough but then he seemed to sense that there was something bigger at play and turned to go and collect the baskets instead.

'I'll go and supervise the hand-washing,' Felicity said, clearly looking for a task to do.

Their mother nodded weakly and Felicity followed the boys up the steps and into the house.

'Are you okay, Mum?' Lily asked quietly.

Her mother gave her a quick, tight nod. Lily could see that that would have to be enough for now.

'Right,' her mother said decisively, marking the end of that chapter and moving on. 'Who'd like a drink? Where are the drinks? Julia? Did you bring them?'

And then she was off. Back to being Lily's organised, efficient, super-calm mother as if nothing unusual had been said at all.

PART FIVE

1

Richard's front door key sat in the middle of the kitchen table. It had been there for three days now, but somehow Felicity was unable to pick it up. It was probably a security risk, she thought, just sitting there in full view of the window, but even that fact didn't seem to make it any easier to move.

And so Felicity left it there, half-hoping that it might evaporate or melt in the meagre autumn sunshine, or maybe even stand itself up on two little legs and put itself away so that she wouldn't have to. Whilst it sat there, it could be that Richard had just forgotten to take it with him when he went to work or to the gym or wherever it was that he might be. But if she picked it up and slipped it into the drawer with all the other spare keys, then she would have to accept that her marriage was over, that she had failed, that everything had slithered out of her control.

She had wondered whether Richard would have left if she hadn't called his bluff, forced his hand. Of course, she would never know the answer to that; and in any event, she had reached a point of no return, no longer able to turn a blind eye to his infidelities, and once those scales had finally dropped there was so very much to see. First there had been the flooding and the cancelled restaurant booking and the subsequent night spent in Leeds. After that, she had begun checking through his jacket pockets on a regular basis, even though it was undignified to stoop so low.

As it turned out, his pockets didn't have any secrets to give up; but a credit card bill just left for her to uncover under a pile of business papers at the very bottom of Richard's locked briefcase (who set their combination to 1234?) told her a romantic tale of epic proportions. Flowers she had never sniffed, classy underwear that wasn't nestling in her drawers, meals in restaurants that she'd never visited. As she'd suspected, rather than staying with colleagues in the company's flat in London, he had been in hotels, one in particular seeming to have become a favourite. Felicity had assumed this meant that his colleagues must know of his tawdry doings, too, and the fact of her shaming made her almost as cross as the affair itself. Was there really any need to humiliate her so publicly? What had she ever done to him to deserve that?

Until that point, she had ignored Richard's dalliances. She had suspected, and he had always got whoever it was out of his system quickly and quietly and then drifted back to her. It was, she figured, better for her to have a husband, albeit one who struggled a little with the small print of his marriage vows, than to be on her own. Plus, there was Hugo to consider. She wanted him to grow up in a family with two parents, just like she had done. She firmly believed in that, even though she knew there were many alternatives. Her son would always be denied the joy of siblings, so ensuring that he had both his mummy and his daddy was the least that she could do for him, even it meant sacrifices on her part.

And as long as Richard was there in the background, a husband of sorts, she felt complete. It was so old-fashioned, she knew, to measure success in terms of one's relationship, but she couldn't help herself. She was an old-fashioned person. The terror of being a woman who was so unappealing that her husband left her for another struck a chord so deep inside her that its chimes reverberated through every cell in her body.

But if his infidelities were no longer a secret, if other people knew what he was up to – well, that put a different slant on things. Felicity could keep up appearances with the best of them, but she wouldn't be made a fool of. A scale had been tipped.

She had waited until Hugo was safely tucked up in bed and out of earshot. Richard was at the kitchen table, flicking through his iPad. She sucked in a deep, calming breath and began.

'I found your credit card bill. The one that catalogues the sordid history of your current affair.' She stood facing him, arms folded, legs wide, feet solid on the expensively tiled floor.

'You went through my things?' he said. He almost sounded hurt at this betrayal of trust. Felicity ignored his comment and just stared at him, and he appeared to change tack under the scrutiny of her gaze. 'It was nothing,' he continued. 'I'm sorry. It's over now.'

It wasn't. She could tell by the tone of his voice, the panic in his eye, the new aftershave that played around her nostrils.

'Please don't lie to me, Richard,' she replied. She was surprising herself by how very calm she felt as her world tumbled down around her. 'I know that isn't true. I can always tell when your affairs are over, and this one is clearly ongoing.'

His face registered shock. Had he really thought she didn't know? Then his expression altered, too subtle for a stranger to spot, but Felicity saw it.

'Well, can you blame me?' he asked, a slither of indignation in his tone. 'How long do you expect me to play second fiddle, Fliss? Ever since we had Hugo it's been the same. He is all you're interested in. You don't make room for anyone else.'

'But he's our son!' she shouted, the calm of the moment evaporating instantly at Richard's ridiculous implication. Of course Hugo was the most important thing in her life. Wasn't that why she had endured the agonies of IVF treatment for years? So that they could have a child?

And now that they had realised that dream, it was for her to make Hugo's life as perfect as it could be. That was her job as his mother. Surely Richard knew that? Their marriage was something else entirely.

'And I'm your husband,' said Richard bitterly. 'If I'd known how having a baby would destroy our relationship, I would never have gone along with it.'

'Gone along with it!' she spat back. 'Is that how you see it? Having a baby, having our son, was just a whim to be indulged?'

'Well, no. Of course not. But you must see that since he came along you have become more and more distant. I feel like I'm in the way, an obstacle to be dodged between you and him. There's no room.'

'So, instead of talking to me about how you felt, your solution was just to slip into the bed of someone who would pay you more attention?'

Richard shrugged. 'You have driven me away, Fliss. I'm only human.'

It was pathetic, Felicity thought, to be so needy. She had been starved of affection from him as well, but she hadn't flown into the arms of the first available alternative.

'Pack some things,' she said quietly. 'Leave your key on the table on the way out.'

It had felt like the right thing to do at the time but now, three days on, a numbness had settled on Felicity. She barely recognised herself in this shell of a woman who wandered in and out of her rooms, sighing but not achieving anything. She felt incapable of action, as if someone had removed a vital part of her being and swapped it for jelly. She had told no one. When Hugo had asked casually for his daddy after a couple of days, she had just said that he was at work; Hugo had accepted this, moving straight on to his next question – what was for tea – without a pause.

It was the third Wednesday of the month, but for the first time ever she wasn't looking forward to her evening out with Julia and Lily. They would see straight through her hastily created disguise, would wheedle the truth out of her before the poppadoms and pickle tray had even reached the table. Felicity couldn't bear it. Their sympathy would be bad enough, but what was worse was her own sense of failure. She was not the kind of woman who couldn't keep her husband. She was competent and capable, a successful person who achieved everything that she turned her hand to except, unfortunately, the one thing that seemed to matter the most.

She would cancel. She would tell them that she was ill, or that Hugo was ill. They wouldn't question her, would take whatever she told them at face value as the gospel truth, for what could she, a woman with the most perfect life, possibly have reason to lie about?

And then, with the spooky synchronicity usually reserved for communications between the twins, her mobile buzzed. It was Julia.

Mum has heard from Marnie. She's coming to visit! Heaven help us. See you soon x

There had been little mention of Marnie in the five months since their mother had returned from Greece. After the initial flurry of questions, none of which had been furnished with satisfactory answers, the three of them had just let the subject drop. And now, here was the prodigal daughter of sorts deigning to visit them in their quaint little northern town. Well, it was about time. Their poor mother, being made to wait for news from her like she was nothing – that was unforgivable, to Felicity's mind.

This news put a different slant on things. There was no way she could miss tonight now. Felicity shook herself into action. She needed to get changed out of her scruffy clothes and put some make-up on. Hugo was at her parents' for the night so she could even have a few glasses of wine if she fancied it. She did fancy it, she realised now. In fact, getting drunk suddenly seemed like an excellent plan. Lily and Julia would be too absorbed in the Marnie news to ask too many questions. She could just pretend that something bad had happened at work, for now.

She would tell them eventually. Of course she would. Just not now.

Felicity turned and left the kitchen. The key sat where it was.

2

As the still-nameless man in the Indian restaurant led her to the Nightingale sisters' preferred table, Julia was certain that she saw an inquisitive eye roam towards her waistline. He was young and polite and well trained in what constituted appropriate behaviour for front-of-house staff, even in the case of familiar diners such as themselves. (Even if this familiarity wasn't reciprocal – the forgetting his name business still troubled her.) He knew, it seemed, not to ask a direct question, but perhaps he hoped that by his surreptitious glance he would prompt an admission on her part, which he could then carry back to the kitchens.

Julia could hear the excited conversation now.

'She is! She told me.'

'But she wears no ring. I thought she was the one without a husband.'

'Maybe she's newly married. I'll check her hand when I take their pickle tray.'

But Julia said nothing. Five months in, she liked to think that her condition wasn't entirely obvious. With clever clothing and poor lighting she thought she could still disguise her bump. At work, seated behind her desk and with patients who were far more consumed by their own bodily state than hers, her pregnancy seemed to be progressing without much comment. Maybe her patients, like the waiter, were too polite to make direct reference to something that seemed ever so slightly off-kilter. Or perhaps she was still at the point where her shape could be mistaken for simple weight gain, and to refer to it might be insulting for her and humiliating for them.

She had recently informed her fellow doctors that she would be requiring a period of maternity leave and they had offered congratulations, some of them more sincerely than others, as no doubt they had thought they were out of the woods as far as Julia and maternity leave were concerned. But no one had asked her, when she was – as far as they all knew – resolutely single, how a baby had managed to slip its way inside her.

Telling her family had been more complicated. The moment she had peed on the stick, and then the second and third ones that she had bought as back-up, the joy of seeing the little blue line had almost been eclipsed by an anxiety about what she had done. This was what she had wanted, had planned for, but holding the proof of her achievement in her hand brought home to her the challenges that her unconventional approach to parenthood would bring. She suddenly felt the need for someone to have her back. Julia wasn't the sort to worry unduly about what other people thought, but it felt vital to have her family on board. The trouble was that she couldn't, hand on heart, predict how they might react to her news.

She had decided to tackle them one at a time, starting with Lily, where she knew any negativity would be the easiest to ride over. They had at least discussed the possibility of a sperm donor baby before, and when Julia drew in her breath and prepared to spill the news, Lily, using their spooky twin telepathy, had known at once what was coming.

'You did it!' Lily squealed. 'Well done, Ju! That's amazing!'

She flung her arms around Julia and squeezed her tight. Then came the inevitable barrage of questions. When was it due? How was she feeling? And finally, more awkwardly, how it had been accomplished? Julia had narrated the story of the evening of conception with Sam, warming to her theme as she went, her confidence buoyed by Lily's laughter.

Her parents, too, had been positive. Though they were clearly curious, they had skipped over the technicalities, but both agreed that Sam would make a wonderful (if not a little surprising) father if that was what Julia had decided she wanted.

Felicity, however, had disapproved.

'I just can't see how you're going to make it work, Ju,' she had said, her eyebrows squeezed tightly into a little knot. 'It's far from plain sailing, you know, looking after a child. It's bloody hard work. I don't know how you'll manage on your own.'

'I'm not on my own,' Julia had said. 'I've got Sam.'

Felicity rolled her eyes at her. 'That's hardly the same. Sam won't be there when it cries in the middle of the night and you're too tired to lift your head from the pillow. He won't be much use at all when he's not even living under the same roof. But that's not the main issue.'

'Oh?' replied Julia. Here it comes, she thought.

'I'm not sure it's right to bring a child into the world like this,' continued Felicity.

'Like what?' asked Julia indignantly.

'Well, without a father for a start.'

'But he or she will have a father. What do you think Sam is?' Whilst Julia hadn't been quite sure of the role that Sam would play when they had first set out on their quest, as the pregnancy proceeded it had become apparent that he had got the balance between involvement and detachment just right; but if she emphasised the involvement part to Felicity, what harm could it do?

'But he's not like a real father, is he?' Felicity objected. She made air quotes around the word 'real' and Julia felt the urge to slap her. 'Think of what will happen at school. It's a licence to bully, you know, a set-up like that.'

Julia had been dumbfounded by her sister's attitude. 'You do know that this is the twenty-first century, Fliss?' she had scoffed. 'I think there's room for more than just the traditional nuclear family with 2.4 children.'

'Well, I think the whole thing is . . .' Felicity struggled to find a word. 'Unsavoury. And I don't even want to think about the mechanics of how you did it. A turkey baster – isn't that what they use?'

Her sister's disdain had been horribly on show, which was rich, Julia thought, as they all knew that Hugo was the product of a number of very expensive rounds of IVF. Maybe that was the root of her issue: the fact that she and Sam had achieved with a small plastic tub and a syringe what had cost Felicity and Richard thousands of pounds and a great deal of heartache.

'No. Not a turkey baster,' she had clarified coolly. 'A perfectly ordinary syringe.'

Felicity shuddered. 'Well, as I said, I have no idea how you think you're going to manage,' she said.

'I suppose I'll find a way,' Julia replied shortly. 'Plenty of single women bring up babies.'

'And I can help,' said Lily, her eyes shining with the excitement of it all, and Julia could have kissed her. 'I've got plenty of time and the new little Nightingale won't mind kicking around with his or her cousins, I'm sure.'

She had seen Felicity flinch then. Her sister had never said but Julia was sure that Felicity desperately wanted a second child – one of each, a perfect pair to complement her perfect life – but then Hugo had been so difficult to come by that she seemed to have decided to stick with a singleton. Even though she always seemed to baulk at the chaos that surrounded Lily and her brood, something in her clearly ached for at least a taste of the noise and rambunctiousness that plenty of children brought with them.

And so Julia had backed off, and the pair of them had agreed to differ. They had steadfastly avoided discussing Julia's decision ever since. When it came down to it, it was nobody's business but hers, and possibly Sam's, and the approval of three out of four of her immediate family would be fine.

And it was nothing to do with the restaurant man, either, so whilst Julia clocked his sidelong glance at her waistline, she did nothing to either confirm or deny his suspicions and just took her usual place at the table to wait for Felicity and Lily.

Lily was next to arrive. She looked slender and beautiful, Julia thought and then said.

'Oh, I'm not really,' Lily replied, as ever keen to dilute any compliment. 'I was saying to Marco just the other night how I seem to be getting rounder and rounder.'

'And what did Marco say?' asked Julia teasingly. She knew exactly what Marco would have said.

'He said that I was being silly,' she replied quietly, dropping her head slightly and peering up at Julia through her fringe.

Julia cocked her head to one side and raised an eyebrow. 'And meanwhile I really am becoming rounder,' she added, letting her eyes drop to her stomach which now, instead of falling away like Lily's, was nudging the table top.

Lily beamed at her. 'Don't knock it, Jules. I'm so envious. I love being where you are right now.'

Julia grinned back. 'Really?' she asked playfully. 'We hadn't noticed.'

Lily shoved her gently on the arm. 'Oh, shut up. I'm just blessed that I met Marco and that making babies comes so easily to us.'

'Making boy babies,' Julia corrected, and Lily allowed herself to look wistful for a second.

'Yes. You'd think, given Mum had three – well, four – girls and Marco has two sisters that we might have managed to make at least one girl. Still, I wouldn't swap my boys for all the tea in China. What about you? Will you find out what it is?'

Julia had thought about this endlessly. Sam was keen to know, but Julia had stuck to her guns and refused to ask. She wanted the baby's sex to be a surprise, but she did at least know that she wasn't carrying twins, which was a relief. That particular genetic time bomb seemed to have been passed to Lily and not her.

'No, I don't think I will find out,' she said. 'As long as it's healthy then that's all that matters.'

'And happy,' added Lily. 'Don't forget that.'

As if on cue, Felicity came in, dodging her way around tables and diners to reach them. Now she really *was* looking thin, Julia thought, and every single one of her thirty-eight years and then some. The gentle layers of fat that used to fill out her face had melted away leaving wrinkles and troughs that hadn't been there before, and new shadows fell on her features as a result. Of course, she hadn't told them what was worrying her, but Julia and Lily had assumed it had to do with Richard. Neither of them had seen him since the family picnic in the summer. They perhaps wouldn't have expected to; they all lived busy lives, and Felicity hadn't seen Marco either, as far as Julia was aware. Still, her instincts told her that Richard had been avoiding them, although she couldn't put her finger on exactly why.

'Hi,' said Felicity. She fell into her seat as if she'd walked a hundred miles to reach it. 'How are you both?'

'Good, thanks,' they chorused, still unable, even now in their fourth decade, to quite separate their thought or speech patterns from one another.

Felicity steadfastly avoided looking at Julia's lower body but for now, at least, they had something more pressing to discuss.

'So,' she began, once the drinks had arrived and their standard food order had been placed. 'What's going on with Mum and Marnie?'

'I only know what I've said,' said Julia. 'Apparently she's been in touch, and she wants to come for a visit.'

'About time, too,' said Felicity. 'It's so cruel to have kept Mum waiting all this time. How long is it since she went to Greece?'

'Five months,' said Julia.

'Precisely,' replied Felicity. 'Five months of not knowing, of beating herself up and thinking the worst. It's unforgivable. It really is.'

'I'm not sure that Mum's been doing any of those things,' chipped in Lily. 'And she's had fifty years to get used to the idea of Marnie. Poor Marnie has had so much to deal with. I'm not surprised she's taken her time.'

Julia had to agree, even though she knew it would rile Felicity. 'Lily's right. I'd much rather she got everything straight in her head before she met us all. It should make things a bit easier, wouldn't you say?'

Felicity shrugged. 'When's she coming?'

'Saturday, apparently. She's seeing Mum and Dad first.'

'Short notice. It's like Greece all over again. She obviously thinks that we have nothing better to do than run round at her whim . . .' Julia threw Felicity a look and she stopped mid-sentence. 'Well. I'm just saying,' she added defensively. 'It might not have been convenient.'

'And are you around for lunch at Mum's on Sunday, so she can meet the rest of us?' Julia asked.

Felicity shuffled a little in her seat. 'Well, as it happens, Hugo and I are free on Sunday.'

'Well, there you go then. No problem,' said Lily.

Julia noticed that Felicity hadn't confirmed Richard's attendance, but she let it go. All would become clear in that regard soon enough.

'Is she going to stay with Mum?' asked Lily.

Julia shook her head. 'Hotel in town apparently.'

They each pulled a face at one another, collective eyebrows raised.

Then Lily spoke. 'Well, I suppose that makes sense. It'll be a lot to take in this first time. It's good that she'll have somewhere to retreat to.'

'Retreat from what exactly?' Felicity asked. 'It's not like we're ogres or anything.'

'No. Of course not. But still . . .'

They sat in contemplation for a moment and then Felicity said, 'If I'm totally honest, I'm still struggling with the whole idea. We've got a sister that we never knew anything about. Does that not strike you as odd? I mean, four Nightingale sisters, not three. I can't quite get my head around it.'

'The thing I find the hardest is that Mum has carried this on her own for all those years,' said Lily. 'A baby at sixteen and then having to give it up. Can you imagine how scary that must have been? And how painful.'

'At least she had Dad to talk to,' Julia said. 'She's not been entirely on her own.'

Lily pulled a face that said she wasn't entirely sure how much use her father might have been in these rather odd circumstances. 'But still. She could have talked to us. We would have understood,' she pressed on.

'Would we though?' asked Julia. 'I'm not so sure. I haven't even had my first baby yet at thirty-five. I've got no idea how it would have felt to be a teenage mum, especially in the sixties. Plus things are so very different these days. If one of us had got ourselves pregnant so young we would either have had an abortion . . .' Lily flinched. 'Or Mum and Dad would have helped us to bring it up. No one would ever have suggested just handing it over to someone else.'

'But even now, a teenage pregnancy is frowned upon by some people,' said Felicity. 'I can't really imagine the scale of the disgrace back then.'

Julia suppressed a giggle. 'I know it's not funny and all that. But Mum! Having sex under age! Can you imagine?'

She and Lily exchanged a look and then Lily was giggling too, the pair of them rocking in their seats with tears rolling down their cheeks. Felicity rolled her eyes.

'Oh, grow up, you two,' she said, but Julia noticed that she couldn't help a little smile too.

'I wonder what Uncle Ralph was like,' said Lily, when they were back in control of themselves. 'He was older than Mum, wasn't he?'

'A couple of years older,' confirmed Julia.

'No doubt a bad influence,' said Felicity primly. 'I mean, Mum was under age. That's illegal whichever way you look at it.'

Julia shook her head and tutted at Felicity.

'It's kind of romantic too, though,' said Lily. 'First love and all that. There's always something very special about that first person, that first time.'

'Ew! Lily! This is Mum we're talking about,' said Felicity. 'And anyway, I'm not sure that there is anything at all romantic about it. As I see things, Uncle Ralph took advantage of a young girl when he should have known better and then failed to face up to his responsibilities.'

'By inconveniently dying?' asked Julia. 'Look. Unless Mum tells us a bit more, we can't know what went on between the three

213

of them back then. But Marnie is real and she's coming to stay. That's what we need to get our heads around now. Whatever we think of what happened, she's our sister and we need to make sure that Mum sees us welcoming her. We don't want to make things any worse.'

However, Julia knew that saying that and actually doing it were two very different matters.

3

Marnie was coming and Cecily had fallen into something of a tailspin.

When the letter from her eldest daughter finally arrived, Cecily had almost stopped letting herself believe that it ever would. The possibilities had chased themselves around her mind like mini assassins, each doing away with her latest idea and replacing it with something worse.

1. Marnie would get in touch when she got back from Greece.

2. Marnie would get in touch when the dust had settled on the Greece trip.

3. Marnie would get in touch when she had discussed what she had learnt about Cecily with Sofia.

4. Marnie would get in touch when she'd spoken to her adoptive family about everything. (Although Cecily was under the impression that she didn't speak to them about anything.)

5. Marnie would get in touch when the schools went back. (Cecily wasn't sure how this could be a significant date for Marnie, but it had always been important in her world so it featured on her list.)

6. Marnie had banged her head and had amnesia, thus forgetting that they had met in Greece.

7. Marnie had contracted a terminal illness and couldn't bear to tell Cecily.

8. Marnie had contracted a terminal illness and was too ill to get in touch.

9. Marnie was dead.

10. Marnie would get in touch to send them a Christmas card.

It was ridiculous, Cecily knew it was, but she couldn't help her mind desperately seeking reasons for Marnie's silence. Her lack of contact since they met was surely a little peculiar, no matter which of the options Cecily picked to explain it.

She had initially expected to hear something from her within a couple of weeks of getting back from Kefalonia, and each day that passed beyond that just served to make her doubt her own judgement. Maybe things between the two of them had not gone as well as she'd thought. Perhaps Marnie had been disappointed by her, had decided that she'd seen enough and felt no need to pursue a relationship any further. It was up to her, after all. It might be that her curiosity had been sated and that she was happily getting on with her life without Cecily in it.

She had stopped asking Norman what he thought after a couple of months. His jaw would tighten before he answered her repetitive questions, a tiny tell-tale and no doubt involuntary movement that gave his frustrations away more than any of his actual words did. He was obviously tired of listening to her endless speculation on the question of Marnie's silence. In some ways, his annoyance with her was almost a blessing, as it allowed her to secretly indulge her wilder musings without incurring his scorn.

The letter finally arrived almost exactly five months after the first one. Spotting the unfamiliar envelope on the mat, Cecily had instinctively known what it was. She picked it up and stood, weighing it in her hands and trying to work out how she felt. She had been so focused on Marnie actually getting in touch that she hadn't given any thought to what she might say when she finally did. Maybe it would be bad news, and not good. There was always the possibility that, following their brief but intense meeting in Kefalonia, Marnie had decided her life would be better without her birth mother in it. This long-awaited letter could actually be a particularly cruel 'Dear John'.

Well, she would never know unless she opened it.

Norman was in the sitting room poring over his jigsaw puzzle. It had been on the table in there for six months. He seemed to attack it with gusto every once in a while and then lose interest and abandon it. She had asked several times if she could clear it away, but he had just shaken his head vehemently.

'No, no. I will finish it,' he had said. 'Summer isn't the best time for jigsaws. There are too many other things to be doing. But after the clocks change . . . I'll have more time for it then. Let's just leave it out.'

And so she had done, dusting it delicately from time to time, paranoid about accidentally sweeping a piece or two on to the floor to be eaten by the vacuum cleaner. She even found herself hovering over it occasionally, hunting for a particular shape or colour, even though jigsaw puzzles had never been her thing. They seemed so pointless. If you liked the picture, then why chop it into pieces just to reassemble it? You could simply put it in a frame from the very start.

'It's all about the challenge,' Norman had tried to explain. 'Pitting your wits against the designer.'

But Cecily remained unconvinced.

'There's a letter,' she said now as she walked into the sitting room.

Norman looked up from his puzzle. 'What kind of letter?' he asked and then, when he saw her face, he added, 'Oh,' in a tone that showed that he understood.

'Do you think it's really from her?' Cecily asked him, although he couldn't know any more than she did.

'Well, there's only one way to find out,' said Norman.

Cecily hesitated and then propped the letter against the carriage clock on the mantelpiece. 'I'll just go and make us a cup of tea first, and then . . .'

'Open it, Cecily,' Norman said, his voice gentle but firm.

She looked at her husband and then at the letter. He was right. She had been waiting for so long. She shouldn't put it off.

'All right,' she said quietly.

She plucked the letter up again and sat down at the table next to Norman. Just having him there felt comforting, although there was nothing he could do to help, not really. She broke the seal and pulled the letter out of the envelope. She could see before she read a word that it was very short. Was that a good or a bad thing? Her eyes skipped across the words but it took a moment or two before they settled into an order that she could recognise.

Dear Cecily

*I would like to meet you and your family. I shall be
in Harrogate this weekend and will have some time
free. Please TEXT me to let me know if this would
be convenient and to make arrangements.*

    Yours sincerely,

    Marnie Stone

When she got to the end of the letter her eyes flicked straight back to the top and she began to read again, this time out loud so that Norman could hear. When she had finished, she turned to look at him.

'Well? What do you think that means?' she asked.

'It means that she's coming to Harrogate and wants to call in,' replied Norman simply.

'But why is she coming? And where will she stay? With us or in a hotel? And when she says she wants to meet us, does she mean all at once or do I set up a kind of appointment system so she doesn't get overwhelmed? And why is "text" in capitals?'

'I think the only way you can know any of that is to text her and find out. Where's your mobile?'

'In the drawer in the kitchen,' she said quietly. 'But I'm not very good at texting. Do you think I should ask Lily to help, or Julia maybe?'

'Hello! I'm here. I do know how to text, you know,' said Norman, eyebrows raised indignantly.

'Yes, of course. Sorry, Norman. I'm just nervous.'

'The main thing,' said Norman reasonably, 'is that she's coming. The rest is just detail. Now go and get your phone and we'll compose a response.'

Norman's calming voice was like balm to her racing heart, smothering and soothing it until its beat felt more normal in her chest.

'But do you think . . .' she began.

'I don't know, Cecily. Go and get the phone. And the charger. The battery's probably flat.'

Cecily stood up and made her way, trance-like, to the kitchen, and returned moments later with the phone in her hand. She passed it to Norman who pressed something on the side. The screen lit up.

'Well, that's something. It's not dead,' he said. 'Right,' he looked at Cecily, his eyes calm and focused. 'What would you like to say?'

'Oh, I don't know.' Cecily felt uncharacteristically flustered by the seemingly simple task. 'I can't think.'

'Well,' said Norman. 'How about *That would be lovely. What time would you like to come?*'

'Does that sound a bit negative?' Cecily asked.

Norman shook his head. 'I can't see how,' he said.

'I mean, don't you think we should be more positive about the arrangements? Make a firm suggestion, perhaps? Or might that sound like I'm trying to take control? I don't want her to think that, but I don't want her to think we aren't bothered, either.'

'I'm not sure what's wrong with my suggestion,' Norman replied, but Cecily wasn't really listening as she tried to think through the implications of any message that they might send.

'How about, *That sounds lovely. Would you like to come on Saturday for a cup of tea and then I could invite you and the family for lunch on Sunday?*'

Norman's brow creased and he tipped his head to one side. 'Do you think that might be a bit much, for a first visit?' he asked carefully. 'I mean, all of us for lunch – a tad overwhelming maybe?'

Cecily considered this. Would it be overwhelming? Possibly, although they were a very friendly bunch. But she had been waiting to hear from Marnie for so long that she couldn't bear not to make the most of this opportunity. Plus, they didn't know why she was coming to Harrogate now, or if she would ever come again. This might be the only chance they got to introduce her to her sisters and nephews for a very long time. A strong, almost visceral urge was telling her that she had to strike whilst the iron was hot.

'No,' she replied decisively. 'I hear what you're saying, Norman, but I think we should give her options. She can always say no.'

Norman shrugged. 'Well, that's true enough. So. What am I saying?'

His attention focused back on the phone and Cecily dictated her words slowly. '*Hi Marnie. This is Cecily* . . . She won't recognise the number so I'd better make that clear.' Norman nodded. '*Thank you for your letter. It would be lovely to see you. Why don't you come for coffee with Norman and me at our home at two on Saturday and then you might like to meet the others here for lunch on Sunday, say twelve for twelve-thirty.* How does that sound? Is it clear enough?'

'It'll be the longest text I've ever sent,' replied Norman. 'Not that that's a problem,' he added quickly.

He finished typing out the message, slowly and methodically. Cecily saw his mouth making the shape of each word as he worked.

'There,' he said when he'd finished, and he held the screen out to her so that she could see.

Cecily read her message. 'Do you really think she will be overwhelmed?'

Norman shrugged.

'Should I ask her for the Saturday first? But then what if she makes other plans for the Sunday or goes back to London or wherever she's travelling from? No. Let's offer her both. She can always pick and choose which parts she fancies.'

'All right.'

'And what about where she'll stay? Should I offer her a bed here?'

Norman shook his head. 'You don't have to cover everything in the first message. If she wants to stay she can always ask or you can offer it in a follow-up message.'

'Yes, you're right, of course,' replied Cecily, more to convince herself than to agree with Norman. 'And she can always ask me about anything she's not sure of.'

'She can,' said Norman, his voice calm. 'So? Shall I send it?'

Cecily bit her lip. 'Yes,' she said, nodding decisively.

Norman pressed send, and the message was gone.

Cecily's heart pounded in her chest. This was it. Marnie was going to come here and see where she lived and meet Norman and the girls. It was everything she could have hoped for.

The phone beeped almost at once and it made Cecily jump. Norman picked it up from where it lay on the table between them and peered at the screen. Then he held it up so that Cecily could see. There was a message from an unknown number.

OK, it read.

4

The house looked cleaner and more tidy than it had done in years, although it appeared that some kind of hurricane had passed through the shed. However, Cecily very much doubted that Marnie would look in there and if she did, she would just blame Norman for the disarray.

There had been an unusual degree of dithering on her part over what she would offer by way of refreshment. To start with, she had thought she would bake. After all, that was what she always did when they had guests. But then she had wondered whether Marnie's adoptive mother was a baker. She didn't want to set herself up in competition with her. If the adoptive mother didn't bake then Cecily producing home-baked goods might send out the message that she considered herself to be a superior sort of parent, and that would never do.

So she had walked down into town and bought a selection of treats from Betty's – nothing too flashy; some shortbread, a few fondant fancies and a couple of fat rascals. Fat rascals were always a talking point as few people knew of the tasty, scone-like treat outside Yorkshire. She'd also bought a variety of fruit and herbal teas and a packet of freshly ground coffee. She and Norman would be drinking them up for months to come.

They would sit in the sitting room, she had decided. She had toyed with using the kitchen, which might feel less formal, but the units were so shabby. She didn't notice all the chips and scrapes in the laminate herself, but if she considered the space through a stranger's eyes it suddenly appeared sorely lacking. She didn't want Marnie to think that she didn't care or hadn't made an effort for her; it was more comfortable to sit in the sitting room anyway, and more homely.

She cleaned the insides of the windows with vinegar and newspaper the way Peggy had shown her all those decades ago in the Mother and Baby Home. Her mind had drifted towards Peggy often over the last five months. She had not seen hide nor hair of her erstwhile friend since the day she lost her baby, and had wondered only in the most general terms what might have become of her in the intervening years. But those distant days had been brought into sharp relief by retelling the stories to Marnie, and since then her thoughts had gathered around Peggy more closely. Did she go on to have a family of her own, too? Cecily assumed that she would still be living in Oldham somewhere. Would she even recognise her if she walked into the room? Cecily liked to think that she would know her anywhere, but then hadn't she thought that about her own child? And look how well that had turned out.

The windows were sparkling but her hands were black with newsprint. She should have worn gloves, but it was all right. There was still plenty of time to have a shower and get changed. What she would wear was another decision that she had spent more time mulling over than was entirely necessary. She wanted to make a better impression than she had done in Greece. Her cheeks still burned pink when she thought about what she must have looked like the first time Marnie ever set eyes on her, fresh from her ocean swim. Eventually she had settled on a navy dress that Lily complimented her on whenever she wore it. It was, or at least so she hoped, timeless and elegantly simple, and did not seem to be trying to shout out who she was or wanted to be. With her hair carefully blow-dried and a little make-up strategically applied, she decided that she would be presenting her best self to her daughter.

By one-thirty she was ready, and there was nothing else that she could do to make their home any more welcoming for their guest. She couldn't relax, though. She fretted about the kitchen, picking things up and putting them down again. She over-watered the house plants and hid a pile of unattended post in a cupboard out of sight.

At one forty-five Norman ambled into the kitchen. He was wearing an aged pair of corduroy trousers, shiny at knee and rear and bagging from over-washing. He looked like he was ready for a day on an allotment.

'You can't wear those,' Cecily snapped, aware that her voice sounded shriller than usual but not quite able to control it.

'Why not? They're clean,' said Norman. His tone was border-ing on tetchy. Today was not the day for him to slip into one of his cantankerous moods so she didn't want to provoke one, but at the same time he ought to at least try to make a good impression on Marnie.

'I know, Norman darling, but they are a little bit tired. Why don't you wear those lovely grey ones we bought in the sales? They are much smarter. There's no need to change your shirt.'

The shirt was not far from its last legs either, but Cecily knew that she would never get him to change his entire outfit. Norman let out a little huff but went back upstairs.

Cecily wondered about boiling the kettle ready. She wouldn't make the drinks yet – that would be silly – but if the kettle had already boiled it would speed the whole process up when Marnie arrived. Then she remembered learning how to make tea with the Brownies. There was a rule about using freshly drawn water and not reheating the old, although Cecily had never been sure why it could make any difference. Best not to risk it, though. She didn't want to offer bad tea. Instead she checked the tea tray. The cakes were still in the box provided by the shop, complete with curling ribbon. It looked so pretty that it seemed a shame to open it and throw it away, and also she wanted to show Marnie that the world was really quite civilised in the north. But now she wondered whether the box might be a bit pretentious and make it look as if she was trying too hard.

The clock on the mantelpiece struck two. Thank goodness for that. Cecily was going to drive herself mad with all this overthinking. She decided to go and wait in the sitting room. Surely that was the natural thing to do, although she had thought so deeply about the whole visit that she could no longer remember what normal behaviour looked like.

In the sitting room, however, she did not like to sit on the freshly plumped sofa cushions, so she hovered about instead. She even took a look at Norman's jigsaw. It would become a picture of Monument Valley in Arizona, according to the image on the box lid. It seemed to be mainly oranges and blues, and Cecily couldn't see how Norman could possibly distinguish between them. She bent over the table to view the pieces, and after a couple of minutes she pulled out the wooden chair and sat down. Now she looked more closely she could see that the oranges were of different hues depending on where the sunlight hit the rock. That was presumably how Norman could tell the areas apart.

She focused on a clump of gorse in the foreground that seemed to be slightly more green than the rest, and then scanned the scattered pieces for that particular shade. Almost at once her eyes settled on what she thought must be a fit, but when she put it next to the ones that Norman had already found she couldn't see how it would sit with them. What a waste of time a jigsaw was.

The clock chimed quarter past and she looked up to check, surprised that she seemed to have lost fifteen minutes to the puzzle. Marnie was fashionably late. Cecily wished that she knew what had brought her to Harrogate in the first place. If she were in a meeting, for example, or had been taken for lunch somewhere, it might be more difficult to extract herself, which could account for the delay. Or maybe she was lost. The house wasn't difficult to find once you were on the road, but if you knew nothing of Harrogate then you could get yourself snared up in the one-way system and that could take an age to get out of.

She turned her attention back to the puzzle, but now that the spell had been broken it no longer held her attention. The sitting room door opened and Norman stuck his head round.

'No sign?' he asked.

'Not yet,' she replied, her voice sounding slightly overwrought. 'I'm sure she'll be here very soon. Young people have a different sense of time, don't they? Just look at Felicity. She's always late.'

Norman grunted and disappeared again. Maybe she could put the television on to kill some time, but they never watched the television during the day, and especially not on a Saturday. What if Marnie heard it from the doorstep? She'd think that they had no standards.

Instead, Cecily picked a book up from the table and started to flick through it. It was a David Attenborough volume that Julia had bought Norman for Christmas and was filled with huge coloured plates showing the wonders of the natural world. She stopped at a picture of a hammerhead shark, which was spread in startling detail across two pages. Its teeth looked so sharp that she put a hand out to touch them, and then was a little surprised when the pads of her fingers hit smooth paper. It was such an odd-looking creature, with its eyes stuck on the ends of its peculiar head like that. Briefly Cecily wondered what evolution had been thinking. She flicked

227

over a few more pages. Seals and penguins and coral. It really was a beautiful book. She couldn't think why she hadn't made the time to look at it properly before.

Then the doorbell rang and she jumped.

She was here.

Cecily snapped the book shut and put it back on the table. Was this excitement she was feeling, or nervousness? Maybe a little of both. Her baby was here to see her. Her firstborn. Her little girl, so watchful as a baby with her shock of dark hair and her questioning brown eyes. Was she really so very different now that she was a grown-up? Cecily had no way of knowing what had happened to her over the past fifty years, although she hoped that Marnie would share that with her in time; but from this moment on they could concentrate on rebuilding the bond that she had nurtured in the light-filled nursery of the Home.

She stood, her hand on the latch. Then she took a deep breath, fixed a wide smile on her lips and opened the door.

'Have you got this parcel? We were out when they tried to deliver it so they left a card, but they haven't bothered to write the number of the house they took it to so I'm having to knock on everyone's door until I track it down. It's a new hosepipe so a big box, I imagine. I thought it would be easier to get it delivered than trailing down to the garden centre to pick one up, but now I'm thinking maybe not.'

Her neighbour, Mr Flanagan, stood on the doorstep brandishing a delivery card like a referee, and Cecily felt completely wrong-footed. For a moment she was so confused that she couldn't understand what he was saying, and he stared at her, his face switching from outrage to concern.

'Are you all right, Mrs Nightingale?' he asked. 'You look a bit out of sorts.'

Cecily looked beyond Mr Flanagan to see if Marnie was standing behind him on the drive, but there was no sign of her.

'Yes. I was just expecting it to be someone else,' Cecily said. 'I'm sorry. We don't have a parcel for you.'

'Then it must be next door. Typical that it's at the very last house I try. Thanks anyway.' He turned and headed back down the drive waving the delivery card over his head and still chuntering to himself.

Cecily took one last look down the drive and then closed the door. Norman was at her side.

'It wasn't her,' she said sadly, and she felt Norman tuck his arm around her waist and lead her back towards the sitting room. 'What time is it?'

'Twenty-five to three,' replied Norman.

'She's not coming, is she?' Cecily said, her voice so quiet that even she had difficulty hearing it.

'Oh, she's not that late yet. She's probably just been held up. Let's not get downhearted. Shall I make us a cup of tea whilst we wait?'

But Cecily shook her head. Tears pricked in her eyes and then fell on to her cheeks. 'No. She's not coming. I can feel it. She's changed her mind.'

'Oh Cecily, my darling girl,' said Norman. He put his hands on her shoulders and turned her to face him. Cecily leant into him, pushed her face into the soft cotton of his shirt, and cried.

5

Julia decided to walk to her parents' house for Sunday lunch. The late autumn air had a nip in it and she dug out her favourite scarf and wrapped it tightly round her neck. Her coat didn't quite meet across her stomach any more, but the scarf was so voluminous that it would keep her warm. And the baby seemed to do a good job of that, too, acting like a little hot water bottle right at her core. It was a good half an hour's walk, but she assumed that Marco or Richard would give her a lift back, so she set off with confidence.

She needed time to think. She had been unsure about this lunch with the new long-lost sister even before yesterday's events. Now she was really unsettled. She had rung her mother the previous evening to find out how the meeting with Marnie had gone, only to learn that Marnie had failed to show. To be fair, there had been a text message which, of course, her parents hadn't thought to look for until she had suggested it. Marnie had been unavoidably delayed but would be there for lunch the following day as arranged. That was it. No explanation. No apology. Nothing.

Her mother had made excuses for Marnie, emphasised that these things happen and it wasn't important, but Julia had heard the crack in her voice and the effort that she was making to sound bright. Of course it was important. It was possibly the most important thing to happen to Cecily since Julia had been born.

Part of Julia disliked Marnie before she had even met her for putting her mother through that, yet struggling against that emotional response was her more rational side. Perhaps Marnie had actually been unavoidably detained. No one seemed to know what she was doing in Harrogate, so there was a real chance that she was here on business and that her time wasn't her own. In that case, she had done what any normal person would do and texted to say she couldn't make it. Was it her fault that Julia's parents were technologically incompetent? This was a perfectly sensible explanation for what had happened and gave Julia no cause at all to blame Marnie.

And yet she did. This was what she needed to think about as she walked.

It was a grey day, the sun cloaked by thick, impenetrable cloud. She could smell the fallen leaves rotting on the pavements, musty and sweet. As a child she would have kicked through them, but now the thought of what might lie hidden beneath put her off. Somewhere someone was having a bonfire, the wood smoke drifting across the road and into her nostrils. She seemed to be so much more sensitive to smells now she was pregnant, so much more sensitive to everything, in fact; and it had crossed her mind that all the anger she was feeling towards Marnie might merely be a result of her rampant hormones. But she had various potential explanations for her animosity. It might be a delayed form of shock at discovering that Marnie existed at all, or simply that Marnie had upset her mother, which would be enough all by itself.

To a certain extent, it didn't really matter why Julia was cross, because she would have to keep it hidden. No purpose whatsoever would be served by her showing any hostility towards Marnie today. She was just going to have to suck it up and be a grown-up. And this walk was going to help her with that. She had been tempted to ring Lily and chat it through with her, but then she'd changed her mind. Lily, always so very sensitive to everyone's feelings, would have enough to deal with today without taking Julia's woes on board as well, and so she had decided to keep her concerns to herself.

Always assuming Marnie bothered to show her face. And if she didn't? Well, the rest of them would have a lovely Sunday lunch and just carry on as they always had: a happy, lively family, complete and perfect.

By the time she reached her parents' road, Julia was feeling a little better about it all. This was not her battle. Her job was to be nice to her new half-sister/cousin and support her mother as best she could. And she could, and would, do that.

Lily's people carrier and Felicity's car were already parked on the drive as she walked up it. She was last. Or maybe the last bar one?

She climbed the steps, opened the door and let herself in.

'Hi,' she called. 'Sorry I'm a bit late. I decided to walk, and it took a bit longer than I expected.'

Actually she wasn't at all late. They were all just early.

As she hung her coat and scarf up, Hugo came racing out of the kitchen with Lily's twins hot on his heels. They pushed past Julia and out into the garden, leaving the door swinging wide. She closed it gently behind them. The smell of roasting beef wafted through the hall and a hunger pang twisted her stomach. Her mother's home-cooked food. Perfect.

'We're in here, Julia,' she heard her mother's voice call from the sitting room. Julia let out a sharp breath and opened the door.

They were all there: Marco and Lily, the baby in her arms, sitting on one sofa and her parents and Felicity on the other. There was no sign of Richard, Julia noted, but something told her that this wasn't the time to mention that. And there, in the armchair where her father usually sat to watch the television, was a stranger. Except she wasn't a stranger exactly. She looked like an older, rounder version of Felicity, with the same dark hair and wary brown eyes. She and Lily had always looked more like her mother, fair and long-limbed. She could see nothing of her mother in this woman. But she could see her sister. Of that there was no doubt at all.

Her mother stood up. She looked lovely in a dress that she often wore on Christmas Day, but her cheeks were pinker than usual and she seemed anxious, her movements tight and jerky.

'Julia darling, this is Marnie.'

There was a beat when Marnie didn't move, but Julia watched her eyes as they roamed up and down her in an assessing but not exactly judgemental fashion. Finally, Marnie stood and held out her hand.

Julia smiled. 'Lovely to meet you, Marnie,' she said, taking Marnie's hand and shaking it. The gesture felt old-fashioned and awkward. The natural thing to say next was how she had heard so much about her, but that would be a lie, so she said nothing else.

'Thanks,' said Marnie and then she sat back down.

'I was just explaining,' said Felicity as Julia took a seat, 'that Richard has had to go away again and so can't be here. He sends his regards to everyone though.' Felicity didn't meet anyone's eyes as she spoke.

So Julia was right. There was more going on there.

'That's a shame,' she said quickly to cover any tension. 'And I saw Hugo as I came in. He looked happy as a sandboy. Nothing like an afternoon romping about with your cousins, is there?' As soon as the words were out of her mouth Julia could see how ill-judged they were, but there was nothing she could do about it and so she turned to Marnie to brazen it out. 'Do you have cousins, Marnie? Or siblings for that matter?'

'Apart from you, you mean?' Marnie asked. There was no warmth in her voice. 'No. I'm an only child of only children. It must be nice for them to have so many of you all living so close.'

Julia examined her face as she spoke, scanning it for any sub-text, but if there was one it wasn't apparent. She couldn't work her out. Was she angry with them, or just uncomfortable at the situation? Had she come just to challenge them or did she deserve the benefit of the doubt? Julia wasn't sure.

'Yes,' said Lily. 'We're lucky that we all live so near one another, although it can be a blessing and a curse. We're in each other's pockets a lot of the time.' She gave a little smile and shrugged her shoulders but she was blushing furiously, clearly worrying that she had made things worse. Lily had always hated conflict and she looked so small and vulnerable that Julia had to fight the urge to go and sit next to her in a show of sibling solidarity.

'And soon there'll be another,' her mother added. 'Julia is expecting in the spring.'

'And where's your husband?' Marnie asked coolly. 'Is he away too?'

The question hit Julia like a body blow, but she recovered herself quickly. 'No husband,' she said. 'I'm having this baby, just me.'

Felicity's lips tightened ever so slightly but it was enough for Marnie to notice, and Julia thought she saw something pass between the pair of them.

'Unusual decision, to bring a baby into the world on your own,' Marnie continued. 'I'm of the view that a child needs two parents.'

Was she challenging Julia now, so soon after they'd met, or was she just stating her opinion? It was hard to tell.

'Well, I got tired of waiting for Mr Right,' she said. 'And decided to take matters into my own hands. I'm a GP,' she added, as if this fact alone was justification for her decision.

Lily, leaping to Julia's defence, spoke next. 'Sam, the father, well, we've all known him forever. He was at school with me and Julia. He's so lovely. I'm sure he'll make a great dad,' she said.

Marnie turned her dark eyes back on Julia. 'But you're single, you say. Not with him.'

'Sam's gay,' said Julia simply. She wasn't justifying her decisions to this woman, no matter how closely related they were.

Her mother stood up. 'Norman, could you come and carve, and then I can serve lunch.'

Her father pushed himself up from the sofa and Julia did the same, unable to trust herself any longer. 'I'll come and help,' she said and she followed them out.

'How are you doing, Mum?' she asked when they were in the kitchen. 'She's very direct, isn't she?'

Her mother nodded. 'She can be, yes. But I don't think she means any harm by it. That's just her way.'

Julia nodded.

'And did she explain what happened yesterday?' she asked. She could hear the irritation in her voice, and her mother clearly did too.

'That's water under the bridge now, Julia,' her mother said firmly. 'Let's focus on the here and now, shall we?'

After several journeys backwards and forwards, the food was all laid out on the dining table and the family was summoned. Everyone took their usual places. Richard not being there was handy as it meant that there was a space for Marnie, and the conversation was light as they served each other with roast beef and potatoes, vegetables and gravy.

Once she was happy that everyone had what they needed, her mother sat down.

'I hope this is up to your standards, Marnie,' she said, although roast dinners were something of a speciality of hers and not a morsel was less than perfect. 'Marnie is a chef,' she explained. 'Her food at the hotel in Kefalonia was absolutely delicious.'

'You're not a vegetarian, though?' Lily asked, and for a minute Julia saw a look of horror cross her mother's face, this possibility apparently not having occurred to her.

'No,' Marnie replied. 'I'm not sure how good a chef you can be if you can't eat half the foods you want to cook with.'

'I'd not thought about that,' replied Lily. 'I suppose there are cooks who are vegetarians, though. Boys, try not to eat with your fingers. Marco, could you just help Leo cut up his meat?'

Marco leaned over obligingly and did the necessary cutting.

'So, Marco,' her father said. 'How's business? Still selling plenty of pizzas? Marco is in the food business too, Marnie. He runs an Italian restaurant in town.'

'He has a whole chain, Dad,' added Lily.

Marnie looked like this was of no interest to her whatsoever.

'He serves the best pizzas this side of Napoli,' Julia said, anxious to defend her brother-in-law. She grinned at him and he winked back.

'Is all good, Norman,' he said, his accent drawing out the vowels. 'We busy at half-term, too. I'm looking at a new place in York. Is early days still but it looks promising.' Marco stuck out his lower lip and nodded his head approvingly.

'It's always hard to keep standards up when you grow a business,' said Marnie. 'Easy to topple over into mediocre.'

'Well, I'm sure Marco won't let that happen,' replied Julia tightly. Who did she think she was, this woman who had dropped herself into their family and was making no effort whatsoever to fit in, or even be polite? Well, they didn't have to invite her into their fold, Julia thought. She'd do well to remember that she was very much on trial.

'So, Marnie,' Felicity said as she finished her meal and placed her knife and fork together decisively. 'Why don't you tell us all what you've been doing for the last fifty years?'

Way to go, Felicity, Julia thought, and she sat back to let things unfold. She noticed her mother shifting in her chair, ready to intervene if necessary, but Marnie seemed to appreciate the directness of Felicity's approach.

'Well,' she said, wiping her mouth on her napkin. 'I was adopted by Christine and Stanley Stone who lived in a back-to-back in Ashton-under-Lyne. They had no other children. They ran a pretty tight ship. Lots of rules for me to live by. I did my best but by the time I'd done my O levels things weren't really working out with them, so I left and got myself a job working in McDonald's in Manchester. Stayed there for five years and then went to catering college part-time. Got a qualification and then I worked as a sous chef at the Midland Hotel. Stayed there for a bit and then worked in various other restaurants. Then I moved to London where I met Sofia, and now I do mainly agency work and help her with the retreats. We do four a year at that hotel that you came to, Cecily.'

'And are your parents still around?' Felicity asked.

Marnie shook her head, the corners of her mouth turning downwards as if this was just one of those unfortunate things. No love lost there then, Julia thought. Were they dead, though, or just not part of Marnie's life? Somehow Julia had the impression that it was the latter, and that made her wonder just exactly what was going on. Could Marnie be looking for a ready-made family to slot herself into after her own had imploded? This explanation didn't feel right to Julia, though. If Marnie was trying to ingratiate herself with the Nightingales then she was going about it in a very strange manner.

'I'm a great cook,' continued Felicity, with characteristic immodesty. 'You obviously passed that gene on to me too, Mum.'

Julia glanced at Lily, who had had exactly the same response to Felicity's comment. Their eyes met, and Julia saw her twin's eyes widen ever so slightly. The discussion of shared genes was surely a step too far.

'Oh, I'm not sure cooking is an inherited skill,' said Cecily, and gave a quick, high-pitched laugh.

'And what about you, Norman?' Marnie asked, diverting the attention from herself. 'What did you do?'

'I was an engineer,' he said. 'Ran a factory making parts for industrial ovens. Long gone now, though. All the parts are imported from the Far East these days.'

'And what about my dad – Ralph, was he called? What did he do?'

Norman eyed her as if deciding what he was going to do with the question. Julia could sense her mother's tension rising, along with her colouring.

'He didn't get the chance to do much before he was taken from us,' Norman replied curtly.

'Ah, yes. Cecily told me. And that's how you two got together? At my dad's funeral. Handy.'

Julia wasn't sure how much more of this she could take. She clamped her jaws together to stop herself speaking.

'Would anybody like any more of anything?' her mother asked weakly. Julia could tell from her expression that she was finding the encounter bruising. There was a general murmuring of 'no thank you' and 'that was delicious' and so Cecily picked up a vegetable tureen and headed out of the room.

'I'll clear the plates, Mum,' said Lily, leaping up so quickly that the baby, who was now snoozing on her shoulder, sprang awake and started to grizzle. She passed him to Marco and then began to move around the table, collecting dishes with quick efficient movements. Nobody else spoke.

'Boys,' Julia said, speaking to them collectively, 'what are you going to do after lunch?'

Frankie spoke for them all, like a junior shop steward. 'We're going to build a den in the garage. Granny's given us some sheets and we can fasten them up like we did last time to make tents.'

Julia nodded approvingly. 'Good plan,' she said.

'And Marnie,' Felicity ploughed on. 'What brings you to our neck of the woods?'

God bless her, thought Julia. Felicity had got this covered. There were times when her 'take no prisoners' approach to life was very useful.

'I'm here for a conference,' Marnie replied. 'It's on next week at that big conference centre down in the town. I was supposed to be here yesterday so I could see Cecily and Norman, but the trains were all to cock so I didn't arrive until late.'

Julia noted the excuse. It was a perfectly plausible one. The trains from London were notoriously bad, but she wasn't feeling ready to cut Marnie any slack just yet. 'Are you staying in a hotel?'

Marnie nodded.

'Maybe we can meet up again during the week,' Felicity suggested, and Marnie shrugged but nodded.

'If you like,' she said. There was a hint of a smile for Felicity.

Julia was confused. This woman was so antagonistic one minute and then trying to build bridges the next. She couldn't understand it, but Felicity seemed to have the measure of her.

Then Felicity was fishing her phone out of her handbag and scrolling down. 'I have something on tomorrow night,' she said, 'but I'm free on Tuesday. Shall I pop down to your hotel after work and then we can go get something to eat?'

Julia noted that none of the rest of them seemed to be involved in this plan. But did she care? No. Not really. Let Felicity pour oil on troubled waters, and when she had sorted it all out she could report back and they could have another go at playing happy families.

And then Cecily reappeared, carrying a home-made Black Forest gateau and a jug of cream.

'Pudding?' she said with a fixed smile.

6

Felicity had been looking forward to meeting Marnie all day. Something new to focus on other than the car crash that was her marriage was exactly what the doctor would have ordered, had she actually told the doctor, or indeed anyone, what had happened with Richard. She had taken her car home and got a taxi back into town, and now she was waiting in a bar not far from the conference centre, a large glass of wine on the table in front of her.

To begin with, Felicity hadn't been at all sure about Marnie. She had led the vanguard of complaints about her failure to contact their mother following that wild goose chase across Europe in the summer. She had been righteous in her indignation. It wasn't fair for this stranger to raise their mother's hopes and then dash them back down, seemingly on a whim. It was unkind; cruel, even.

But then she had met Marnie and something in her had shifted.

Initially, it was probably something to do with how alike they looked. Felicity had always been the odd one out in the family. She didn't particularly resemble either parent, carrying a mere smattering of shared features, but only in certain lights. The twins, although not identical, were both fair and willowy like their mother, whereas she had always been stockier and dark. She was the spit of her Uncle Ralph, apparently, but Uncle Ralph had died long before she was born and looking like him had never helped her feel like she belonged. Swarthy, that was the word her father had once used to describe her. He had meant it kindly, but the description made her think of Heathcliff in *Wuthering Heights*, which had only added to her general feeling of isolation.

Of course, it didn't really matter who she looked like. They were all cut from the same cloth. It was just that she was more Nightingale and the twins were more Hardcastle. That was the luck of the biological draw, but now there was another Nightingale on the scene who seemed to be evening up the numbers a little, and Felicity liked it.

However, her growing liking of Marnie wasn't just based on the simplistic matter of their appearances. Something else about Marnie spoke to Felicity in a way that she didn't yet quite understand, and it was this that she wanted to pursue. There was something about her half-sister's directness, her apparent lack of concern about upsetting people and her no-nonsense approach to life that appealed to Felicity. It took a certain kind of guts to behave as Marnie had done, and Felicity could respect that.

And so there she was, sitting on her own in a bar on a Tuesday night with a large glass of wine. It was her second large glass of wine, in fact. The first one had barely touched the sides.

Then Marnie arrived, peering around the room from the doorway cautiously, as if worried that she was about to be the subject of a cruel practical joke. She was dressed in well-worn jeans and an old sweater, not the kind of outfit that Felicity would don to do the gardening let alone attend a conference, but then if this was some sort of catering gathering maybe the sartorial bar was set a little lower than Felicity was used to. She waved; Marnie altered her course and moved towards her, eyes wary but her steps confident.

'Hi,' Felicity said, her voice louder than she had intended. She adjusted her volume. 'Great to see you. Can I get you a drink?'

'No. I'll get my own,' replied Marnie stiffly, and then disappeared off to the bar without asking Felicity if she wanted anything. Felicity considered this, but concluded that as her own glass was full, it hadn't been impolite.

Marnie returned with a pint of something brown in a tall glass. Felicity assumed it was a bitter of some sort, although she never drank beer herself.

'I like to try the local brew wherever I go,' Marnie said as she sat down opposite Felicity. 'The barman said this was the most local. Mary Jane?'

Felicity giggled. 'Like the shoes? What an odd name for a beer,' she said. 'Does it taste okay?'

Marnie took a deep drink and then nodded her head slowly. 'It's good,' she said.

Now that they were here, away from the rest of the family, Felicity wasn't entirely sure what they would talk about, so she decided to start simply.

'How was your day?' she asked. 'Is the conference going well?'

Marnie shrugged. 'It's okay,' she said, diving for her pint again. It was almost half gone now. At this rate she would have caught up with Felicity within moments of arriving.

'And it is a catering conference?' Felicity tried again.

'Something like that.'

The conference was not going to be a rich seam of conversational treasure, then. She picked a different topic. 'And what do you think of Harrogate?'

'Seems nice.'

It was going to be a very long evening if this carried on. 'Yes, I like it. It's just big enough that there's always something going on, but not too big that you become anonymous. It's funny that all of us ended up living here. I'm not sure that was the plan. We left to go to university – well, Julia and I did – but then we just seemed

242

to float back again. Did you go to university?' Felicity remembered too late that university hadn't featured in the potted life story that Marnie had given them. 'No. You already said that. Catering college, wasn't it?'

Marnie nodded and finished off her pint. 'Another?' she asked.

Felicity, whose drinking had slowed now, was only halfway down her glass and so she shook her head and watched as Marnie went to the bar for a second time.

When she returned she seemed slightly more relaxed. 'Do you know what's weird?' she asked as she sat back down.

Felicity shook her head, not really knowing if this was a continuation of the previous conversation or a starter for ten.

'My whole life I've never looked like anyone else. People mention family traits in conversation all the time. You know, my mum's eyes, my dad's curly hair. That kind of thing. I don't suppose you notice if you have some, but I never did. My parents were small and mousey and I was big and dark. I just didn't fit. And then I meet you and we look just the same. You are so obviously my sister. It's weird,' she repeated.

Felicity's forehead creased as she tried to understand the significance of what Marnie was telling her. She supposed it must feel strange, after fifty years of not knowing where you belonged. She didn't look like the twins, but she'd always known that they were her family.

'I mean, just look at your hands,' Marnie continued.

Felicity pulled them out from under the table and studied them. She had always taken good care of her hands, having regular manicures and wearing gloves in the cold, but despite this they weren't attractive. Her fingers were short and fat like sausages, and even though she kept her nails long to try to add some length it didn't really disguise that fact. She noticed now that there was also a pale band on her third finger where her wedding rings had been.

Today had been the first time she had been out without them. No one had noticed.

Marnie put her hand on the table next to Felicity's. At first glance it was hard to see the similarities. Marnie's nails were bitten low and the tops of her fingers were swollen from years of chewing. There were kitchen scars, too – an aged burn mark across the back and various callouses, but fundamentally Felicity could see what Marnie meant. The shape of the hands, the way the knuckles sat, the curve of the nails in their beds. They were the same.

'I've never had that before,' Marnie continued. 'I have never looked at another human being and recognised part of me in them.'

'No,' Felicity agreed thoughtfully. 'I don't suppose you have.' She took a mouthful of her wine. She was feeling beautifully relaxed now as the wine began to take control of her muscles and loosen them. 'Actually, I do understand that,' she continued. 'I was always the odd one out, too. There was me and then the twins came and they were a pair and I was left out. No one was interested in the singleton any more, especially with Lily being premature and the different birthdays thing. Suddenly the twins were all anyone cared about. And I've always been the high-flyer. I know Julia's a doctor but I'm the one with the big job, the nice lifestyle and everything. But Lily still gets all the attention. She did when we were kids because they were all worried about her, and she still does because she's got a ludicrous number of children and she's just so calm all the time, so everyone is in awe of her.' Felicity sat back in her chair. 'Well!' she said in surprise. 'I'm not sure where that little diatribe came from.'

Her glass was empty now, but she probably shouldn't have another. Not on a Tuesday. 'I'm just going to the bar,' she heard herself say. 'Can I get you anything?'

Marnie lifted her empty glass.

When she got back with the drinks Marnie, instead of looking at her sideways as she had done up until then, started to openly stare at her, her eyes scanning each feature in turn.

'Our noses are different,' she said. 'Yours is kind of lumpy. Mine is a bit flatter.'

Felicity had never been told that she had a lumpy nose before and she bristled slightly, but she didn't say anything.

'What happened to your rings?' Marnie asked then, apropos of nothing at all.

'I threw my husband out,' Felicity replied without even thinking about it. 'He'd been having an affair and I'd had enough.' She was surprised at how easily the words came to her.

'But you haven't told the others?' Marnie asked. 'They were expecting him to be there on Sunday, weren't they?'

'I haven't told anyone, actually,' Felicity said. 'You're the first.'

Marnie paused as she considered this. 'And are you okay?'

Felicity gave a small, tight nod. 'It was the right thing to do,' she said.

'It was,' agreed Marnie. 'The man's a bastard. You should have done it years ago.'

Felicity looked at her. She was right. She should have given him his marching orders the first time he had strayed.

'I . . . I mean, men like that,' Marnie said, stumbling over her words slightly as if she thought she might have overstepped some invisible line. 'They never change.'

'No,' agreed Felicity. 'They never do.'

For the first time Marnie looked slightly uncomfortable, which struck Felicity as odd. She seemed to have no qualms about saying exactly what she thought, so why was Felicity's marital status suddenly such an awkward topic?

Then she changed the subject again. 'And I was surprised about Julia,' Marnie said. 'The single mother thing.'

Felicity pulled a face.

'You don't approve?' Marnie asked.

'Well, it's not for me to say,' replied Felicity. 'But I really don't think she has any idea what she's letting herself in for. I think she just looks at Lily and thinks having kids is a breeze. Well, it's not. It's hard work.'

'And it's hard enough to be a kid without setting them up to be bullied,' Marnie said, picking at what was left of her nails with her teeth as she spoke. 'Imagine what will happen when the kids at school find out that it started in a syringe.'

'Well, precisely,' said Felicity emphatically. 'I mean Hugo was IVF, but at least he has a real daddy. In the traditional sense of the word, I mean.'

'I think it's best for a child to be brought up by two parents, preferably ones who like each other,' Marnie said.

Felicity pushed away the fact that she and Hugo were now a single-parent family. Her case was different. She had at least tried for the traditional ideal, even though it hadn't worked – through no fault of her own, she might add. Julia appeared to be setting out on her own from the outset. How was that fair on the child? To Felicity's mind, her sister's decision was self-indulgent. Having a child was not like getting a puppy, and there were reasons why it took two to conceive. Yes, Sam was her friend but it wasn't as if they were a couple or had any intention of ever living under the same roof.

'Exactly,' she agreed, with a decisive nod of her head.

She liked that Marnie shared her view on this. She felt vindicated, rather than being a lone voice crying out in the wilderness. Her opinion on this was as welcome as a sausage at a vegan's table with the others, but she could express her real thoughts with her half-sister. It felt like a new safe space for her.

They sat in silence for a while, both lost in their own thoughts.

Then Marnie stood up. 'I must go,' she said. 'But this has been good.'

Felicity, initially flustered by the sudden change, gathered herself together. 'It has. Will there be time to meet again before you leave? Did you say the conference was all week?'

Marnie didn't reply at once, her eyes focused on a space above the bar door. 'There is no conference,' she said. 'I made it up.'

'Oh!' Felicity wasn't sure what she thought about lying. Did it alter how she looked at Marnie? But then she remembered about Richard. She lived with lies all the time. 'When are you going back home?' she asked. 'I'd love to spend more time with you. And the others. I'm sure they would like to see you too.'

Marnie shrugged. 'I don't know. I'll text. Nice evening. Thanks.'

And then she was gone.

7

'Do you fancy a little run out this afternoon? We could go to Bolton Abbey, have a wander by the river and then a cup of tea afterwards.'

Norman was trying to cheer Cecily up, God bless him. They had not seen Marnie since the Sunday lunch and now it was Wednesday. Cecily knew that she was in town for her conference and was probably frightfully busy, but she was so anxious to talk to her daughter again, to find out what she had thought of her sisters and little nephews.

Cecily hadn't exactly been sitting by the telephone but she had found herself putting off going out to run errands, just in case it rang whilst she was gone. It hadn't occurred to her until Norman pointed it out that the number Marnie had for her was for her mobile, which she could just take with her. Then she checked the mobile obsessively. Each time she looked, her heart did a little flutter and then sank again when there were no new messages.

She hadn't forgotten that Felicity had arranged to meet Marnie for a drink. Cecily was desperate for news as to how that had gone, too, but she didn't like to ring Felicity at work and Felicity had not yet rung her. And so she was stuck in limbo. She had even thought about ringing Marnie herself, but she worried that that would look too pushy. Marnie was cautious enough, and the last thing she wanted was to drive her away. She was well aware that she would have to be patient and just had to wait. However, it appeared that Norman thought she was making a very poor job of being patient.

'We could even run to a couple of sticky buns,' he added with a crooked smile. 'Come on, Cec. You can't skulk about around here all the time. I'm sure Marnie will be in touch in due course. She'll have a lot to think about after Sunday.'

'But what if she goes back to London without telling us?' Cecily asked him. It was a thought that had been haunting her: that they might have scared her off.

Norman took her hand in his and gave it a little reassuring squeeze. 'If she does that then there isn't much we can do about it. But at least you have a contact number for her now.'

Cecily felt a little lighter when he said this. 'Yes. That's true. But still. Do you think I should invite her round again?'

Norman took his anorak down from the coat pegs and shrugged himself into it. Then he placed his tweed trilby on his head firmly and reached for her coat. He held it open for her.

'I think we should go for a nice walk in the countryside and forget all about it for a while,' he said. 'If you carry on fretting like this you're going to make yourself ill.'

Cecily allowed herself to be manoeuvred into the coat like an old lady. She did not want to go out but she could see that Norman was taking charge, and that it would just cause more trouble if she resisted. And they could take the mobile with them. Just in case.

There were very few cars in the car park when they arrived, and Norman edged into a space right at the front. It wasn't a great day for a walk. She could hear the wind whistling through the tops of the trees, although the air in the valley bottom felt still and damp. The last few shrivelled leaves were clinging on to the uppermost branches, and intermittently one would relinquish its grip and float elegantly down to the grass. It was nearly winter.

She shivered against the cold and fastened her coat tightly around her, wishing all the time that she'd just said no to Norman. Then they set off down the path that trailed alongside the river. The water ran dark and brown without the sun on it to make it sparkle.

As they walked, Norman slipped his gloved hand into hers. 'I thought I might dig those watercolours out of the attic,' he said. 'Have a bit of a dabble.'

Cecily thought that it was probably the wrong time of year to be painting, the light being so dingy now and the days increasingly short, but she didn't want to pour cold water on his plan so she simply nodded.

'That's a good idea,' she said, even though it wasn't.

They walked along in companionable silence for a while. Cecily's thoughts were all running along the same track towards a single destination – Marnie. She seemed incapable of twisting her mind around anything else. She worried about what Marnie thought, what her plans might be, how she saw herself slotting into their family, how the others might let that happen. Ideas spiralled round in her head, each thought blurring into the next like coloured inks in water until all she had left to cling on to was her child's name – Marnie.

'Do you think she liked us?' she asked Norman. She could feel his shoulders tense at her side and his gait seemed to become slightly stiffer.

'Who? Marnie? It's hard to tell,' he said noncommittally.

'But what did you think?' Cecily pushed. 'Do you think we made her feel welcome?'

Norman was quiet for a couple of steps. 'I think you did your very best,' he said eventually.

Cecily stopped and turned to face him. 'What do you mean by that?' she asked.

Norman smacked his lips together before replying. 'Well, if you want my honest opinion, she didn't seem very relaxed when she was with us.'

Cecily's spine straightened involuntarily as she felt herself prepare to defend Marnie. 'Well, would you be relaxed?' she asked indignantly. 'Thrown into a room of strangers all staring at you like you're an exhibit in a zoo?'

'I'm not sure that that's what we did . . .' Norman began.

'Well, how would you describe it?' Cecily snapped.

'The lunch was your idea, remember,' he replied, his voice far gentler than hers had been. 'You could have met up one to one.'

'Oh, so it's my fault that we've driven her away, then?'

Norman let out an exasperated sigh. 'Cecily, you need to get some perspective here. I'm not saying anything of the sort, and I'm sure we haven't driven her away. It's been two days and she's probably busy with this conference. And didn't she meet Felicity last night?'

Cecily shrugged and set off again, her pace a little faster.

Norman was soon back at her side. 'I know you're anxious, Cec, but us falling out about it isn't going to help.'

'I just want to know that she's all right, that she's glad that she came to find us.'

'I'm sure she'll tell us, given time. She doesn't seem to have any difficulty in saying what she thinks.'

Cecily was immediately thrust back on to the defensive. 'What?'

Norman took a breath before replying. 'Well, she was pretty quick to have a go at Julia,' he said. 'How Julia chooses to live her life is frankly none of Marnie's concern. It might have been better if she'd kept her opinions to herself.'

'Is she not entitled to a point of view, is that it?' Cecily snapped.

'No. That's not what I meant. I just think that in a situation where you are meeting new people, there are ways of dealing with things you don't agree with. I found Marnie's attitude a little confrontational for my taste, that's all.'

They walked on a little further. It was now obvious that they were arguing, and as they passed another couple coming in the opposite direction Cecily noticed that they dropped their conversation as if to overhear what was going on. Normally Cecily would have been embarrassed to be caught in a public disagreement, but now she did not care.

'So are you saying that you didn't like my daughter, your niece?' she asked.

She had gone too far now, she knew she had. But she also knew from years of marriage that Norman was able to ignore the more unreasonable things that slipped from her lips. He had decades of experience in moderating her, in keeping the peace. Diplomacy was one of his skills and she loved it about him. No matter how aggressive she was feeling, it was almost impossible to get into an argument with Norman and he never fanned the flames of her anger.

'Actually,' he said now, 'I'm not sure I did like her that much, no. If you want me to be honest, I found her confrontational and at times downright impolite. And whilst I can make some allowances for the extraordinary circumstances, there can be no excuse for rudeness.'

Cecily opened her mouth to reply but no words came out.

Norman, by contrast, had no such trouble. 'In fact, she reminds me rather a lot of her father. He wasn't always the golden boy that you seem to think he was. He hardly stood by you in your hour of need, did he? It grieves me to say this, Cecily, but Ralph couldn't get away from the mess he had made quickly enough. How often did you see him when you got back home after having Marnie?'

'That wasn't his fault,' Cecily spluttered. 'He had to go to university.'

'That was months later. I'm not saying that he didn't love you. I'm sure that he did, in his own way. But he was selfish. He looked after number one and he didn't really care who he stepped on as he did it. And on Sunday I got the impression that it wasn't just his physical features that Marnie had inherited.'

This was more than Cecily could bear. Not only had Norman criticised Marnie, who had done nothing wrong, but then he had taken a pot-shot at Ralph, too. Poor dead Ralph, who wasn't there to defend himself. As far as she was concerned that was unforgivable. She turned on her heel and stormed back the way they had come.

'I'd like to go home now,' she called over her shoulder without turning to face him.

'But we haven't had our tea yet,' Norman called back.

Well, he could whistle for his tea. There was no way that she would be sitting down with him any time soon. Except, that was, for the long, silent drive back to Harrogate.

8

'Can you mind the kids tonight, Marco?' Lily asked.

Marco was sitting at the kitchen table, his laptop squeezed into in a small island of space in the sea of book bags, lunch boxes and half-built Lego models that the boys had scattered since their arrival home from playgroup and school.

He pushed his dark hair away from his face as if it was irritating him just by being there, but he smiled warmly at Lily. 'Sure. Where you go?'

Lily loved that even after twenty years of living and working in the UK, her husband still hadn't mastered verbs. It didn't seem to hold him back, though. If anything, Lily always thought that the quirks of his spoken English added to his charm, and it certainly gave him an air of authenticity as he strolled around the tables of diners in his restaurants. He took pride in remembering interesting little details about the lives of his regular customers, and that made them return time and time again. It was a strategy that paid dividends for the business, but also came as naturally to him as swimming comes to a seal.

'Fliss thinks we should invite Marnie round to Mum's again so we can have another meet-up before she goes back to London.'

Marco raised both eyebrows and furrowed his forehead, which told Lily he wasn't sure this was a great plan.

She decided to leap in and head his objections off at the pass. 'Look, I know it didn't go brilliantly on Sunday . . .'

'She was rude, Lily,' he said simply.

Lily knew this was true. 'Well, maybe a little,' she replied. 'But let's look at it from her side. It was the first time she'd met us. It was only the second time she'd met Mum. It must have been a bit full-on for her. And I think she's had a difficult time. She said that she didn't get on with her parents and left home at sixteen . . .'

'So did I, but I not rude to your sisters,' Marco objected.

'I know, I know.' Lily ran a hand down his back. 'But you come from a massive and very loving family, like I do. It sounds like Marnie didn't have anything like that. Mum said that her parents didn't even tell her she was adopted until she went to secondary school. Can you imagine what that must have felt like? Suddenly realising that there was a reason why you didn't quite belong, but that no one had bothered to tell you. It must have been really tough.'

Marco tipped his head to one side in acknowledgement.

'And then to come and meet us, the family she might have had. Well . . .' Lily paused. She had tried to imagine how life might have been if Marnie and not Felicity had been their eldest sibling. If she was being entirely honest, she would have to admit relief that that wasn't the case; not that she would ever say that out loud. They were where they were, and as far as she could see, it was up to them to make Marnie feel as welcome as they could. They would have to make allowances for her brusqueness and hope that, in time, she softened at the edges a little. What was it they said – you can't choose your family? 'So, you're sure you don't mind me going out?'

Marco snaked his arm around her waist and pulled her into him. 'Of course. You go do what you need with your family. I stay here and guard our sons from danger.'

Lily bent down and kissed him gently just as a howl of indignation sounded from the boys' playroom.

She pulled herself free. 'Now what?' she laughed, shaking her head indulgently at her sons.

An hour later she was sitting at the big pine table in her parents' kitchen, enjoying a cup of tea with her mother. Julia and Felicity were coming straight from work and would arrive a little later, and Lily relished this little bit of one-to-one time, just the two of them.

Her mother, however, was cross. 'Your father is being very unhelpful about Marnie,' she complained. 'We rowed about it this morning.'

'That's not like you two,' Lily replied. 'You hardly ever row.'

'I know, but he was being such a pig.'

Lily waited. She didn't want to intrude on her parents' argument unless her mother chose to share it with her.

She did. 'He said that he thought Marnie was rude.'

'Yes. So did Marco,' confessed Lily. 'I said that she'd had a lot to deal with and that we had to give her time to adjust.'

Her mother beamed at her. 'Well, precisely. As far as I can tell she had quite a tough time growing up. It can alter you, a thing like that.'

'Of course it can,' agreed Lily. 'There's no way of telling how it might affect you.'

'And that just makes me feel worse. I didn't want to give her up, Lily. They made me. I had no choice in it at all. But I can't help thinking that maybe if I'd fought a little bit harder . . .'

Lily reached out for her mother's hand and squeezed it gently beneath her own. 'You can't think like that, Mum. You were sixteen, just a child yourself. Your parents did what was right for everyone at the time. You mustn't feel responsible for how anything turned out. It just isn't your fault.'

Lily saw tears gathering, a sheeny film across her mother's eyes. She could count on the fingers of one hand how many times she had seen her mother cry, and it upset her to see her thrown when she was generally so calm and collected.

'I know that,' she said. 'And it's what your father has told me over and over for years. But actually meeting Marnie . . . Well, it brings it all back.'

Lily was fascinated by the idea that her parents had spent decades discussing this huge issue whilst none of them had had the first idea about it. She had so many questions, but she would ask them when the time was right. And that was not now.

The front door opened and in came Julia. They heard her pop her head around the sitting room door to speak to her father.

'We're in here, Julia,' her mother called, and moments later Julia appeared. She seemed to have grown in the three days since Lily had last seen her, but maybe it was just that her stomach muscles were unable to cope after a tough day of holding everything up.

She flopped down on a chair, her face drawn. 'How do you do this being-pregnant thing over and over again, Lils? I'm knackered, and I've only got me to worry about.'

Lily gave a modest little shrug.

'Thank your lucky stars that you're not carrying twins, Julia,' her mother said, and she gave Lily a conspiratorial little wink.

'Well, there is that,' Julia agreed. 'So, Fliss said that she and Marnie got on well yesterday, so that's good. Hopefully she'll have built us some bridges. It was all a bit awkward on Sunday.'

Bearing in mind how fragile their mother was, Lily didn't want the conversation to slip into another character assassination of Marnie. 'We were just saying how hard it must have been for her,' she said. 'But hopefully it'll be easier today, and meeting Fliss is bound to have helped.'

Julia opened her mouth to speak, but Lily knew exactly what she was going to say and hushed her with a glance. Julia closed her mouth. And then the door opened again.

'They're here,' said their mother, leaping to her feet and smoothing her skirt with the flat of her hand. She looked so uncharacteristically anxious, Lily thought, and just for a moment she felt a flicker of resentment towards Marnie; but she shook it away. It wouldn't help.

'Shall we sit in here?' her mother asked in a low voice. 'Your father's in the sitting room and anyway it feels a bit cosier in here somehow. Would you put the kettle on please, Lily? Julia, you stay where you are. You look exhausted.'

Julia smiled gratefully, and Lily busied herself with cups and teapots.

Then the door opened and in came Felicity with Marnie close behind. They looked so alike, Lily thought, although Marnie looked a good deal more than twelve years older than Felicity. Where Felicity's dark hair shone in glossy waves, Marnie's was frizzy and unstyled. She also wore no make-up. There were broken veins on her cheeks and deep grooves running from nose to mouth and around her eyes where Felicity had only slight creases, expertly disguised by foundation and highlighter. Marnie's was the face of someone whose life had been a challenge which was, Lily realised now, very much in contrast to the other four Nightingale women.

Their mother went straight over and moved to hug her, but Marnie pulled away. It wasn't a huge gesture but it was enough to stop their mother up short, and instead she just put her hands on Marnie's shoulders.

'Welcome, Marnie. So lovely to see you. I hope everything's been going well at the conference.'

Lily noticed a look that passed between Marnie and Felicity, but Marnie just nodded. 'Fine thanks.'

'And you two had a nice time last night?'

This time Marnie nodded rather than replying and so Felicity stepped in to fill the gap. 'Yep. We had a proper old chinwag, didn't we? It was great.'

'Well, sit down, sit down. The kettle's on. Would you prefer tea or coffee, Marnie?'

Marnie pulled a face that suggested that she'd actually prefer something stronger. 'Tea,' she said.

The urge to say 'please' for her, as she did with her children, was so strong that Lily had to put her hand across her mouth to stop the word from accidentally escaping.

Then they were all sitting at the table with steaming mugs of tea and a packet of shortbread fanned out on a plate before them. Nobody spoke. Julia, often the person to provide conversational gambits, seemed to have decided that she wasn't going to oblige this time; she sat, hands curled around her mug, and examined the table top.

Lily finally took the plunge. 'You mentioned someone called Sofia when you were here before.'

Her mother, grateful to have got things started, leapt on Lily's words. 'Oh, Sofia's lovely,' she said. 'I met her at the retreat. She's so beautiful too, and slim and very bendy with all that yoga. Is she part-Spanish, Marnie?'

Marnie nodded her head. 'Seville,' she said, as if that were the answer to everything about Sofia.

'And you two work together?' Lily pressed on.

'Yes. And sleep together.'

She said it so bluntly, as if challenging Lily to criticise her, and it took Lily by surprise. All she could manage at first was a crisp 'Oh!' She hoped that she didn't sound all narrow-minded and suburban, because she really wasn't; it was just that she hadn't been expecting such a bare reference to Marnie's sex life. It wasn't how conversations generally progressed in her world. And then she added, 'That's lovely,' which she suspected actually made things worse. She could feel her cheeks burning. 'And whereabouts in London are you?' she managed, to move things on.

'Finsbury Park,' replied Marnie.

Lily was generally good at chatting with strangers. It was one of the very few things that she thought she did well, but this was like getting blood from a stone. She knew next to nothing about London and she hadn't even heard of Finsbury Park, let alone what that might say about the pair of them. 'Is it nice there?' she asked weakly.

Marnie shrugged. 'Suits us. It's nothing flash but it's handy for Sofia's studio.'

'Oh, that's good then,' Lily replied. She wished Julia would help out but she seemed determined not to.

'Do you do yoga too, Marnie?' their mother asked, and Lily was relieved to be able to step down from the hot seat for a moment.

'I don't go to her classes. But I do some. When I get time.'

'I've never really tried yoga,' said their mother, 'apart from that class in Greece, but I enjoyed it very much. You go, don't you, Lily? And didn't you and Richard both start going once, Fliss?'

The atmosphere shifted very slightly, and Lily saw Julia look up.

Felicity opened her mouth. 'Yes, but we didn't go for long,' she said dismissively.

'And you won't be doing any more now that you've given him his marching orders, eh Felicity,' said Marnie.

Confusion leapt from face to face like a forest fire. The only person who didn't look confused was Marnie, and she was grinning.

Julia put her mug down and straightened her spine. 'We pre-scribe yoga a lot at work,' she said, her tone sharp. 'It's good for all kinds of conditions. Back and joint pain, obviously, but also anxiety and other stress-related issues. Meditation and mindfulness, too.'

'That's interesting, Julia,' their mother said, taking Julia's lead and steadfastly avoiding looking at Felicity. Lily looked, though. Her sister's cheeks had flushed scarlet and she was biting her bottom lip. Lily glanced down at her sister's left hand but she had it well hidden beneath the right one.

'My yoga teacher was telling me about this technique,' Lily said, also keen to give Felicity time to recover, 'where you just hold the same pose for five minutes and then move on to the next one. She runs classes by candlelight. It sounds so relaxing. I'm planning to go. I just need to make the time.'

'Well, you're so busy with the children, Lily. I don't know how you find time for anything else,' their mother said. She looked longingly at Felicity as she spoke, and it was obvious to Lily that all she wanted to do was comfort her. Now was not the moment, though.

'Did I tell you that I've signed up for an upholstery course, Mum?' Lily added, more to distract her mother than anything else. 'I'm really looking forward to it.'

'Not sure why you'd bother,' said Marnie, 'when you can clearly afford to buy new stuff rather than just tarting up old.'

Julia bristled. 'That's hardly the point, is it?' she snapped. 'I think that's a great idea, Lily,' she continued more gently. 'I've got that hideous old chair that the cats trashed. You can practise on that if you like. Heaven knows it could do with a new lease of life.'

Lily wasn't sure how much more of this she could stand. Generally she used the children as a way of escaping situations that she didn't like, but she couldn't just run away from this and leave the others to deal with it by themselves.

But then Felicity spoke. 'So, when are you going back to London?' she said to Marnie, her face closed and hard. 'I suppose you could leave at any time, seeing as the conference isn't actually real.'

Now it was Marnie's turn to look uncomfortable, but only for a split second. 'Actually, I'm going tomorrow. It's been nice, this little wander into the frozen north, but I need to get back to my real life.'

Lily saw a look of panic cross her mother's face, but then something else replaced it. Resignation, maybe? Sorrow?

'Well, you must come and visit us again, very soon,' her mother said. 'You know where we all are now and our door is always open. You know that, don't you?'

Marnie looked at her untouched cup of tea and then looked up at their mother. 'I do,' she said carefully.

Lily worried about what would come from her mouth next, and she could see Julia sitting a little forward in her seat as if she thought she might have to protect her family from a physical attack.

Marnie was looking straight at their mother as she spoke, as if the rest of them had just faded into the floral wallpaper. 'It took me a long time to decide that I wanted to find you, Cecily,' she said. 'I always knew that I didn't fit with my adopted mum and dad. I didn't really match up with their expectations and neither did they with mine. But just replacing them with another set of disappointing parents? I wasn't sure that that would do me any favours either.'

For a moment, Lily thought that Marnie was going to tar her parents with that same brush, accuse them too of being somehow lacking, but before she could leap in to defend them Marnie continued. Her voice was low but despite the bitterness of her words, Lily couldn't detect any anger in it.

'I've never felt whole, complete. It's like some part of me has always been missing. I've floated through life not really getting close to anyone. Well, until Sofia, that is. But I wasn't sure I could march in on someone else's life, your lives, and expect you to welcome me with open arms. But then I thought, why should it always be me that gets the shitty end of the stick? So I sent that letter. I think I wanted you to be damaged by what you did to me, just like I was.

262

I was looking for some pain, something to prove to me that giving me up hurt you as much as it hurt me. And obviously I needed you to tell me what was so wrong with me that you wanted to give me away in the first place.'

Lily heard her mother start to speak. 'There was nothing wrong with . . .' she began, but Marnie put up a hand to silence her.

'I can see that now,' she continued. 'So I'm going home. I've seen what I needed to see here.' She stood up. 'You have my number, Cecily, so if you really have to get in touch with me for anything then you can.'

Then she strode across the kitchen and out into the hall. Lily heard the front door open and close. And then she was gone.

A stunned silence filled the space as each of them digested what had just been said.

Then Julia spoke. 'I'm sorry, Mum, but who the hell does she think she is? She drops on us like a bloody atom bomb, does the most damage she possibly can, and then saunters off without a care in the world. Nothing that has happened to her is the fault of any of us. She's got a chip on her shoulder so big that I'm surprised that she can even stand up straight, but that doesn't give her the right to come here bandying her accusations around. You were a child when you had her, Mum. A child. And none of it is anything to do with the three of us, so I just don't get why she needs to be so vile.'

Their mother opened her mouth to speak, but Julia shook her head. 'No, Mum. Don't defend her. As far as I'm concerned the whole episode is over, and if I were you I would be thinking along the same lines. Close the book, Mum. Move on.' She slumped back in her chair as if the effort of giving her speech had drained her entirely.

Lily's gaze flicked from her mother to her twin and back again, and she was about to say something, although she had no idea what, when her mother spoke. 'I'm sorry, Julia, but I can't agree.

Just because Marnie looks at the world differently from us doesn't make her wrong. None of us has the first idea about what she has been through or what it took for her to get in touch with me after all this time. I'm not about to abandon her simply because she has sharp edges to her. She is my daughter. Mine and Ralph's. I can't just abandon her.'

'You did once,' said Felicity darkly.

Lily gasped. 'Fliss!' she said. 'You can't say that.'

'Well, it's true,' Felicity continued. 'It's all very well, Mum having this attack of conscience now, but the time to do something about this was fifty years ago. I'm afraid the damage has been done and I can see no point wasting any more time or effort in trying to sort it out. You can't make a silk purse out of a sow's ear.'

Lily looked from her mother to her sister and back again. They were staring at one another. At first their mother looked shocked and upset by what Julia and Felicity had said, but then her face hardened. 'Neither of you has the first idea what I went through. How could you? You weren't there and you cannot possibly begin to understand. You don't even have a child, Julia.'

Julia curled her arm around the swell of her stomach as if she was trying to protect her baby from hearing what was being said.

'So,' continued their mother, 'I don't know what you think gives you the right to speak like that to me. How Marnie and I deal with this is up to us. Obviously I would prefer that you all got on, but actually it has nothing to do with you, and what you think makes very little difference. I'd like you all to leave now. I want to talk to your father. I'll see you all at the weekend.' She stood up and looked, stony-faced, at each of them in turn. She meant it, it seemed.

Lily was horrified. She couldn't bear arguments and certainly not amongst the four of them – not something like this that was so raw, so personal, so damaging.

Julia pushed her chair back noisily and stood up. 'Fine,' she said, her tone cold. 'If you want to choose her over us then that's up to you, Mum.'

Their mother seemed to weaken a little at this suggestion and her expression softened. 'I'm not choosing. It's just that . . .'

But Julia put up her hand. 'It's okay,' she said. 'I get it. I'll speak to you soon.'

And then she left the kitchen. Lily heard her go into the sitting room to their father and there was the murmur of low voices.

Lily was torn. Should she stay and make sure her mother was all right, or show solidarity with her twin? And what about Felicity? Had she really kicked Richard out, and why hadn't she told them? Instead it appeared that she had chosen to share that with Marnie, a woman she barely knew and who had just single-handedly decimated their family.

Lily chose Julia. 'I'll ring in the morning, Mum,' she said as she turned to follow her twin out, but something held her there; she wasn't quite able to leave.

Felicity had also stood up now and was putting on her jacket. Lily saw her bare ring finger as her hands flashed backwards and forwards. Their mother stepped towards her and made to put her arm around her, but Felicity sidestepped her embrace.

'Not now, Mum,' she said simply, and then she too left the room.

'Oh, Mum,' said Lily when there were just the two of them left.

A fire was burning behind her mother's grey eyes and her lips were pursed tightly into a little knot. 'I'll speak to you tomorrow, Lily,' she said shortly, and then she turned to put the tea things in the sink. Lily was dismissed.

9

Cecily couldn't remember ever feeling as angry she did right then. She had to get out. It was dark and cold but she didn't care. She couldn't stand to be in the house for another second.

She grabbed her coat and struggled her arms into it, wrapping a scarf that Lily had knitted for her so tightly around her throat that it might have been a noose.

'I'm going out,' she said, without popping her head into the sitting room. Norman would only try to talk her out of it and anyway, she didn't want any kind of conversation. Not now. She didn't want to talk to anyone. She just wanted to get out.

'But it's dark,' objected Norman. 'You shouldn't go out on your own. Would you like me to come with you?'

She could hear him getting to his feet but she didn't wait. 'No, thank you,' she said crisply, and then she left, slamming the front door behind her.

Outside it was dark and so cold that she felt it burn the inside of her chest as she breathed in. She should fasten the coat before she set off, but she worried that Norman would catch her so she let it flap open and headed down the drive with no clear idea of where she was going. At the end of the road she turned right, away from the town and towards the open countryside, took a couple of steps and then turned round and headed down the hill instead.

She might be angry, but she felt safer walking towards people rather than away from them. But then again, what she wanted was solitude. She needed time to simmer with her anger and her hurt. She turned round again and went back the way she had come, striding past their gate and out into the night.

How could they have been so unkind and uncaring towards Marnie? She was her daughter and their sister, for God's sake. Cecily was furious that each one of them, even Lily, seemed to have closed ranks against Marnie and had refused to see her side. Yes, Cecily had to admit that Marnie was proving more difficult to get to know than she had hoped. She didn't seem to be slotting into the Nightingale family quite as easily in real life as she had done in Cecily's daydreams, but that didn't mean that she didn't belong. Just because she had not embraced them all with open arms and squeals of delight didn't mean that she had no place amongst them.

If her girls would only stop for a moment and put themselves in Marnie's shoes, then they would surely be less quick to judge. This was never going to be easy, for any of them, but that was no reason to turn back for port at the first sign of rough seas. She thought she had brought her children up to be more resilient than that.

And it wasn't just the children. Norman wasn't being as helpful as she had hoped, either. Maybe they had all been talking to one another behind her back? Actually, that would make sense. It would certainly explain why they all seemed to be singing from the same hymn sheet when it came to Marnie, as if they had all decided what the party line was to be without bothering to tell her.

Cecily was approaching the end of the road now and there was not much ahead of her except wide open fields. Perhaps she would have been better walking in the opposite direction after all. There was an old wooden bench concreted into the pavement at this point. It wasn't clear why it was there, but there it had sat for as long as Cecily could remember. She plonked herself down on it and tipped her head back to look up at the sky. It was a rich, velvety brown out here, away from the worst of the light pollution from the town. And there were stars out, too. She could see the belt and sword of Orion and the W of Cassiopeia. There was even something low and very bright, which was probably a planet. Norman would know. He always knew things like that.

Her anger was subsiding now, the hot red burn of it fading to a gentle glow. Marnie wasn't blameless in all this. Cecily could see that, too. Marnie seemed to be going out of her way to cause trouble amongst them, making spiteful comments that felt designed to rile. And what was that about Felicity and Richard? A shared confidence betrayed? That was never a firm foundation for a friendship. Felicity had done her no harm and yet that was how she had treated her, by embarrassing her in front of them all. Cecily could see why Julia had become so defensive. But then again . . .

A car approached, slowing down as it drove past her. The passenger window rolled down and the familiar face of a young neighbour appeared.

'Are you all right, Mrs Nightingale?' she asked.

'Yes, yes. Quite all right, thank you. Just waiting for a lift,' lied Cecily.

'Well, as long as you're okay,' said the neighbour, and then the window rolled back up and she continued on her way. People were so kind, Cecily thought. They looked out for one another. And she supposed, when she thought about it, that that was what her family were doing, too. They were looking out for one another. In this new and confusing reality they were just keeping each other's interests at the forefront. Could she really blame them for that?

The night felt so very chilly now. Cecily gave a huge and involuntary shudder and pulled the scarf even more tightly around her neck, although it was doing a poor job of keeping the savage cold at bay.

Maybe she was being unfair. The anger that she had felt so keenly just moments ago was really being driven by her disappointment, not just that all her children seemed unable to get along, but also, if she was really honest with herself, that Marnie was as she was. It was hard for her to think it, but Cecily had to face the unpleasant fact that Marnie just wasn't very likeable. Yes, allowances could be made for the fact that she didn't seem to have had a good relationship with her adoptive parents, but it was more than that. Fundamentally, there seemed to be something dark at Marnie's core. This was what Norman and the girls were seeing, and were unable to get beyond.

But Cecily was her mother. If you couldn't rely on your own mother to love you, warts and all, then what hope was there? The solution here was surely to get Marnie to trust her, and then, once their relationship was sound, to resell her to the others. It would be easier, Cecily felt certain, once she had got to know Marnie herself, to then showcase her best parts to the rest of the family. She had gone at it all far too quickly. Norman had tried to warn her, and he had been right. It had all been too much too soon, and so Marnie had reacted badly. Cecily could kick herself. This was obviously her fault for trying to force them to play happy families before they were ready.

That was no problem, though, she thought positively. Yes, some damage had been done but that didn't mean it couldn't be undone.

Her teeth began to chatter. She needed to get back home or she was going to make herself ill. The cold had permeated through to her very bones and she could feel the stiffness in all her joints as she levered herself up from the bench. She set off back towards the house, her legs now moving far less fluidly than they had done when she'd set out. That was what she'd do. She would spend some time getting to know Marnie herself, build a proper relationship and then, and only when she was sure that the time was right, she would reintroduce her. That was the way to go.

The cold was making her ears hurt and she freed up a bit of scarf to bring over her head as a makeshift hat. Heaven only knew what she must look like. Someone was walking along the pavement towards her and she felt her heart rate quicken a little. She was perfectly safe on her own street. It wasn't even that late, but still, a stranger was alarming.

'Come home, Cecily,' said the figure. 'You're going to catch your death out here.'

Norman. Her darling Norman, who had been there always. She pulled her hand out from under her armpit where she had been trying, in vain, to keep it warm, and offered it to him. He took it in his and lifted it to his lips to huff gently on it.

'How did you know where I'd gone?' she asked him, all remaining traces of her anger disappearing like smoke into the night.

'I've been married to you for forty-one years,' he said kindly. 'I think I have the measure of you.'

'I don't know what to do, Norman,' she said. 'The girls all hate her.'

'They don't hate her. She just makes it quite hard to like her. But I'm sure in time we could all learn to get along. We can try, at least.'

'She's going back to London tomorrow,' said Cecily.

'That's probably no bad thing. We can let things simmer down for a while. Next time I'm sure it'll be a little bit easier for everyone.'

'But what if there is no next time?' Cecily asked desperately.

Norman was silent for a moment or two. Their footsteps rang out into the quiet night.

'Well, we'll just have to make sure that there is,' he said.

PART SIX

1

Thursday 13 June. Marnie's fifty-first birthday.

Across the decades, Cecily had marked all her 13 Junes in some way. Some years she had gone on a little outing, not mentioning to anyone the purpose of the trip or the significance of the day, but marking it by giving herself a little treat. Other years she had written letters to her daughter. Having nowhere to send them they had usually ended up in the bin, and often they were so tear-stained by the end that they would have been illegible anyway.

This 13 June was different. She no longer had to imagine what had become of her baby, hope that she was happy, healthy and fulfilled. This year Cecily knew where, at least approximately, Marnie was and what her life was like. She did not have to torture herself with those terrifying 'what ifs' that only actual knowledge could subdue. But did that make the day any easier to endure? Cecily wasn't at all sure that it did.

There had been no news from Marnie since she had left their kitchen and walked out into the chilly night seven months before. In the early days, Cecily had hoped for some news of her each morning, but no letter had hit the doormat. She had even remembered to check her mobile phone for text messages but the little screen remained resolutely blank. Marnie's silence was not surprising the second time around, but it was just as disappointing.

However, Cecily had kept her hopes with regard to Marnie to herself for fear of causing friction in her family. Her new strategy, to get to know Marnie herself first, meant that she couldn't allow the girls to moan about her. The more they did, the harder it would be to turn the whole situation around. Cecily couldn't control how the girls talked to one another, but at least she could reduce the chances for unkindness when they were with her.

In fact, her silence on the subject of Marnie's visits had been so deafening that after a couple of weeks Norman had raised it himself, but she had dismissed his enquiry with a little shrug. She had told him only the barest bones of the conversation that had taken place in the kitchen, knowing that he already took a dim view of his niece. She didn't want to colour matters any darker for him as, with the passage of time, even she had to admit that Marnie's behaviour that evening had fallen short of what could be considered acceptable. So she had kept her lips sealed.

Now, seven months later, he tried again.

'Have you heard anything from Marnie?' he asked tentatively as they washed up the dishes after supper. 'I mean, how exactly did you leave things between you?'

'We didn't, really,' she replied. 'She just said that I had the mobile number if I needed to get in touch with her for any reason.'

'And have you? Got in touch, I mean?'

He passed her the casserole dish that he had been washing up. It still had a sticky trickle of gravy down the outside. She should hand it back to him to be washed again, but instead she chose to ignore the dirt, making a mental note to rewash it later. She wiped the gravy off with the tea towel and then put the dish away.

'No,' she said. 'She made it sound like I should only use the number in an emergency.'

'Oh, I'm sure that can't be right,' said Norman charitably.

Bless him for at least trying to see the positive side. Cecily had thought about this long and hard, however, and she was certain that that was what Marnie had meant.

'Isn't it her birthday today?' he asked.

A powerful gush of love for her husband washed over Cecily, and she had to take a deep breath to steady herself. She hadn't been aware that he knew which day Marnie's birthday fell on, let alone that he might notice when that day arrived. She put the tea towel down and went to stand behind him at the sink, wrapping her arms around his waist and squeezing tight.

'Yes,' she replied simply. 'She's fifty-one.'

Norman turned himself round so that they were facing one another and then returned her hug, resting his chin on the top of her head like he used to do when they were young.

'I don't even have an address to send her a card,' Cecily said, her voice cracking slightly as she spoke.

'I'm sure she knows you're thinking of her,' he said, but in truth neither of them could know any such thing.

They stood there holding one another for a moment or two, Cecily enjoying the sensation of safety that Norman's arms instilled in her.

'I imagine it's been hard,' Norman said then. 'Knowing that she's out there but not having any contact.'

Cecily nodded, her head banging gently against his chest. 'In some ways it was easier before she got in touch, when I had no idea where she was or what she was doing. Now that I know she could contact me but chooses not to, well, what does that say about us?'

'I think that probably says more about her,' Norman replied. 'I imagine she had some demons to exorcise and meeting us possibly did that for her. Maybe she just needed to answer some questions for herself.'

'Maybe,' Cecily agreed. But then an unfamiliar stab of irritation with Marnie needled her. 'It feels very one-sided,' she said. 'She came here, met us and the girls, saw where we lived and how our lives were, but we have no idea about what her life is like. It doesn't feel very fair. Sometimes I think about what I'd do if I did know where she was. I might even go down there and just have a nose about, without telling her. All I want is to see where she lives and that she's happy and safe. Is that so wrong?' Cecily let out a long sigh and she felt Norman's arms close tighter around her.

He was quiet for a moment. 'Well, we could do that,' he said. 'Go and have a nose about, I mean.'

Cecily stepped away from him so that she could see his face. 'Of course we couldn't,' she said. 'All we know is that she lives, or even lived, in Finsbury Park. It's a big place, you know. We couldn't just hang about and hope to bump into her. That would be ridiculous. A real fool's errand.'

Norman nodded his head in agreement. 'Yes,' he said. 'It would be. If I didn't have her address, that is.' A little smile of triumph tickled his lips.

Cecily was confused. 'What do you mean? Her address?'

'It's not that hard to find people any more, Cec,' he said. 'I know her name, and we had the name of the yoga company from when you went to Greece, so I just did a search on the internet and a few clicks later I found her. I have her address in Finsbury Park and the address of that yoga company.'

'Are you sure that's legal?' Cecily didn't know whether she felt horrified or elated.

'Of course it's legal. They are public records. So how about we take a little trip down to London and have a beetle about? There's no need to let her know that we're there. But at least you'd be able to picture her world. I thought it might make things a bit easier for you,' he added, a little shamefacedly.

'Her address?' clarified Cecily. 'In Finsbury Park? Well, I don't know. What do you think? It's an awfully long way to go.' But even as these words came from her lips, Cecily knew that there was no way she would be able to keep away.

'That doesn't matter,' Norman said. 'What else do we have to do with our time? It might be fun. We could go on the train first class and have a spot of lunch somewhere nice. We might even fit an exhibition in if we get our timings right.' He was smiling at her broadly now, clearly delighted with his achievement.

'But what if we bump into her? I'd die of shame.'

Norman's head twitched from side to side as he considered. 'Well, that might be a little bit awkward but it's a free country. There is nothing to stop us.'

Cecily wasn't at all sure that it was a good idea, but the chance to see where Marnie lived was overpowering her natural caution.

'We can go in disguise if it makes you feel any better,' Norman said, laughing now. 'Big hats and dark glasses. She'll never know it's us and anyway, it's highly unlikely that we'll bump into her.'

'When would we go?' Cecily asked, allowing herself to be swept along by Norman's enthusiasm.

'Whenever you like. How about one day next week? Why don't I look at the trains and see what's available?' Before Cecily knew what she was doing, she had nodded her agreement and the plan was hatched.

2

There were many things that Julia's highly fecund twin sister had failed to mention to her about the realities of having a baby, and none of them were good. Baby Tamsin was barely three months old and already Julia was more exhausted than she thought it was possible to be and still function. Her time as a junior doctor had nothing on this. At least when she'd struggled through those long and relentless shifts there was time off at the end when she wasn't at work. Not so with this job. Apparently, you couldn't just walk away from being a mother for a few hours and then show up again when it was your turn.

Julia remembered, rather shamefacedly now, all those women who had sat before her in the surgery and wept about what had seemed, at the time, the most trivial of concerns. These were not the women with postnatal depression, but the ones who just wanted to talk about how very hard having a newborn baby was. Once Julia had been certain that there was nothing more than the baby blues at play, she had made sympathetic noises as she glanced at the clock on the bottom of her screen and assured the women that matters would improve soon enough.

Now that it was she who was strapped into the baby roller-coaster rather than them, she wanted to know how long the ride would go on for and precisely how many more loop-the-loops she was expected to endure. When she had asked Lily, her eyes so heavy that it took a superhuman effort to keep them open and even then only as slits, her twin had just smiled and told her that she understood the first twenty-one years were the worst.

Everything seemed to take so long in this new reality. She would get the baby quiet, cuddled, changed and fed, and just have time to grab a slice of toast and half a cup of tea before it all began again. It was like some nightmarish train journey, going round and round a circular track but with nowhere to disembark. How Lily dealt with five of the little blighters was totally beyond her. Julia had always had a respect for her sister's mothering skills, but now that she had a slither of her own experience she had elevated Lily to the status of a demi-god.

Not that she was complaining. Despite the near-death exhaustion and the lack of showers or food or any adult conversation that wasn't about babies, Julia was the happiest she had been in as long as she could remember. Hours could pass with her lying on the carpet next to Tamsin, just watching her exist: the way her tiny chest rose and fell, how she bashed herself in the face with plump little fists over which she still had very little control, the face she pulled just moments before she began to cry. All these things were magical to Julia, and each day she thanked the universe for giving her the chance to absorb them.

Sam was being brilliant, too. Even though he was building himself a role in Tamsin's life that was bigger than they had agreed when they set out on this adventure, his presence was in no way obtrusive. He turned up like the cavalry with home-cooked meals that he heated up and served for her on proper china. He cleaned her flat without suggesting in any way that the job needed doing, and best of all he kept her vases full of sweet-smelling flowers and her cupboards full of loo roll. He was, in short, a godsend.

He had arrived that evening with a copy of *Mother and Baby* magazine and a punnet of fresh raspberries, which had probably cost the earth but which were exactly what she fancied. During her pregnancy, Julia had flicked through a couple of baby magazines at the surgery dismissively, thinking it all a little unnecessary, but now that Tamsin was here she devoured them, even noting when the next edition would be available so she knew when to look out for it.

She was lying flopped on the sofa in her pyjamas, getting dressed having proved too much for her that day, when she heard his key in the lock. Again, this invasion of her privacy was something that she would never have tolerated before, but now she was just grateful that she didn't have to get up to answer the door. Tamsin was asleep, lying face down across her lap and pinning her to the spot.

Sam smiled indulgently at them both. 'Shall I put our little bundle of joy in her carry cot?' he asked, and Julia nodded weakly.

Carefully he plucked the sleeping baby up, supporting her head in his hand, and placed her gently in her bed. He arranged the blanket on top of her delicately, but she didn't stir.

'She needs changing,' said Julia, although just opening her mouth was using up more energy than she had to spare. Her eyelids drooped and then closed entirely.

'There's no rush,' Sam said calmly. 'It can wait until she wakes for a feed.'

Julia nodded. Then something occurred to her. 'Oh shit!' she said, without opening her eyes. 'What day is it?'

'Tuesday the nineteenth,' he said. '2019,' he added with a grin.

'Oh, ha ha! I'm not that bad. Yet.'

'So what have you forgotten?'

'Nothing, but it's the Nightingale sisters' curry night on Wednesday . . .'

'The third Wednesday in the month. As if anyone could ever forget,' Sam said.

'I can't go,' said Julia, slumping even further down into the sofa cushions. 'I'm too tired. I just can't.'

'Well, that's okay. I'm sure they'll understand,' said Sam reasonably.

'But I have to go,' Julia wailed. 'Lily has never missed a single one and even Fliss managed, and she had a C-section. If I don't get there I'll never live it down.'

'You'd better go then,' said Sam.

'But I can't,' repeated Julia. 'I'm so tired that I'll just fall asleep in my curry.'

Sam moved towards the sofa. 'Budge up,' he said, and gently shuffled Julia along until he was sitting side by side with her. 'It's not tonight. You've got a whole day to catch up on some sleep and you don't have to stay late, just show your face.'

Julia nodded. All she wanted to do was cry forlorn tears at how very pathetic she had become, but even that felt too much like hard work. 'What about Tamsin?' she asked, her voice sounding petulant now.

Sam patted her on the hand as if she was an old lady. 'Well, you can either take her with you in the car seat or I'll come here and look after her.'

'But what if she needs feeding?' Julia was not looking for solutions any more, just problems.

'Well, if she needs feeding I'll bring her to the restaurant and you can feed her there. Simples.'

Julia flopped back on to the cushions again. Her eyes refused to stay open.

'But you'd better stick to korma. We don't want to send her into shock!'

'What would I do without you?' she asked him, her eyes still shut. 'How did I ever think I could do this on my own?'

'You're doing brilliantly, Jules. No one said that it was going to be easy. You knew that.'

Julia nodded weakly, tears just nanoseconds away.

'And you're not on your own. You have me and Lily and Fliss and your mum and dad. You are totally surrounded by people who love you and want to help. All you have to do is ask.'

Without having to look, she knew exactly what expression would be on Sam's face. Asking for help wasn't the Julia Nightingale way. But, she supposed, just because she had never done it before didn't mean that it couldn't be done. Then, as she contemplated the idea, sleep came and stole her away.

3

Cecily had forgotten how much she enjoyed a train journey. They had taken the slower train partly because it was cheaper, but mainly because they were in no real rush. Norman had bought a newspaper at the station and then disappeared behind it as soon as the train pulled out of Leeds, leaving Cecily with her thoughts. She still wasn't convinced of the merits of this plan, but her desire to find out a few more precious details about Marnie and her life had squashed her fear of being caught snooping. At least Norman was right in that regard. London was a huge place. Even if they stood right outside the address that he had tracked down, the chances of Marnie coming out at that precise moment were tiny. So that wasn't the problem, Cecily reasoned. What was worrying her went far deeper than that.

It was the fear of rejection that was gnawing at her panicked mind.

Cecily already felt as if she were teetering on the brink of losing Marnie. She barely had a grasp on her as it was. What had they had so far? Four encounters, none of them terribly satisfactory for either of them, but as things stood, Cecily was able to tell herself that there would be more. Marnie was taking her time to integrate herself into their lives and that was totally understandable. She had been living a life that was entirely separate to Cecily's for more than half a century. A person couldn't just undo all that overnight. It took time to build trust, to knock down prejudices and preconceptions. It was a slow process but one that they had begun, albeit falteringly.

But if she and Norman just turned up in her home territory unannounced, just how much damage could that do to the already fragile relationship? From what she had seen of her daughter so far, Marnie seemed uncompromising and unforgiving. A mistake at this stage could prove fatal.

The stations flew by, the train slowing and occasionally stopping at various points, and soon they were in the outskirts of London, the station names familiar simply by virtue of her general knowledge. As they approached King's Cross the doubts that Cecily had managed to subdue grew again, tall shadows rising up like the buildings on either side of the train tracks, threatening to engulf her.

Finally, Norman put down his paper and swigged the end of his coffee as he peered at the scene outside the windows. 'Nearly there,' he said. 'That was a pleasant journey.'

Cecily nodded without much conviction, her mind totally absorbed by her other, much larger concern. 'Norman, I'm not sure we should do this,' she said. 'We could just go and have a pootle around the V&A, have lunch in the café. There's bound to be an exhibition on that we fancy. Why don't we do that instead?'

Norman furrowed his brow and considered her for a moment. 'We could,' he said slowly. 'But I think this is important for you, Cecily. This not knowing is eating away at your insides. Until you have the full picture you're not going to rest, are you?'

He was right. Of course he was. He knew her better than she knew herself.

'But I'm frightened,' she replied simply.

'I know. But faint heart never won fair lady,' he said, and then he pulled a face at the inappropriate expression. 'You know what I mean,' he added with half a smile. 'The point is that we're here now. There's no need to go knocking on any doors. We can simply put Marnie's life into context for you and then we'll leave and I promise we won't ever come back, not if you don't want to. But I think you need this, Cecily. We need it.'

'All right,' she agreed, but only because she knew that seeing something of Marnie's life beyond her was the stronger draw.

They caught the Piccadilly Line tube up to Finsbury Park. Norman offered to pay for a cab, but Cecily felt that seeing the place as Marnie would see it was somehow important. She had never been to that part of London before, and when they emerged from the tunnels into the light she couldn't help but be disappointed. She'd had no particular expectations of the place but when she saw the cheap shop fronts with their garish colours and their wares displayed in plastic baskets on the narrow pavements, she knew that Marnie's existence must just be ordinary, unremarkable, like millions of other people's.

Norman had brought their battered copy of *London A–Z* and was peering at it. People flooded round him as if he were an island in a fast-flowing river. He looked up to confirm a street name and then snapped the book shut.

'Right. It's over the road and up that one.'

As they walked away from the main road, the houses became bigger and far more genteel. Front gardens contained plants rather than bicycle parts, and the doors were freshly painted. This always surprised Cecily about London, how you could seem to slip from one place to something totally different and yet barely move.

After a little navigation they found themselves on a wide tree-lined street. The houses were terraced and uniform, each three stories high with render to the first floor and then sandy-coloured

London brick above. Rows of chimneys dotted the roofs like so many sandcastles.

'Well, there it is,' said Norman. 'Number thirty-six.'

They were standing on the opposite side of the road and Norman pointed directly at the building, making Cecily uncomfortable. Her hand shot up to push his down, and he gave her a brief look of irritation before his face settled back into something kinder.

Cecily looked up and down the street and then across at the house. It looked nicely kept. The front garden, such as it was, had been pared down with no grass to maintain and huge terracotta pots instead of flower beds, but it was neat and clearly cared for. None of the windows had grotty nets hanging at them and there were no stickers or posters attached to the glass. It looked like the home of perfectly respectable, and affluent, adult occupiers.

At some point it had been divided up into flats, judging by the number of bells that adorned the door frame.

'Number two,' said Norman, instantly reading her thoughts. 'It looks nice enough,' he added.

Well, that was one fear dismissed. Cecily had worried that Marnie was living like a student in a cheap bedsit in a rough area, but this was nothing like that. That said, it was nothing like their beautiful family home in Harrogate, either. Cecily remembered now the little dig that Marnie had made at poor Lily about her upholstery course. The contrast between their lives and hers was clearer now that she was here. Marnie must have wondered how different her life could have been had she not been given away. Who would blame her if a little flash of resentment shone through from time to time? It didn't matter how many times Cecily told herself that it was not her fault, that she had been just a child and had things done to her rather than making choices for herself; the thought that Marnie might compare and contrast would forever haunt her.

'I want to go in,' she said in a voice so quiet that she barely heard it herself.

'What?' asked Norman. 'I didn't catch that.'

'I want to go in,' she repeated, a little louder this time.

Norman looked at her, his eyes narrowed. 'But you said . . .'

'I know what I said, but now that we're here it feels important that I tell her. She needs to know that we think enough of her to have found her and made the effort to come to see her. And if she's angry, then that's her choice, but at least she'll know that I care.'

Norman pursed his lips as he considered this. 'Okay,' he said doubtfully. 'If that's what you want.'

Cecily nodded. Her heart seemed to be clamouring to be released from her ribcage and every hair follicle was pricking her skin, but yes. That was what she wanted, she realised now. That was what she wanted more than she had wanted anything in a very long time. She crossed the road and walked up to the door.

The doorbell to flat 2 was the second from the top. A handwritten label read Molina/Stone. With a trembling hand Cecily reached out and pressed it. She did not hear it sound, but that meant nothing. She waited. What would she say if Marnie answered the door? She had no idea, but it didn't matter. The seconds ticked by and no one came. She pressed the bell again, this time for a little longer. She took a step back from the doorstep so she did not appear to be crowding whoever answered, but the door remained resolutely shut.

'There's no one in,' she said, her shoulders suddenly too heavy to hold high. 'She's not there.'

'Let's go and get a cup of coffee and come back,' said Norman cheerfully. 'We walked past a nice café. We could grab a sandwich or something if you like.'

He was trying so hard to keep things light for her. She nodded and then turned and followed him back down the short path. She was not sure why she felt so crushingly disappointed. They were here out of the blue and it was the middle of the working day. It was hardly surprising that the flat was empty, but having made the difficult decision to knock, Cecily now felt cheated out of her meeting.

'Do you think we should leave a note?' she suddenly asked, and began scrabbling around in her handbag to find a pen.

Norman shook his head. 'We'll just go and get a drink and come back. We can leave a note if she's not here next time.'

Cecily nodded. She really did not know what was best and she allowed herself to be led away.

'I think the café was down this way,' said Norman.

There was a woman walking down the pavement on the other side with three dogs on leads. They were all different breeds and so of wildly different sizes, but each was a similar caramel colour and had a matching purple lead. They looked slightly comical, like something out of a rom com.

'She's got her hands full,' joked Norman and Cecily was about to agree, but then she saw who it was.

'Sofia. It's Sofia,' she said. 'With the dogs.'

Without thinking, Cecily stepped out into the street. Norman tugged at her arm, pulling her back as a van flew past them, missing her by inches.

'Careful!' he said.

'Sofia,' Cecily shouted, checking the road more carefully now and crossing to her side. 'It's me. Cecily.'

Sofia looked at first confused and then delighted to see her. 'Cecily,' she said, placing a kiss on each cheek as she drew close enough. 'What are you doing here?'

The dogs, excited by this unexpected encounter, danced around her legs, the smallest one yapping madly.

'We came to see you,' Cecily said. 'Well, Marnie actually, but there's no one in.'

'Is she expecting you?' Sofia asked. 'She didn't say anything.'

Cecily shook her head. 'We're here on a whim. This is my husband, Norman. Norman, this is Sofia, the yoga teacher from Kefalonia.'

'And Marnie's partner,' Norman added, reaching out to shake her hand. 'Lovely to meet you.'

'She's gone to the supermarket,' Sofia said. 'But she'll be back in a minute. Why don't you come in and I'll let her know that you're here?'

Cecily felt a rush of something between excitement and guilt. When they had set off it had been on nothing more than an exploratory mission, and now they were going to be waiting in Marnie's house when she got home. Cecily's stomach twisted at the awkwardness of it. And yet . . . Marnie's house, her world outside them. Wasn't that exactly what she had been hoping for a glimpse of?

4

Sofia led the way, the dogs at her heels. At the front door she dug a key out of her pocket and let them in, leading the way up the stairs. It smelled of communal space, slightly musty and with the hint of stale food and dog. It was dark, too, with all the doors leading off firmly shut against intruders. They trooped up, one after another, and then stood in a line on the stairs as Sofia unlocked the door to the flat.

'Here we are,' she said. 'Home sweet home.'

Cecily thought that there was an edge to her voice that she hadn't heard before, a slightly fake enthusiasm as if she was trying a little too hard to be jolly. It was probably the surprise, Cecily thought. After all, she and Norman had just accosted her in the street totally out of the blue. It was not surprising if she was a little thrown. Perhaps she had left the flat in a mess before she went out, not imagining that anyone would see it. Well, that didn't matter. Cecily wasn't here to inspect the state of their home. She would take them as she found them.

But the flat was tidy. The door opened into a corridor that led to the sitting room. It looked lived in, but not at all cluttered. The walls and floorboards were painted white and the light bounced around, making the room feel fresh and airy. The high Victorian ceiling and large sash windows added to the effect. A huge green parlour palm stood in a pot in one corner and there were framed posters advertising art exhibitions on the walls.

The dogs, now that they were home, had become even more excitable and the smallest one bounced up and down enthusiastically. Cecily had never been very fond of dogs, but Norman adored them and he was straight there, rubbing their ears and talking to them in that strange sing-song voice that people often use to talk to animals and small children.

'Sit down,' said Sofia as she took the leads off the dogs and hung them on the back of the door. 'Marnie won't be long, but I will just text her and let her know that you're here.'

A shot of panic hit Cecily. That might scare her off. What if she took one look at the text and ran for the hills, not returning home until she was sure the unwanted guests had returned from whence they came? Then she checked herself. That was silly. Marnie was fifty-one years old. She was hardly going to run away from her own flat.

The dogs were now chasing each other around, the big one, some kind of pointer, clearly irritated by its smaller, more excitable housemates. They seemed to take over all the available space with their tails wagging and their snouts into everything as they explored the new scents that the two of them must have brought in with them. Cecily wasn't at all sure that the flat was big enough to accommodate one dog, let alone three. She shrank a little further into the edges of the room. Norman was still fussing them vigorously and seemed, if anything, to be adding to their excitement.

She took a seat on one of the sofas, placing her handbag primly on her knee rather than risk putting it on the floor, where the dogs might steal it.

'I'm so sorry to just descend on you like this, Sofia. That wasn't the plan at all.' Cecily left the obvious question of what exactly the plan had been hanging.

'Don't worry,' Sofia called cheerfully from another room. 'It's so lovely to see you. I'm sure Marnie will be delighted.'

Cecily was less sure of that.

'Can I get you both a cup of tea? Coffee?'

'Coffee would be fabulous,' replied Norman. 'Great place you have here, Sofia. Have you been here long?'

And so they chatted, the two of them, making easy conversation whilst Cecily waited, listening intently for signs of someone arriving. She didn't have to wait long. Sofia had just appeared with two steaming mugs of coffee when they heard a key in the lock and the front door opened. Cecily felt sick, like a child caught stealing from its mother's purse when they had thought it was the perfect crime. She had no idea how Marnie was going to react to their being there. She didn't know enough about her to predict whether they were about to face delight, anger or withdrawal, and she braced herself for whichever it might be.

The dogs raced from the room to greet the new person and the sound of barking and yelping increased as the door closed. Cecily could hear Marnie greeting each dog in turn, making a fuss of them and laughing. It was the first time Cecily had ever heard Marnie make anything approaching a joyful sound, she realised. The dog greetings seemed to go on forever, but then finally Marnie appeared, a jute shopping bag in each hand.

'Well,' she said coolly, 'this is a surprise.'

Cecily's mind went blank. Any words that might have been waiting to be spewed out in feeble explanation of just how she and Norman had found themselves on her street, right outside her flat, had fled. Her mouth opened and then closed but nothing came out.

'And for us,' Norman replied, filling the gap. 'When we decided to take a trip down here with the sole purpose of spying on you, we didn't imagine for a moment that we might actually bump into you.' His eyes twinkled as he spoke and the edges of his mouth turned up in a wry smile.

It was enough. Marnie shrugged, but she didn't seem angry. 'So were you just going to have a look at where we lived and then go back?' she asked, one eyebrow raised questioningly.

'Pretty much,' replied Norman.

'Fair enough,' said Marnie. She moved towards the table in the corner which they clearly used as a desk rather than a dining table and sat on a hard wooden chair, her spine straight and alert. The dogs stayed at her heels and settled at her feet, all vying with one another to get the prized spot closest to her legs.

'They're beautiful animals,' said Norman, nodding at the dogs. 'A bit of a handful, I should imagine.'

And then Marnie smiled, a wide-open smile that seemed to light her face from within. 'They are my beautiful babies,' she said, ruffling each dog's ears in turn. 'And I love them with all my heart, don't I, my darlings? Mummy loves you very, very much.'

And it was obvious that they loved her, too.

'Yes,' said Sofia. 'I barely get a look-in around here. But it's all right. I know my place.'

Marnie looked up at her and winked, and Cecily saw the depth of affection that there was between them. This was Marnie in a whole different light. Gone were the sharp edges and the spikes. Here, in the safety of her own environment, she seemed softer, more at ease with herself, happy. It made Cecily's heart sparkle in her chest.

'And how are the rest of the family?' asked Sofia.

Cecily had the impression that Sofia was used to dealing with the social niceties for Marnie, but the fact that she knew to ask must surely mean that Marnie had shared something of them with her.

'They are well, thank you,' Cecily replied. 'Julia had her baby, a beautiful little girl. They called her Tamsin.'

'Don't you mean "she"?' Marnie asked.

Cecily didn't follow at first, but then remembered how Marnie hadn't seemed to approve of Julia's methodology. 'Yes, I suppose I do,' she replied. 'Although Sam has turned out to be far more hands-on than either of them intended at the outset. It's good,' she added. 'We all adore Sam.'

Marnie nodded knowingly, as if this changed her initial view of the arrangement. 'And how's Felicity? Has she let that husband back in?'

Cecily shifted a little in her seat. Marnie could be so brutally direct and it knocked her sideways every time. 'No. It's just her and Hugo now.'

'Good thing too,' added Norman, and Marnie nodded.

'He's always been a shit,' she said. 'Felicity's well out of it.'

They must have had a very open discussion, the two of them on that evening out that they had shared, Cecily thought. It was strange that Felicity had chosen to be honest with a stranger about the state of her marriage, but not told her sisters or her mother. But then again, maybe it wasn't that very strange after all.

'And Lily, well, she's just Lily,' Cecily said, bringing her inventory to a close. 'And how about you? Did you have a nice birthday?'

Marnie's eyes widened just a tiny fraction as if Cecily had surprised her, but then her face fell back into its usual, unreadable expression. 'Very nice. Not that there's much to celebrate about being fifty-one.'

'Oh, I don't know,' said Norman. 'Wait until you get to seventy-one.'

They all smiled, and then took sips from their mugs to cover the gap in conversation.

'Could I just use your bathroom?' asked Cecily. 'We came straight here from the train and the facilities at King's Cross . . .' Her face twisted to express what she thought of station toilets.

'Of course,' said Sofia. 'It's just down the hall.'

Cecily put her mug down and headed for the door as Norman began to ask questions about the dogs.

Outside, the hallway was dark and all the doors except the one leading to the kitchen were closed. Cecily was going to have to open each of them in turn to find the bathroom. Hopefully, she thought, it would be the one at the far end.

Gingerly she pushed open the first door. It was their bedroom, a huge pine bed with pale blue bedding and white pillows. A small selection of soft toys sat in a little line next to the headboard. They must be Sofia's, she thought. She couldn't imagine Marnie with such frivolities. But then she remembered Marnie with her dogs, her clear and joyful laugh, and allowed herself to think that at least one of the toys might be hers.

Surreptitiously peeking at this intimate space was making her feel uncomfortable so she pulled the door to and opened the next one along. It was the bathroom and she let out a little sigh of disappointment, but she went in and locked the door behind her.

When she came out, she could hear laughter coming from the sitting room, although she couldn't make out any of their conversation. Norman was so good at putting people at their ease. It was such a talent of his.

She just had time to peep behind the third door. It felt wrong, but surely this was what everyone did when they first went into someone else's house? They were always doing it on television shows. She pushed open the door.

It was a second bedroom, with a small double bed against one wall and a single wardrobe in the far corner. It was quite dark, the blind having been pulled two-thirds of the way across the large window. She was just going to slip back to the others when she noticed that there were lots of black and white photographs all in matching black frames laid out across the bed. Unable to resist this window into Marnie's world, Cecily stepped into the room to take a better look.

It took a couple of seconds for her brain to make sense of what her eyes were seeing. It was a photograph of her and Norman. They were standing together in the front garden of the house in Harrogate, Cecily pointing up at something and Norman following her line of sight. Judging by her hair and what she was wearing, it must have been taken the previous November when Marnie had come to Harrogate to meet them all.

Cecily smiled to herself. There was something quite endearing and almost childlike about this stolen photograph, snapped when neither of them had been aware. She remembered how she had longed to take a photograph of Marnie when they had been in Kefalonia. Marnie had clearly been thinking along similar lines.

Her eyes strayed to another image. It was her again, but this time she was carrying that red leather handbag that she had been so fond of, the one that Felicity had made her throw away because it was so decrepit. But surely she had done that years ago; certainly long before Marnie had visited.

Then there was a photo of Felicity and Richard leaning over a pram and rearranging the blankets. Hugo's pram. And then Julia and Lily tripping down the front steps, arms linked, Lily's head turned back to speak to whoever was in the house. They couldn't have been more than twenty-five.

Cecily couldn't believe what she was seeing. These were photos of her family taken years before Marnie had contacted her. She took a step to her left and then, when she focused on the image in front of her, her hand shot up to her open mouth. It was her girls in a paddling pool, Julia's head flung back in delight, and Felicity, who

296

had clearly just been splashed, pulling the indignant expression that was so familiar to Cecily even now that Felicity was an adult. They could have been no older than five.

Then the room filled with light as the door opened fully, and Marnie entered.

'I thought you might be in here,' she said.

Cecily turned to look at her, desperate for an explanation that would help her make sense of what she was seeing. 'What is all this?' she asked, gesturing to the photos on the bed.

'My family photo album?' replied Marnie with a shrug. 'Do you like it? Actually, I was just taking it down. Time for something new on the walls.'

'But . . .' Words failed Cecily.

'I found you,' Marnie said simply. 'When I was eighteen. I found you.'

'But . . .' said Cecily again. 'But the letter? Your fiftieth birthday? Greece?'

'That was Sofia. She said that the time had come to introduce myself. So I did. I'm still not sure it was the right thing to do, but it's done now.'

Cecily pulled her eyes away from Marnie and back to all the photographs. They settled on one of the house. It was dark, but the window of the sitting room was lit by an enormous Christmas tree standing in the bay, the lights and baubles twinkling. She could just make out the shadow of a girl stretching up to touch a branch that was out of her reach.

Tears ran down Cecily's cheeks, but when she turned to look at Marnie her daughter's eyes were dry. 'But why did you never knock on the door? If you knew where we were, came often enough to take all these pictures . . .' She gestured to the gallery of images. 'Why did you never speak to us?'

Marnie shrugged. 'This was your world. I could see that, even when I was eighteen. There was no place in it for me.'

'But there was,' Cecily interrupted her. 'There was,' she repeated insistently. 'Oh . . . if only I'd known. All these years, me waiting, hoping, praying that you would get in touch and you were there, all the time.'

Norman's voice was approaching now. 'Cecily?' he was saying. 'Sofia was just saying that . . .'

He appeared in the doorway but when he saw her, he stopped. 'What's going on?' he asked, his voice more wary. 'Are you all right?'

'Norman, look!' said Cecily. 'Look.'

Norman moved towards the pictures and peered down at them. It took him a few seconds before he registered exactly what he was looking at. 'Well, I'll be damned,' he said.

Then he started at one end of the bed and looked at each image in turn, taking them all in quickly and without comment until he reached one towards the end. Then he said, 'I never did like that coat of Julia's. It made her look like a hobo.'

It was Julia when she was at university and had come across an Afghan coat in a vintage market. It was a hideous garment and had always had a slightly unwholesome smell about it, no matter how many times Cecily washed it. Cecily peered at the image and then she wasn't sure if she was laughing or crying. Norman was at her side and wrapped his arms around her. She pressed her face into his shoulder, the familiar feeling suddenly very necessary to her continued existence.

'And isn't that . . . ?' He stepped away from Cecily towards the window and picked up a silver ball on a stake. It was the missing one of the three that Cecily had bought at Chelsea that year.

'Oh, yeah,' said Marnie, finally looking slightly shamefaced. 'Sorry about that. I couldn't resist it. It was a nightmare to get back on the bus, though.'

5

The four of them sat in Marnie and Sofia's sitting room, a bottle of wine open on the table in front of them. Cecily was beginning to feel that she could think in straight lines again but then, just when she thought she had a grip on what had happened, another question would pop up in her head and she would feel herself lurching dangerously towards some invisible edge.

'Would you ever have told us?' Norman asked. 'Or would you have just let us go on thinking that this' – he searched for a word to describe what it was – 'this relationship was all new?'

Because she knew her husband so well, Cecily could hear the faint undertone of anger in his question, but Marnie either wasn't aware of it or didn't care.

'Not sure,' she replied nonchalantly. 'Probably not.'

Norman rubbed his hand over his jaw and narrowed his eyes, regarding Marnie coolly. She returned his stare, but without offering anything in her expression that Cecily could read.

'Well, that doesn't matter now,' Cecily said quickly, anxious to avoid any confrontation between the two of them. 'The main thing is that we are all connected and we can move forward together.'

She threw a smile, wide and broad, at her daughter, but Marnie didn't return it and Cecily felt herself shrink back into her chair. She was so at sea here. It was too much to take on board. Marnie had been there, watching them for over thirty years, without ever making contact. The thought that she might have passed her in the street outside the house – in fact probably had, judging by some of the photographs – made Cecily feel sick. She had always believed that she would know her child anywhere, and had constantly had an eye open for a familiar feature in a crowd. Now she felt stupid. Marnie had been close to her so many times and yet she had failed to even see her, let alone realise who she was. What kind of mother did that make her?

'Actually,' said Marnie, 'I'm not sure about that either. The moving forward part.' She leant back in her chair and put a hand down to scoop up the smallest of the dogs and settle it on to her lap. 'I'm not one for happy families,' she continued, running a hand gently over the dog's velvety ears. 'I don't really have the tools for it. I admit I was curious. Who wouldn't be? When I first found out that I'd been adopted I used to dream about my real family being rich or famous or royal. You know, all that normal kid's stuff. And as soon as I was old enough to find you then I did it straight away. It helped that you've never moved from that tumbledown old house. That made life much simpler.'

Cecily gave her a weak little smile. At least she and Norman had done something helpful in all this, even if it was inadvertent.

'But actually, it's never been much more than curiosity for me. I needed to know who you were so that I could put lids on the various questions I had, but once I'd done that then that was more or less job done for me.'

'I don't believe that,' said Norman sternly. 'If that had been it, then you wouldn't have visited us so many times over the years. There must have been more to it.'

Marnie tipped her head back and looked up at the ceiling as she contemplated Norman's words. Then she nodded. 'Yes,' she said. 'You might be right there, Norman. I guess I did find you all kind of addictive. On the bus to Harrogate I used to hope that my visit would coincide with an event of some sort, a birthday party or a wedding or something. Christmas was an easy one. And Easter. They were sweet, those egg hunts you used to do in the garden.'

Cecily couldn't identify her feelings as Marnie said this. Part of her was sad that her eldest child had been there to witness these family occasions but never been part of them. But another part felt humiliated and even angry that she had been spied on. There was something very challenging about what Marnie had done, even though she had managed to keep it hidden from them all until now.

'But the future?' Marnie continued. 'I'm not sure that I see you all in my future. That's why the photos are coming down. I know where I came from now. I understand, and so I can put it to one side.'

Sofia, who had sat in silence until this moment, sat forward in her seat as if she had something to say about this, but Marnie waved her back down.

'It's okay, Sof,' she said, giving Sofia a grateful smile. 'I think we've been moving forward to this place from the moment you gave me to someone else to bring up, Cecily. I'm glad I've met you. And don't get me wrong. I think you're lovely and I'm sure you would have been a good mother. But that wasn't how things were and having you there now, a constant reminder of the fact that I wasn't the winner, that I got the consolation prize, well, I'm not sure that's helpful or healthy. It's probably good that you did a bit of spying of your own today. It means that we all know everything, it's all out in the open, no secrets. But now, I think we should say goodbye and then we can draw a line under it and both move on as we were before.'

She stood up then, the little dog jumping to the floor. She retrieved the leads from where they hung and the dogs all bounced around her, each wanting her attention.

'I think I'll take the dogs out now,' she said. 'I expect you'll be gone when I get back.'

It was all happening so quickly, but instead of wanting to prevent it, to fight back to stop her child walking out of the flat and out of her life, Cecily found that what Marnie was saying made a kind of sense to her. Marnie had been a square peg in a round hole, right from the moment she had turned up at their house for Sunday lunch. Cecily had known that at once. She had been prepared to work at it, to file down Marnie's edges so that she sat closer with her sisters, but it would never have been a perfect fit; it would always have been a compromise. She could see why Marnie did not want that and if she was honest, it wasn't what she wanted, either. They had met, they had taken from each other what they needed, and now it was time to let go.

Norman stood up too, and offered a hand to Marnie. It seemed so formal, but Marnie looked at him gratefully and took his hand in hers.

'It's been a pleasure to meet you, Norman,' she said.

'Likewise,' said Norman, and then took a couple of steps back so that Cecily could take his place.

Tears trickled down Cecily's cheeks, but she smiled at Marnie. 'I just want you to know that I have always had four daughters, not three,' she said. 'I am honoured to have you as my child and you will stay in my heart forever. Just as you have always been.'

Then, before Marnie had time to step away, she threw her arms around her. Marnie stood there stiffly and unresponsive for a moment, but then Cecily felt her raise her arms and wrap them around her in a tight squeeze. The dogs, for once, were still.

6

Cecily struggled up the steps into the house with four bags of groceries. It would have made much more sense to take two trips from the car but instead she had gathered them all up at once and attempted just one. She pushed the door handle down with her elbow and just managed to carry herself and the bags over the threshold before she dropped one. There was an ominous thud. That would be the chocolate spread for Hugo's birthday cake hitting the floor. Felicity had said she would just buy a cake like everyone else did, but Cecily was having none of it. No grandchild of hers was having a party with a shop-bought cake, not whilst she was breathing.

She opened the bag and peered nervously inside but everything seemed to be intact. Then she carried them one at a time through to the kitchen. The others were all arriving at three o' clock so that gave her plenty of time to get the cake assembled and decorated.

Each time they hosted one of these gatherings for a grandchild's birthday, Cecily worried that it would be the last time, that jelly and ice cream and party games at their grandma's house wouldn't be sophisticated enough and that she would be rejected for the bright lights of the bowling arcade or the swimming pool. But each time they seemed to come back for more. And now there was Tamsin, too. She hadn't even had her first birthday yet. There would be plenty more Nightingale family birthday parties to come.

But none with Marnie. It had been two months since they had said goodbye for what looked as if it would be the final time. Cecily had wept on the train home, not caring who saw her, with Norman's arm wrapped tightly around her shoulders. For weeks she hoped that Marnie might change her mind, get back in touch and arrange to come and try again, but in her heart she knew that that wouldn't happen. There was no place in Marnie's life for her or her family.

There was a place in Cecily's life for Marnie, however. Cecily still thought of her daughter often, but now she had real details to help her imaginings. She could picture Marnie in her mind's eye, could visualise the flat, how she lived. She no longer had to imagine the best, or the worst.

But she also knew something else. Marnie was happy. She had Sofia and her dogs and their life together. And whilst knowing that wasn't the same as having her firstborn in her life, it certainly made their separation easier to bear.

Norman wasn't in the kitchen, so she made her way into the sitting room. She found him kneeling on the floor, the contents of the hoover bag on the carpet in front of him.

'What on earth are you doing?' she asked as she took in the scene.

'I finished the jigsaw,' he said, his voice triumphant.

Cecily saw that there was indeed a complete picture of Monument Valley sitting on her table. Except for one piece of sky. The green baize of the mat shone through where there should have been cobalt blue.

'There's a piece missing,' she said unnecessarily. 'You've been doing that puzzle for over a year and all that time there was a bit missing. What a waste of time.'

Norman stood up, his hands grey and dusty. He shook his head.

'It's not been a waste of time,' he said, taking her in his arms. She flinched a little as his dusty hands touched her dress, but then she relaxed into his embrace. 'I have still had the pleasure of building it and we can see what it is even without that piece. It really doesn't matter that it's not there. In some ways I quite like it. Nothing's ever quite perfect, is it? And now that I've finished, I can start a new one.'

'Well, maybe if you worked a little bit quicker, bits wouldn't go missing . . .' she chided him gently. 'And couldn't you have put some newspaper down before you started that?'

'No need. I'm just going to hoover it all back up again,' said Norman with a wink.

'You'd better get on with it then. The children will be here soon,' said Cecily, and then she went back into the kitchen. The cake wouldn't ice itself.

ACKNOWLEDGMENTS

In 1968, the number of babies being placed for adoption in the UK reached its peak. When I read that I knew at once that I wanted to tell a story about it because those children are a similar age to me. I read a book published by The Children's Society called *Adoption, Search & Reunion: The Long-Term Experience of Adopted Adults* by David Howe and Julia Feast, and was particularly interested in what motivated adopted people to get in touch with their birth families. We all have a view, I imagine, on what we think we would do if we were in that situation but, of course, there is far more riding on these decisions than just curiosity. And from these thought processes, Marnie and the Nightingale family emerged.

When researching what life would have been like for Cecily in a Mother and Baby Home, I found an MA project online (http://www.motherandbabyhomes.com/the-homes), which was written using interviews with a number of women who spent time in the homes, and this gave me a valuable insight into their day-to-day experiences.

Slightly less harrowing was the research I did into yoga retreats, and I am very grateful to Juliet Hammond who agreed to come with me to a retreat in Spain so that I wouldn't be on my own. Then I simply superimposed our Spanish experience on to my own memories of Kefalonia. Isn't the imagination a wonderful thing?

As ever, I would like to thank my wonderful editors Victoria Pepe and Celine Kelly for their wisdom and kind words, and to everyone at Amazon Publishing who work so hard to produce the final book.

Thanks also to my children, who have learned to deal with the many and varied vicissitudes of the novel-writing mother, and to my husband John, who is always there for me no matter what.

If you have enjoyed *The Last Piece* then please consider leaving me a review on Amazon or Goodreads, and if you would like to get in touch then visit my website (imogenclark.com) where you will find links to all my social media pages. Thank you for reading.

ABOUT THE AUTHOR

Photo © 2017 Karen Ross Photography

Imogen Clark lives in Yorkshire, England, with her husband and children. Her first burning ambition was to be a solicitor, and so she read law at Manchester University and then worked for many years at a commercial law firm. After leaving her legal career behind to care for her four children, Imogen turned to her second love – books. She returned to university, studying part-time while the children were at school, and was awarded a BA in English literature with First Class Honours.

Her first three novels, *Postcards from a Stranger*, *The Thing about Clare* and *Where the Story Starts*, all reached the Number 1 spot in the UK Kindle charts, and her books have also been Number 1 in Australia and Germany. She has been shortlisted for the Contemporary Romantic Novel Award 2020. She is also the author of a Christmas novella, *Postcards at Christmas*, which is a sequel to *Postcards from a Stranger*.

Imogen loves sunshine and travel, and longs to live by the sea someday.